# DECEPTIVE DESIRES

## ELLIE HALLARON

Cover design by Ellie Hallaron

ISBN: 979-8-9990397-2-9

First edition, 2025

*Deceptive Desires*

Book Two of the Syndicate Series

For rights, permissions, or inquiries, contact:

EllieHallaron.Author@gmail.com

*To all the lovely ladies who want your hero to be the monster who will give you the world even if it means taking it from someone else, who will kill with the same fingers he puts inside you, and whose obsession runs to the point of psychosis, I wrote Roman Montclair for you.*

# Content Warning

This is a dark romance intended for mature audiences. It contains themes that some readers may find triggering, including stalking, robbery, drugging, murder, torture, violence, and manipulation. The heroine is a sweet, kindhearted woman who has zero red flags... Now her héroe, known as the 'Monster Montclair' to others, is a walking red flag. He's dark, dangerous, and deranged, but never to her. He never planned on love, but now that he has his sunshine, he'll never let her go.

This is not a safe romance, but it is a satisfying one.

If you crave love you never saw coming, desire you never expected, and passion you'll feel through the pages...

Let me introduce you to Roman Francis Montclair.

# Prologue
## *Roman*

I stalk my prey through the silence of the night.

The dumb fuck doesn't even realize it. He thinks he's invincible. They all do.

I can tell he's new at this. He isn't covering his tracks, isn't checking his six, isn't doing anything.

The silence I've perfected over more than a decade allows me to gain on him without him realizing.

"You must be lost," I whisper darkly in his ear.

"What the fuck!" he shrieks in surprise. I'm thrown aback by how light his Russian accent is. But it's still there, like I knew it would be. "No. I'm fine."

"You don't seem to be fine. You seem to be in the wrong side of town." I pause. "You seem to be in *my* side of town."

"What, man? Look, I'm heading back."

"No, you're not. You're coming with me."

It's the only warning I give before I hit his head twice. His eyes flutter as he crumbles to the ground.

I pick him up with ease, despite his build. He must be six feet tall and frequent the gym, but I still have a good five inches and sixty pounds of muscle on him.

I deposit him in the trunk of my black, bullet proof SUV. No way am I letting his filth contaminate my backseat.

I turn on the radio and bask in the sound of eighties rock.

A smile takes over my face.

What's a better way to spend a Tuesday night than with some light torture and ACDC?

Once we get to one of our warehouses, I remove his shirt and hang him by his arms on the chain hanging from the ceiling. His toes barely brush the ground. *That'll get painful rather quickly.*

I splash cold water on him to wake him up.

"Why are you in our territory?" I ask calmly when his eyes flutter open.

"Who the fuck are you?" He growls at me.

A devilish grin breaks out, transforming myself into something vicious.

This is my favorite part.

"Let me introduce myself. I'm Roman Montclair. And you are?"

He freezes, then tenses as fear washes over him. His eyes widen, and he pales two shades.

"I take it you've heard of me."

Of course he has. Everyone who lurks in the shadows has heard of my irredeemable, ruthless reputation.

He swallows and nods.

"Let's try this again. Why are you in our territory?"

He curses me in Russian.

The first snap of my fist meets his stomach, and I hear a rib crack. The sound is music to my ears. *Beautiful.*

"Tell me what you know," I demand.

No response.

Another hit to the same spot. The pained howl he lets out soothes me.

*Tonight's going to be fun.*

I don't go to the table full of equipment to my right, instead choosing my fists. I love to get my hands dirty. There's something about not having a barrier between me and the pain I inflict that fills me with satisfaction. It's pure, unadulterated me. And I crave it.

"Really? That's how we're going to play this?" I chuckle. Maybe he needs more encouragement.

I approach the table and select my pure gold brass knuckles. Maybe this'll loosen his tongue.

When he sees me approaching, he blanches further.

I go for his sternum this time, and the crunch is exhilarating. It calms the pounding in my head. The hum that's never quiet enough.

"Fuck! Fine! I was trying to get men to come to our clubs," he wheezes out.

"Why?"

"Business is down. Not as many people are coming to us. They're choosing your places more and more."

I smirk. That's what I like to hear. Our nightlife has been pumping.

"Is that all?"

I can always tell when someone's lying. I can pick up their tells within seconds of meeting. Reading body language is my whole career.

This man isn't lying. His story also matches the other men I've interrogated.

"That's all. We just want more business."

I believe him. Well, I believe that's what he knows. But I know there's more. They're just keeping it quiet.

"Thank you for your time."

"So, I'm free to go?" There's hope in his voice.

And as much as I want to squash it, I know Dom doesn't want more Bratva death on his hands.

"Yes. But first, you need to be reminded of the consequences of encroaching on our territory. The mafia never has these issues, but you dumb fuck Russians can't seem to learn."

I grab a small knife from the table, the one I finish every interrogation with. This knife has seen plenty of bloodshed but has never ended a life; that's not its purpose.

I see it in his eyes. He knows what's coming next. The reminder to not fuck with the Syndicate or you're leaving with my mark.

I use the knife to cut open a lemon and inhale the refreshing scent. I drag the knife through the acidic juices and return to his side. Lemon in one hand, knife in the other.

I find a space free of tattoos on his side on top of the ribs I just broke.

"This is going to hurt," I warn him, glee dripping into my voice.

To give him credit, he just nods and hangs his head. Smart man. He knows if he fights this, I might change my mind about letting him live.

I start to carve into him. One line down, then a curve, and a diagonal. Three straight lines. Then four more.

*RFM*

My initials. Roman Francis Montclair.

Carved into his ribs.

It's my signature.

Most think it's to feed my vicious nature, but it's really a tagging method. I interrogate far too many men to keep track of them, so I tag them with my initials.

If I catch one and they have my initials on them, I look at how healed it is and what size it is. The bigger the carving, the more severe their crime. And if it's still healing, that means their offense was recent.

It determines how I handle them next.

It's an effective method.

Now this next part, that's to feed my vicious side.

I run the knife off on the lemon, trying to get rid of the red liquid. Dried blood is a bitch to clean.

Then, I press the lemon half into his side and squeeze, letting the acidic juice burn him.

I revel in his cries, as a smile forms on my face.

This was a good one. He didn't even piss himself.

"You'll be staying the night here, just like this. And tomorrow, one of my men will let you out."

I use the other half of the lemon to clean my hands and cut through the smell of blood. The lemon does a good job of hiding the stench.

As I head out, I relive the moment.

This is where I thrive. My brothers don't do the grunt work, so I do. And I love it. I love the thrill of the confession. I love getting it out of them. The games we play. The way I get them to sing. The crunch of bone, the sounds of begging, the smell of blood. It fuels me.

I do it all for the Syndicate.

It's the criminal organization my family runs. My dad passed it down to Dominic, my eldest brother, when he retired. Dom's the head. The cold, ruthless bastard runs it with an iron fist. Our second brother, Matthias, runs the legal operations,

Syndicate Enterprise. It's our cover. When people look up Montclair, SE comes up. It's one of the biggest security and defense companies in the nation. Our youngest brother, Sebastian, is a computer genius. Bash works on both sides of the operation. Helping create things for Syndicate Enterprise and using his skills in more nefarious ways for the Syndicate.

And that leaves me. I'm the enforcer for the Syndicate. I have a crew under me, but I like to get my hands dirty too. I lead by example. The streets are my home.

Which leads me here. To this Russian fuck who was in *our* territory, soliciting *our* customers, outside *our* clubs. Which isn't fucking allowed.

I know they're up to something. But after the *situation* with Matthias's fiancée, Margot, we're trying to keep our alliance intact. Dom wants me to keep an eye out under the radar and not provoke the Bratva. But I know those fuckers are up to something. I'm going to get to the bottom of it.

And if it's anything like tonight, I might just do it with a smile on my face.

# Chapter 1
## *Cecilia*

A melodic tune wakes me from my dreams. I crack my eyes and am greeted by the rising sun. I turn off my five thirty alarm and sit up in bed.

*This is going to be the best day ever.* I tell myself, as I do every morning.

Every day has the possibility of being the best day ever, it's up to me to make it happen. I want every day to be even better than the previous. That's how you have a happy life. Seek out good, and good will seek you out. Mamá taught me that.

I throw on a pair of soft leggings and a sports bra then throw my long brown waves into a messy bun. I grab my yoga mat and lay it down by the window in the living room.

I sit in the classic Sukhasana pose, cross-legged with my hands resting open on my knees. I close my eyes and focus on my breathing. I deliberate on today's affirmations and land on, *I am open to what the world gives me. Whatever is thrown in my path today, I will handle with grace and kindness.*

I roll my neck and shift onto my hands and knees, arching and curling my back in the Cat-Cow pose. Flowing through Downward Dog to a Sun Salutation sequence. I keep it a light morning, still sore from yesterday's advanced yoga class I taught.

After a short thirty-minute session, I end in Child's Pose with my forehead to the mat, arms extended forward. I slow my breathing and let my mind empty. The quiet morning calms me.

Once I feel myself release all remnants of sleep, I wipe my mat and roll it back up.

*Time to start the day!*

I hop in a hot shower and wash the sweat off. I blow dry my hair and pull it into another bun, this one neat and professional, perfectly appropriate for work. After applying my makeup, I get dressed in my scrubs. While I'm much more comfortable in linen pants and flowy skirts, I can't exactly wear them at work.

I make my way into the kitchen of our petite apartment. I turn on the electric kettle. Today feels like a guayusa tea kind of morning. I take a pottery mug Mamá and I made, and scoop in the homemade mixture.

While the water heats, I make breakfast. A fried egg on avocado toast. A perfectly balanced way to start the morning.

As I sit at the counter eating, Gracie walks in. I can't help the laugh that escapes at the sight of her. Really, I should be used to her adverse reaction to mornings after a year of living together and even more years of being friends, but her messy hair, along with her death glare at the coffee pot elicits a giggle.

"Good morning, sleepyhead," I sing to her, the smile invading my voice.

"Fuck off. This is child abuse!" she grumbles as she makes her way over to the coffee machine.

Already knowing what she's referring to, I counter. "Gracie, you're twenty-four years old. You're a graduate student, and not to mention, a graduate assistant as well. Pretty sure CPS doesn't include you in their protection."

"Whatever. Then this goes against labor laws!" she pouts.

"Waking up early is not a violation of any labor laws in the state of Massachusetts." I check my phone. "Plus, seven thirty isn't early."

"You wouldn't understand. You're a freak! You wake up before the sun. You know, that's a sin." She glares at me jokingly.

I laugh at her, but when she reaches for the creamer, I sigh. "Why do you do this to yourself? You know it's only going to hurt your stomach."

She's lactose intolerant but consumes dairy anyway. Then she always has *stomach issues* and complains to me about it. I'll always support her, but I hate seeing her hurting.

"Maybe my body will decide today's the day it can tolerate lactose," she says sarcastically. "Just let me enjoy my coffee. I have *the freshmen* today."

We met in college and became instant friends. She's the midnight rain to my sunshine. We're a perfect case of opposites attract.

After the four years were done, I graduated and took the first offer I had. Granted, being a tech at a physical therapy practice doesn't require a degree, but there aren't many options for a Kinesiology major who has no interest in any medical field.

I'm a people-person. I can't sit at a desk all day staring at a screen. The only reason I even went to college was to please my parents. They always dreamed of their daughters living out the American dream. I couldn't disappoint them.

But my dream doesn't align with the current American dream. My dream is to be a stay-at-home mom. There's something so beautiful about starting a family. All I want to do is raise my kids in a loving home. But until I find a man who I want to do all that with, I find peace in yoga.

I teach afternoon classes some days. Helping people meditate and center themselves fulfills me. I think the world would be a better place if everyone took a few minutes a day to focus on their zen.

"Ugh. Off to hell I go," she mutters as she flies out of the kitchen.

"Think positive thoughts! You're almost done with the spring semester! Only two more to go from here!" I hear her grunt and slam her door shut.

With that, I let out a laugh and make my way out the front door.

Today's going to be a great day!

I can feel it.

# Chapter 2
## *Cecilia*

After another day at the clinic, I inhale the fresh, outdoor air as the door swings shut behind me. I make my way down the sidewalk, heading toward my apartment.

One of my favorite patients, Mrs. Orla, came in today. She's in her eighties but is still impressively spry. She attends physical therapy to stay active. She walks two miles a day and can even use the stationary bike.

She brings me homemade goodies every week and always wants the gossip about my dating life. Unfortunately, for both her and me, it remains nonexistent.

She frequently pouts about only having granddaughters, or she'd set me up with a grandson. She's even offered to set me up with her granddaughter who prefers women, but I politely declined, not interested in women in that way. If I were, I'd certainly be interested in her granddaughter, if only to be family with Mrs. Orla.

Mrs. Orla helped keep my day bright even after she left and Dr. Sanders got a little too interested. It isn't out of the ordinary, but he was more persistent today. He's a middle aged, *married* man, but sometimes his stare lingers too long and I'm always the tech he asks to assist him with his patients, even when I'm assigned to other therapists. He brushes against me too often and although I try to tell myself it's in my head, he triggers my fight or flight way too often.

But I won't let any of that stop me from having a good day. I'll find a way to save the day.

It's a mental mindset Mamá taught me. When something's dampened the light of my day, I find a way to Save the Day. Whether it's cooking a delicious dinner, hanging out with my friends, or even just a nice cup of tea, I won't go to bed until I've found something to save my day.

Maybe I'll see if Leo is available to give me a massage. Despite my yoga this morning, I already feel knots forming in my neck. He's one of my closest friends, and his hands are pure magic. He took a masseuse course with one of his previous girlfriends, and although they didn't work out, the skill stuck around, and I reap the benefits. He's now my personal masseuse, and although I've offered to pay him countless times, he always refuses, claiming he just enjoys spending time with me.

Gracie swears he's interested in me, but I just don't see it. He's one of my closest friends; I'd never want to cross that line. And I don't see him that way. He's like a brother to me.

I take out my phone, ready to send him a text as I walk down the sidewalk, when a heavy force hits me.

I'm thrown off balance and start to fall.

I try to catch myself, but I hit my head against a metal pole and am sent flying in the opposite direction.

My eyes squeeze shut, prepared to meet the pavement, when I feel the motion stop.

I don't feel the ground hit me.

I don't feel the ground at all.

My eyes crack open, and my breath catches in my throat.

All I see is a chin.

*The sexiest chin I've ever seen.*

What a weird thought.

*A sexy chin.*

The chin drops down, and deep brown orbs meet mine. Confused deep brown orbs meet mine.

And although I lay stable in his arms, for the second time in as many seconds, I feel my world shift.

# Chapter 3
## *Roman*

"The sexiest chin I've ever seen," a melodic voice says. It's breathy and light.

I drop my gaze to the woman who fell into my arms... literally.

And I'm met with caramel eyes. Warm, tan skin. Pink, full lips. An adorable nose. And a mop of wavy, rich brown hair.

She's the most enchanting thing I've ever seen.

"A sexy chin," she mutters.

I stare at her in confusion. What is she saying?

Then I smirk when I realize she's staring at me, at my chin.

This goddess thinks *I* have a sexy chin.

I go to put her down, but she immediately stumbles and starts to fall. I swing her back into my arms and glance up. Indecision reigns through me.

I watch the figure in black walk further away, increasing the distance between us.

I've been following Ivan Sokolov for days, after even more spent tracking him down. If I lose him now, it's going to put me behind schedule. I planned on nabbing him in a few hours.

The girl in my arms moves to follow my gaze, but winces, and grabs the back of her head.

I look down at her and realize she must've hit her head.

One last glance up at his retreating form, indecision wars within me.

A light groan of pain brings my gaze swinging back to her. To this beauty that I'm holding.

I glance at Ivan and curse when he turns a corner, then I look back down at the siren in my arms.

Nothing comes between me and my work. Nobody does. Certainly not a stranger who I have no intentions of interacting with. No matter how enchanting she is.

But she's too tempting to ignore.

I don't know what the hell I'm thinking, but I can't put her down. She's hurt. *She needs me.*

"I want to lick the tattoos on his neck." She sighs, and her eyes flutter closed as a heart-stopping giggle escapes her lips.

Fuck. She probably has a concussion. She can't fall asleep.

"Sunshine, I need you to open your eyes for me," I say in a gentle tone I didn't even know I was capable of. It just came out naturally for her.

Slowly, her lids flutter, and her face scrunches in concentration as she pries them open.

"Yes, sir," she whispers, and my body reacts immediately.

My cock springs to life as my blood boils. I grind my teeth.

This is not the right time. I don't get off on concussed women. She probably doesn't even know what she's saying.

*But I bet she doesn't go around saying 'yes, sir' to every man she sees. Or telling him she wants to lick his tattoos.*

Then her eyes glance at my neck and the ink peaking from the collar of my shirt, and she licks her lips.

*Fuck.*

Why is she doing this to me?

When her eyes start to droop again, I give her a slight jostle.

"What's your name?" I ask, trying to keep her talking to stay awake.

"Cecilia María Álvarez Rivera." She thrusts her hand in my face, as if to shake for introduction. I adjust my hold on her to one arm, which is quite easy with how light she is, and I shake her hand with my now free one. Tingles shoot up my arms at the contact, and she sighs again. "You can call me Celia."

"Is that what your friends call you?" I ask, trying to keep the conversation going as I turn into an alley, not wanting to cause a scene. Holding an incoherent woman in the middle of the sidewalk may raise suspicion. Not that I've done anything wrong.

Some man knocked into her, and she landed in my arms. I didn't even mean to catch her, but instinct kicked in.

"Nope." She pops the 'p', smacking those luscious lips. "No one's ever called me that. Mi mamá calls me Cecisita. And the rest of my family calls me Ceci María. My friends just call me Cecilia. But Celia... no one calls me Celia." She gasps in excitement. "No, that's not true anymore. You, my sexy héroe, can call me Celia. It'll be your name for me. Just for you."

*Just for you.*

An unfamiliar warmth takes over my chest and spreads throughout my body.

"Hey, hero, what's your name?" She sings it out, and I'm once again mesmerized.

"Roman Montclair," I respond mindlessly. Only to falter when I realize my mistake. I never give my name to strangers. There's little more powerful than knowing someone's identity.

But I'm not too worried about my sunshine. I doubt she's familiar with Syndicate affairs. Unless this Latina goddess is associated with one of the small cartels. I glance down again, but there's no recognition in her features.

"Roman Montclair." She tries it. "Hmm. It's not bad. A strong name for a strong man. But I think I'll stick with héroe. Because you saved me."

I try not to laugh at the irony of the situation. She fell into my arms while I was tailing a man to torture. I didn't even consciously catch her. And now she's calling me her hero.

I've never been someone's hero.

I've never been a hero.

I'm the villain. For the good side. But nevertheless, I'm the monster that lurks in the shadows. The one the other monsters fear.

And now, this goddess is proclaiming I'm her hero.

And for some reason, I want to be. I don't want to correct her. I don't want to prove her wrong and reveal who I really am. For just this one moment, I want to be someone's hero.

No, not someone's.

Her's.

I want to be *her* hero.

"Okay, Celia. Let's get you home. Do you live with anyone that can take care of you?" I ask, gritting my teeth at the thought of a man waiting at home for her. There isn't a ring on her finger, so at least she's not married. But I'm not sure even that would stop me.

*Stop me from what? She's just some girl I'm bringing home and never seeing again.*

"Yes. My Gracie. She's the best. My little Oscar the Grouch. She should be back from school soon. My little Spacey Gracie. She doesn't like when I call her that." Then Celia winks at me, as if letting me in on the inside joke.

*I'm just bringing her home. Then leaving her forever.*

I chant it to myself.

"What's your address, sunshine?"

She rattles it off, and I head in that direction. It's only a mile and a half away, and I can keep to side streets and alleys to avoid judgmental eyes.

"Héroe, you can't carry me that far! It's a hop and a skip away. You'll get tired. I don't want my hero tired."

I scoff, offended. "Sunshine, I could carry you all day and never get tired. You barely weigh anything."

She eyes me skeptically, then brings her hand to my neck. She traces the top of my tattoos lightly, and I hold back a groan. Her touch is so soft, but it sears into me as if it were a flame.

She trails her fingers to the back of my neck and runs her whole hand up through my buzzed hair. She plays with the short spikes with the tips of her delicate fingers.

I keep it short out of convenience, but I wonder if she'd rather it longer, so she had more length to run through.

"I like the prickle."

I smirk.

Of course, my girl likes my hair how I do.

She's perfect.

# Chapter 4
## *Cecilia*

As he said, he had no problem carrying me home. We've reached my apartment complex, and he huffs a breath as he opens the front door and makes his way into the lobby. I swear I hear him mutter something about *'no lock'* then *'safety hazard'* when he bypasses the elevator.

My complex may not be the fanciest, but it gets the job done. It's not in a terrible neighborhood either, so I'm not too worried about the lack of a lock on the front door.

"I'm on the fifth floor. You might want to take the elevator," I explain, and it comes out willowy.

"Sunshine, we're not getting in that death trap. It looks a ride away from collapsing," he says with an eye roll as he takes the stairs two at a time. "And, again, I have no issue carrying you."

*My hero's so strong.*

He grins.

"Here we are!" I squeal, then flinch at the noise. There's a drumline in my head marching and pounding.

I fish in my purse for my keys but drop them before I can slide the key into the deadbolt. Roman squats, grabs the keys, and unlocks the door, all while balancing me in one arm.

He walks in and takes a moment to look around. I study his features, wanting him to love my place. It's tiny, but it's ours. Gracie and I spent a lot of time thrifting and at estate sales collecting décor and furniture.

He nods with what I hope is approval then lays me on the couch. He crouches next to me and just stares for a few seconds. A look of what I can only describe as awe crosses his face.

"I need to check you out," he says worriedly. *You can check me out any day.* He chuckles. "While that may be the case, now's not the time. I'm going to check you for a concussion. Okay, sunshine?"

"Thank you, héroe." I shoot him my biggest grin, and he smiles back.

He gently pries my left eye open and shines his phone's flashlight in it. I flinch back, but he holds my head. *What a strong grip.* He moves on to my left eye and hums in approval.

"Sunshine, follow my finger." It's the only instruction he gives before slowly moving his finger side to side. "No, no. Just with your eyes." I keep my head still and do as he says.

"Whoa," I groan and squeeze my eyes shut.

"What's wrong, Cecilia?" His voice comes out rushed, almost frantic.

"Dizzy. So, dizzy," I mumble.

He hums in disappointment this time. "Okay, you can keep your eyes shut. I want you to touch your nose with your index finger, alternating hands."

I do as he says, but even I can tell how slowly I'm moving.

"Good girl," he murmurs, and I can't stop myself from reddening. "Now, I'm going to give you three words, I want you to remember them."

I nod then wince, opening my eyes.

"Sunshine. Smiles. Spanish." He stares into my eyes as he says them, and I can feel the electricity shift between us.

"Español. Sunshine. Smiles," I repeat with a grin.

"Not yet, sunshine. I'm going to ask you a few questions first. What's your name?"

"Cecilia María Álvarez Rivera. I already told you that." *I hope he doesn't have memory issues.*

He grins and continues. "Good job, Celia. What day of the week is it?"

"It's Wednesday. It's a great day."

"Why is it a great day?" He seems genuinely interested.

"Well, every day can be a great day. Dr. Sanders tried to make it a not great day, but you saved the day. Literally, my hero. But also, you saved my day!" I remind him. He raises a brow in question. "Mamá used to preach Save Your Day. If something upsets you or threatens a great day, find something to save the day. That's you! You saved my day!"

His smile loses its cockiness and transforms into something soft. "I'm glad I could help." He coughs. "Now, where are we?"

"In my apartment in Boston," I answer proudly.

"Good. And who is your emergency contact?" He has a gleam in his eyes when he asks it. It's a standard question to ask if someone is concussed and needs help, but the way he phrases it... It doesn't feel so innocent.

"Gracie. She's my bestie roomie. She should be home soon. Or Mamá if it's serious." I respond timidly, hoping he approves of the answer. I'm not sure why I crave his approval, but I do.

"Hmmm. Not your boyfriend?" he questions not so innocently.

"No boyfriend. I haven't had much luck dating, but that's okay. The universe will send me someone when the time is right." I fully believe it.

"Good girl," he praises darkly, his voice taking on a husky tone. "Do you remember your words? The ones I gave you?"

"¡Español y sonrisas!" I'm proud of myself for remembering.

"In English, por favor, sunshine. It's been a decade and a half since high school Spanish."

I try to do the mental math. I am twenty-four years old. I graduated high school at eighteen. High school was six years ago for me. High school was fifteen years ago for him. He's how much older than me? I can't figure it out. It's been... however many years since high school since my last math class.

"Sunshine, in English please," he lightly reminds me. It's such a sweet tone coming from the gentle giant.

"Spanish and smiles! Those were my words!"

"...And?" he encourages me.

I tilt my head in confusion. "Spanish and smiles. Those were the words you gave me, right?"

"There was also 'sunshine.'" When my smile starts to fade, he quickly consoles me. "It's okay, Celia. You're doing great. I think you have a minor concussion. I'd recommend staying off your electronics for the next couple days and resting your eyes. Your brain has a little bruise."

"Héroe, are you a doctor?" He's taking such good care of me, a complete stranger, that I could see this caring man being a doctor. Saving lives. Helping people heal. Doing good for the world.

"No, sunshine. I work in... security. My brothers and I run Syndicate Enterprise."

"Ah, so you still save people. Keep people safe. You really are a hero." I'm mesmerized.

"Only for you," he murmurs. "Okay, when is Gracie getting here? I don't want to leave you alone, but I have somewhere I need to be."

I grab my phone, intending to check her location, but the brightness blinds me. I quickly switch it off and thrust it in his direction.

"Here, you check my tracking app. I have her location. I like to watch over her, make sure she's safe. And I like to know what she's up to," I explain.

He grabs my phone, ready to check, but turns to me. "What's your password?"

"012345," I murmur, covering my eyes with my arm, unable to stand the brightness.

He huffs dramatically. "That's not a good password."

"No one will try to go into my phone. I only have a password because Gracie scolded me into it," I yield.

"It looks like she's turning the corner onto the street. She'll be here in the next five minutes." His grin falters then his gaze turns to steel. "Who's Leo? And why does he have your location?" he grits out.

"Oh, that's just Leo. He's my friend. He's like a brother to me." His shoulders drop slightly, but he stays tense.

He does something else on my phone, then powers it off and places it next to me, face down.

"I added my contact to your phone. Call me if you need anything." I feel his sincerity in his intense gaze.

"Thank you." I hesitate before asking, "What'd you put it in under? You know, in case I need to call you." I redden at the embarrassment of not knowing his name.

His expression falters for a moment. "It's under 'Héroe.' But did you forget my name?"

"I don't remember you giving me your name. I don't think you did. I'm great with names. And even if I weren't, there's no way I could forget *your* name."

"It's okay, sunshine. I'm Roman. And it's been a pleasure meeting you. You have my number now. Use it."

He stands, and I realize he's been crouching this entire time. *I bet he has thighs like tree trunks.*

He barks out a laugh, covers me with a blanket, then leaves me alone with my thoughts.

*Boy, did he save my day.*

# Chapter 5
## *Roman*

What the hell am I doing?

I don't stop to help strangers. And I definitely don't give my name and number to strangers. And I sure as fuck don't abandon a capture mission of a Bratva member I've been tailing for a week for a stranger.

*But, for her?*

*For her, I think I'd do just about anything.*

I don't know why. It's ridiculous. She's a stranger!

A gorgeous, sexy, goddess of a stranger. But a stranger, nonetheless. I was stupid today, bailing on Ivan, and for what? A beautiful woman?

Beautiful women are a dime a dozen. I've been with plenty of beautiful women. My phone is full of beautiful women who want me. Who aren't concussed.

But she's different. She's pure and warm and kind. Just being around her lightened my soul. She felt like absolution for my heinous sins. Her goodness is infectious.

I didn't want to leave her, but I couldn't be there when the roommate arrived. I'd done enough stupid things today; I didn't need to expose myself to anyone else.

At least, not before I've done my research.

Which I will be doing. I may not be as skilled with a computer as Bash, but I have my ways. With what I do, I have to be good at investigating people.

I'm not leaving Celia alone.

She calls me her hero. I wouldn't be doing a good job of being her hero if I abandoned her.

I don't think I could even if I wanted to.

# Chapter 6
## *Cecilia*

I hear the front door open, and my heart skips a beat, hoping it's *him.*

But instead, Gracie walks in.

"Dude, you know you left the door unlocked? What a day I've had. Just wait-" She freezes when she sees me lying on the couch in the dark. "What are you doing? You never nap. Oh no! Are you sick?" She rushes over to check on me.

"No, not sick. Minorly concussed," I mumble.

"Oh my God! What happened?" she shrieks. I flinch, and she quiets instantly. "Sorry," she whispers.

"A man ran into me then during the fall, I knocked my head into a metal street sign pole. I ended up falling into another man's arms, and he helped me home."

"Hmm. I bet he was just trying to get into your pants," she speculates.

"Okay, Grouchy Gracie. He was a nice guy. I think he just likes helping people," I defend Roman.

"Sure," she says sarcastically with an eye roll. "Okay, what do we need to do? Do I need to get you anything from the store? I'm going to look it up."

She starts searching through her phone, I assume researching minor concussions.

"He said I need to stay away from screens for a bit. I'll call in sick for tomorrow and Friday. I also shouldn't move much."

"Is he a doctor?" she questions.

"No," I mumble.

"Yeah, in that case, no, I'm not just going to listen blindly to him. I'm going to do my own research," she huffs then plants herself on a chair.

After about fifteen minutes of searching through her phone, she finally looks up at me.

"I'm also not going to just accept that you have a concussion. We're going to run some tests. Follow my finger," she orders.

"He already did the tests on me," I try to explain, even knowing it's fruitless. She's more stubborn than a mule.

"I don't care. I don't trust some stranger off the street. Now, follow my finger."

I do as she says, and she nods in approval. We work our way through more tests including some I already did.

It takes about fifteen more minutes of repeated test for her to draw the same conclusion. "Yep, you have a minor concussion."

"Thank you, Gracie," I say teasingly. "Might I also add, out of the three of us, I'm the only one with medical experience. And I can also deduce that I have a minor concussion."

"The three of us? The three of us!" She huffs in exasperation. "There is no *three* of us! There's *two* of us. Only the two of us. Some slimy creep off the streets isn't one of us.

God, I can't believe some stranger knows where we live. What if he comes back and tries to attack us?"

"It's fine. I doubt I'll ever see him again. Boston's a big city." I try to keep the disappointment out of my voice. I know he gave me his number, but I won't bother him. I've already burdened him enough.

Gracie breaks me from my pity party. "Okay, you need to rest physically. No yoga for a couple days. The change in head position won't do you well. No screens. Drink lots of water. And eat healthily." She pauses then shoots up. "Wait, do we have any of your Columbian soup? It's so good."

Caldo de Pollo is a classic Colombian soup. It's a comfort meal and extremely nourishing. Abuela used to make it when we were sick, and she taught me how to cook it as a young girl.

Papá is Colombian. His mom, my Abuela, lives with my parents, so she taught me a lot of Columbian traditions growing up, including how to cook many traditional dishes.

Mamá is Ecuadorian. She raised me to live slowly and prioritize inner peace, gratitude, and patience. We used to wake up early to do yoga together in the mornings. She gardens and grows her own herbs. One day when I have a home, I want a garden just like hers.

It was important to my parents to carry on their cultures and traditions through my sisters and me. I'm grateful they kept me in touch with my roots, and I love sharing my culture with my friends. And they, especially Gracie, love to eat it.

"Yes, we have a few quarts of caldo de pollo in the freezer. We can put one in the sink in some water, so it'll defrost in time for dinner, and we can warm it on the stove. We have avocados to serve in it, but we'll need to make some rice." I start to stand up to do just that but wince.

"Sit down! I've got it," she scolds me and heads to the freezer.

For the rest of the day, she pampers me.

All the while, a certain gentle giant with buzzed hair and sharp features consumes my mind.

# Chapter 7
## *Roman*

With a last swipe of lemon on my hands, the rest of the blood disappears.

I finally got some *alone time* with Ivan, and it proved pretty useless. He confirmed what we already knew.

They have a new product. It arrives in the docks every other Saturday. They disperse it at their clubs. They're making a lot of money off it. It's coming from the motherland. Something pure. Something we can't compete with.

I'm starting to think it's something we don't *want* to compete with.

A grunt from Ivan draws my attention to him.

He's bloodied and bruised, hanging by his arms from the ceiling. His new *RFM* carving is about an inch tall, revealing he was a mid-level catch. Important, but not enough to get me in trouble. The tattoo isn't bigger because he was cooperative. Which is rare for an older Russian bastard.

"One of my men will release you when they're free," I throw over my shoulder as I leave the warehouse.

I make a pitstop at the shower installed in my office in this warehouse. I have several offices throughout the city, since I have many areas around town I frequent, and walking around dripping in others' blood is generally frowned upon.

I rinse off quickly and change into one of the extra outfits I keep here. My usual black t-shirt, black tailored tactical pants, and black boots.

I wear black because it hides blood, and also because color doesn't support the menacing reputation I maintain. And I have to wear something active enough that I can chase someone down or interrogate in, but it has to be mainstream enough I can camouflage in a crowd.

I'm not sure how well I fit in though. With my buzz cut, tattoos, and muscular six-foot five-inch build, I don't think even Matthias's tailored suits would make me look anything less than terrifying.

*You know who wasn't terrified of me? Cecilia.*

Well, she was concussed, so that probably affected her judgement.

No time for thoughts of her though. I have things to do. I need to catch Dom up on what Ivan told me.

...

Despite my better judgement, I stare at the old, decrepit building with no functioning locks.

I had no intention of making a pit stop here. But I also can't even lie to myself and say it was on the way. The detour was miles long.

But I couldn't help myself.

I make my way inside, scowling at how the front door opens so easily to a dangerous man. None of my stealthy break in skills are even needed. She shouldn't be here. It isn't safe.

I stalk past the elevator that seems to be on its last leg. I don't trust it to lift my two-hundred-and-sixty-pound frame without snapping.

I take the stairs three at a time, too eager to slow down.

I stand in front of a familiar red door. A door I've only seen once before.

I could turn around.

I should turn around.

This goddess doesn't need my darkness adulterating her light. She's safer away from me. *That's a damn lie. I can keep her safe.* She's happier without me. *Maybe she needs her hero.* I don't need the distraction. *She could be so much more than a distraction.*

It'd be smart for all parties involved for me to turn around, exit the building, and never look back.

I could never give her a white picket fence life, and she could destroy everything I've built.

I know nothing about her.

I need to leave.

So, I knock on her door.

# Chapter 8
## *Cecilia*

There's a knock at the front door. I rise from the couch, but Gracie beats me to it.

"Sit your ass down. You're still healing," she grumbles at me. Under all her grouchiness, is sisterly love, and that's why she bosses me around. "Do you have anyone coming over? Ugh, please tell me it's not *Leo*." She fakes a gag at his name.

She's not a fan of my guy friend. She never has been.

"The concussion was two days ago, I'm pretty much healed. But thank you for grabbing the door. And no, I have no idea who it could be. I haven't even told Leo about the concussion. I didn't want to worry him. He's a sweet guy. I don't know why you dislike him so much."

"I don't *dislike* him. I *hate* him. I don't trust the weasel." She swings the door open, then her jaw drops. I can't see past the door as to who it is, but she eyes whoever it is up and down and raises a brow. "*Definitely not Leo,*" she practically purrs it. "How can I help you?"

I'm taken aback by her tone. I've heard her answer our door, her phone, and many others with a rude, 'What do you want?' more times than I can count. Why is she being nice?

"I'm here to see Cecilia. Is she available?" the sexiest voice carries into the room.

I instantly straighten. My body reacts instinctively. Goose bumps spread across my skin.

*Roman.*

*He's here.*

"She may be. Who are you? What do you want?" Gracie's flirty demeanor shifts to a protective one. She's not about to let in any man who she doesn't know. Especially not if he could be after me. Gracie is nothing if not paranoid and pessimistic.

"Gracie, please let him in," I plead, not wanting her to make him suffer. He's already such a selfless, kindhearted man. He helped me, a stranger, for no reason except for it being the right thing to do. And now he's back to check on me.

"Who is he?" she addresses me but never turns from Roman. She glares at him, as if trying to uncover his ill intentions.

"He's the one who brought me home and took care of me after the concussion," I confess.

Her head snaps to me, and she raises a brow. "It seems you left out a few *crucial* details. I expect a full, honest retelling soon." She checks him up and down one final time with an eyebrow arched, then steps aside. "Welcome," she says dryly.

Instead of going to her bedroom to give us some privacy, she sits on a stool at the island and faces the living room.

Roman walks in and his eyes immediately find mine. A warm smile breaks out on his face, bringing one to mine.

I start to stand, ready to greet him properly, but he rushes to my side and gently pushes me back on the couch.

"Don't get up on my account. You're still healing, sunshine."

I nod at him and try to force my skin not to redden at the nickname. I try and fail.

I look him over. His buzzed hair calls to me. I still feel the phantom prickle on my fingers. His tattoos peak up his neck from his shirt neckline and down his arms. I want to trace them with my tongue. It darts out and licks my lips instead. I didn't realize just how big he is. He'll tower over my five-foot seven-inch frame. I clench involuntarily at the realization. I didn't realize big, muscular men were my type, but Roman is definitely doing something to me.

"Hey, Celia." It comes out low and gravelly. My eyes shoot up, and up, and up, to meet his, and I find them dark.

The energy between us is palpable. I can feel the electricity.

"It's Cecilia," Gracie corrects from the kitchen, snapping us out of the moment. I turn to see her eating a banana, watching us. She's not even trying to hide it. She's not on her phone or anything.

He takes that as his cue to sit in one of the armchairs. He takes the whole thing up. I'm not surprised when I hear it creak under his weight.

"I know her name. Cecilia María Álvarez Rivera." I giggle as he butchers the pronunciation. He doesn't tear his eyes from mine as he answers her. And suddenly, the room feels hot again.

"I guess high school Spanish didn't help with pronunciation," I tease him. When his face drops a little, I quickly lift him up. I'll never be the one to tear someone down. "It's okay. I'm surprised you remember."

His grin is immediate. "I remember our whole interaction. Every second of it. However, *I'm* surprised *you* remember. With your concussion, I was afraid you forgot me."

"How could I forget my hero? Is that why you came back? To reintroduce yourself?" I ask teasingly.

He brightens at the nickname.

I couldn't help myself. It's too fitting for him. He saved me. He is my hero.

"Well, my phone never rang with a call from my sunshine. I had to come by and make sure you were okay."

"I haven't been on my phone. You're supposed to avoid screens after a concussion," I explain to him.

"So, you haven't been on any screens? You've been taking care of yourself?"

"Yes. I've been just lying on the couch the past few days in total darkness. Abiding by Dr. Roman's orders. I've taken up podcasts." I wink at him.

"Good girl." Shivers shoot down my spine. "How are you feeling?"

"I'm great. I've been healing rather nicely. I think by tomorrow I'll be back to normal."

"Great! What podcasts are you listening to?" His interest surprises me. Not many men actually care about that sort of thing.

"I've been listening to a few. I've rotated between ones about yoga, meditation, gardening, and cooking." I love my passions any way I can get them. Since I can't physically do them at the moment, I at least wanted to listen and see if there was anything I could learn.

"Any good ones you'd recommend to me?"

"Do you do yoga? Or meditate? Those are my favorites!" I get excited at the idea I can share this with him.

"I've never done either, but I'd be willing to try. What about the other ones?"

"Those two are in Spanish. I'd probably need to translate them for you if you wanted to listen to them," I offer, not wanting him to feel bad about not speaking my language.

"That's okay, sunshine. But I wouldn't mind learning from you? If that's something you'd be open to?" He seems almost apprehensive.

"I'd love to teach you! What do you want to learn? Yoga? Meditation? Cooking? Gardening? Spanish?" I'd do anything with him, just to be around him. I can't explain the pull I have towards this gentle giant.

"Anything you'd like. You seem so passionate about it all."

"It's a date!" I say, returning his grin with one of my own. My excitement has me practically jumping off the couch.

Before I realize what I've said, that I've demanded a date from him, he agrees. "Perfect. When you feel better, text me, and we'll set it up."

I blush at my forwardness. I didn't mean to be, but it seemed to work out.

"We can start now if you'd like? I can show you some basic yoga poses," I offer, excited to be around him.

"No, you don't!" shouts Gracie from the island. "No yoga for you until you're completely healed."

She effectively crushes my dream while also reminding me of her presence.

"You heard the boss, no yoga today. I need to leave anyway. I have something I need to do for work. I just wanted to stop by and check on you."

I can't help the rush of disappointment I feel at his words. "Oh, okay. I really appreciate you stopping by. And for helping me the other day. I'm not sure I would've made it home without you, héroe."

My eyes start to droop, the remnant exhaustion from the concussion catching up to me after our interaction. I can't hold back my yawn either.

"Anytime, sunshine." He makes his way over to me and brushes my hair out of my face. He leans down, as if to hug me, and I get a waft of him.

"Mmm. You smell like lemons," I tell him.

He tenses and a dark gleam takes over his eyes, but it's gone in a blink. "It's the soap at work. I had an eventful morning." He looks me over again and smiles sweetly. "Lie down, Celia. It's time for a nap."

"Yes, sir," I say with a wink.

He mutters something under his breath and stares at the ceiling for the five seconds it takes for me to get situated. He then covers me with my blanket and just stares.

"Call me when you're better. We have a yoga date to go on." He grins, then heads out.

He says something I don't catch to Gracie, and she leads him out.

I pretend to fall asleep, so I don't have to answer her questions.

I want to bask in what just occurred.

# Chapter 9
## *Roman*

I walk down the hallway of Cecilia's apartment and scold myself.

I shouldn't have come here. I shouldn't be near her.

She smelled the lemon.

There's no way for her to know what that means. To know the reason I use lemons. What the smell hides.

But it's too close.

I need to let her go.

*Or I could just hide it from her. She thinks the lemons are from work. Which they are. I didn't technically lie.*

Maybe I can make this work. Maybe she doesn't need to know every detail of my life. At least, not yet.

Men and women lie to each other all the time. I'm sure she has her secrets.

The only difference between us is I'm going to find them all.

# Chapter 10
## *Cecilia*

I feel myself waking up from my nap. I peek my eyes open to see if Gracie is still in the living room.

She is.

Sitting across from me. On one of the armchairs.

I quickly squeeze my eyes back shut and focus on taking slow, even breaths. Pretending to be asleep gives me a little more time to figure out what to tell her.

"Dude, I know you're awake. Talk to me. What the hell was that? You forgot to mention he's sexy as fuck, you little shit," Gracie grumbles at me.

Something hits my head and falls to the floor with a thud. A pillow rests on the ground.

"Okay, fine. So, maybe I left out a few details," I concede as I sit up.

"Like every interesting detail! Here I am, concerned that some creep is going to show up and take you in the middle of the night, but a terrifyingly sinful, sexy God of Darkness comes instead!"

"Terrifyingly sinful, sexy God of Darkness? No part of Roman is terrifying, sinful, or dark!" I counter, not standing for Roman slander.

"Babe, were you looking at the same man as I was? The buzz cut, tatted, gigantic, sexy man straight from a delectable nightmare? The man dripping in sin? For fucks sake, he was wearing all black!" She's exasperated.

"He does not look like he's from a nightmare! He's sweet as can be. A gentle giant!" I try to convince her. There's nothing evil about my hero.

"Cecilia, are you being serious right now? That man could be downright terrifying if he wanted to be. I'd never want to get on his bad side. That doesn't mean he's not hot as hell. But 'gentle giant?' Come on, that's ridiculous."

I really don't see it. All he's been is kind and caring to me. I'm not scared of Roman at all.

"And don't think I didn't notice you *not* deny him being sexy as fuck," she says with a grin.

"I guess if tall, dark, and giant does it for you, then yes, he's handsome."

"Shut up! You practically swallowed your tongue when he came in. Now, spill! What all happened? I want every last detail!" she demands.

So, I do. I recount every part to her, and when I'm done, I let her sit in silence, soaking it in.

"Okay, babe. He's so into you. He stopped his day to *carry you home.* Took care of you. Gave you his number. And stopped by to check on you. You lucky bitch."

"Oh, stop. He would've done it for anyone. He's just a good Samaritan. It wasn't about me," I add, but secretly hope maybe I got a special treatment. Maybe he is interested in me a little.

"I seriously doubt that. And based on what I saw, he's definitely interested in you. You have to go on that date with him."

"I'll think about it," I mumble.

I haven't been on a date in so long. I find it hard to put myself out there. And finding someone who matches me hasn't been easy.

"Cecilia, what is there to think about? The sexy god wants to go out with you. He wants you to teach him *yoga* for fucks sake!" She says *yoga* as if it's absurd.

"What's wrong with yoga? Maybe he genuinely wants to learn. It's a great way to center your life and find inner peace," I say, somewhat offended. I love yoga. I know it's not her thing, but it means so much to me.

"I know. It's great for you. But do you seriously think a man that looks like him wants to be around a woman that looks like you just to learn yoga?" I huff and she continues. "That man wants to be doing so much more than yoga with you. Look at you! Yoga is not the only thing on his mind. He wants to do a different kind of exercise with you."

I blush at the innuendo and smile unconsciously.

"HA! See, I knew you're into him!" She points at my face as she says it.

"Fine. Yes, I'm interested in him. Not only does he look handsome, but he also has a heart of gold. How could I not be into him?"

"This is so exciting! I'm so happy for you!"

"I can't believe you're not more skeptical of him."

"Oh, I don't trust him at all. But it's good to see you happy. You lit up talking to him. I think he could be good for you. I haven't seen you look at a guy like that since... ever."

"I know. He's different." I smile, then scowl. "I can't believe you stayed the entire time!"

"I wasn't about to let him into our apartment to murder you." She huffs. "Plus, I was curious. I couldn't let a man looking like him in without knowing the full story."

"Fine. You really think he likes me?" I can't help the hope in my voice.

I've never had this kind of connection with a man before.

And I don't want to lose it.

# Chapter 11
## *Roman*

I'm leaning against the wall across from a worn-down apartment complex. This shitty place needs to be condemned.

I straighten when my target exits the front door.

Long, sexy legs covered in scrubs take a left, and I follow.

I'm disappointed to see her long, brown waves in a tight bun, but she's still gorgeous. She could shave her head and still be irresistible.

As Cecilia glides her way through the crowd gracefully, she's oblivious to the man following her. Decades of stalking my prey has made me invisible to her. She's far too trusting and unaware for how alluring she is. It could be a monster with horrible intentions following her instead of a monster with good intentions.

*But I'll never allow anyone to get their hands on her.*

I follow her as she takes her turns. After about a mile and a half, she ends up in front of a physical therapy clinic. She enters, and I stare through the window. She goes through a door that leads to the area where they handle patients.

I look up the clinic and see their hours end at five thirty p.m. Good, she'll be here a while. I'll come back at four p.m. in case she gets off early.

I retrace my steps and end up back at the decrepit apartment. I walk through the lockless front door and up the steps. When I get to their unit, I stand outside the door for three minutes, listening for noise. When I don't hear any, I knock and step aside out of view of the peep hole. After another three minutes, I decide Gracie isn't home either. I take out my tools and work the lock. It takes less than thirty seconds to get the door open, and I slip inside.

There are two bedrooms, and I enter the one furthest from the front door first. I can instantly tell it's Gracie's. The black comforter was the only clue I needed. I quickly go through her things, taking inventory of what she has.

I peek inside her nightstand and am pleasantly surprised to see a pistol. I doubt Cecilia knows about it, but it comforts me that she has someone protecting her.

There are textbooks on her dresser and a schedule written on a calendar. She's a grad student and a grad assistant. She has back-to-back classes today and won't be back for a few hours. *Perfect.*

Once I have a general idea of who Gracie is, I make my way into the other bedroom. Cecilia's bedroom.

The olive-green comforter compliments the multicolored rug under her bed. She has meditation posters and calming paintings on her wall. Unlike Gracie, her bed is made. She has seven pillows, which take up the top half of the bed. I pick one up and sniff it. I don't stifle my groan at the scent. Her smell is intoxicating.

I go through her closet and see most of her clothes are floor-length flowy skirts and dresses, lightweight linen pants, and those shirts that connect to pants like overalls. I go through her dresser and see a lot of athletic outfits.

I land on her panty drawer. She has a mix of them, but my eyes drag to a yellow lacey thong. I pick it up and inspect it. It looks well used. She's clearly worn it many times. I debate for a minute before pocketing it. I refuse to analyze my action, but I know I'll be using it later.

She has a yoga mat curled next to her dresser, and I sneer at it. I can't believe I asked her to teach me yoga. If my brothers knew about that shit, they'd never let me live it down. If my men found out, they'd lose all respect for me. And if my enemies found out, it'd tarnish the ruthless reputation I've spent so long cultivating.

But for her, I'd do anything. I'd even learn yoga.

I see a folder on her dresser and open it up. The gasp of horror I let out is justified. All her important documents are out in the open. Her birth certificate, social security card, passport... They're all just laying on a folder in her dresser. *I need to get her a safe. Or better yet, she can just use mine.*

I check her passport and see she visited Colombia and Ecuador a few years back. Maybe she has relatives there. She does speak Spanish and has a Spanish name.

After putting everything back exactly how I found it in its nonsecure location, I explore the bathroom.

They share it, but it's obvious whose side is whose. Gracie's is a mess of hair products, face products, and dark makeup. Cecilia's a neat row of hippie headbands, organic face products, and light makeup. There's also perfume.

I spray it and groan. It's her scent. It smells floral and sweet. I check the label, but it's in Spanish. I don't know what 'ylang-ylang con notas de vainilla y ámbar' is, but I'm already making a mental note to stock up on this, so she doesn't ever run out.

I picture her, fresh out of the shower, spraying her naked body with this scent and harden impossibly.

Without giving myself time to be reasonable, I unbuckle my belt, unzip my pants, push down my boxer briefs, and free my cock.

My pants crinkle when I lower them, and I remember the treat in my pocket. I fish out her sweet, yellow panties and spray them with the perfume. I bring them up to my nose and inhale the intoxicating scent of her perfume and her pussy.

With one hand, I hold them to my nose and with the other, I stroke my aching cock.

All I can picture is what she does in this bathroom. She undresses, then showers naked. She proceeds to dry off. Wet hair cascading around her waist. Water droplets dripping down her tits.

After a few strokes, I'm weak in the knees. I bite down on the panties and use that hand to grip the counter. I swipe my tongue on the lace and wrinkle my nose. The chemical taste of perfume is nothing like the sweet scent, and I grab them with the hand that was working my cock.

I wrap them around my length. The rough material adds a prick of pain that only amplifies my pleasure.

I only last three more passes before I'm coming in her sink. The orgasm rips through me. I'm blinded by my release, white dots clouding my vision.

Once I'm able to see again, I notice the cum on her panties. *That won't do.*

I wash them in the sink but use the body wash in the shower. It smells so similar to the perfume and so much like her. Then I spray it twice with the perfume, just to help her scent last. If I want to keep them smelling like her, I'll have to be more careful not to get my release on them.

I fix my clothes and exit the bathroom. I walk back into her living room and note that all her furniture seems worn out. There's no way these two girls could make such dents in the couch in only a few years. They simply don't weigh enough. The furniture must be secondhand.

My nose wrinkles at the thought. She deserves so much better than someone's trash. The amount of germs that are probably on the couch and chairs makes my stomach turn.

I deal with blood and gore on a daily basis, but I don't roll around in other's filth.

I open her fridge and note that it's practically empty except some fruits and vegetables. I frown at the realization that she may not be feeding herself enough. Then I almost choke at the realization that there isn't any meat in the fridge.

*What if she's a vegetarian?*

I don't know if I can be with a woman who doesn't eat meat. Most of my diet is red meat.

*Even if it's Cecilia?*

Fuck, for her I might make an exception.

What if she can't be around someone who eats meat?

I'll just have to hide it from her when I do. That's how this will work. What she doesn't know won't kill her.

I see a stack of open mail on her counter. Bills. I pull them out and note the amounts. No fucking way is she paying over three grand for this shithole. That is unacceptable.

A call from Dom interrupts my thoughts.

"Hey, man. What's up?" I ask, eyeing her pantry.

There's not much in here either. I need to get her fed. She's thin and willowy, but not in a way that suggests she starves herself. But I'm going to keep an eye on it just in case. She needs to take care of herself.

I spot a few tea mixes that look homemade and wince. I don't drink the leaf brew. Coffee is my drug of choice.

"Roman! Are you even listening?" Dom grumbles.

"Sorry. I got distracted. What's up?" I give in.

"What are you doing?" he asks skeptically.

"Don't worry about it. I'm listening." No way in hell am I telling him I broke into a woman's apartment and am snooping around. And not just any woman. A woman who I quit a tailing and am currently ditching my duties for.

"Just wanted to give you a heads up that Viktor wants you to lay off his men." Viktor, the Pakhan of the Bratva, wants *me* to lay off *his* men. Fat fucking chance.

"No," I grunt.

"Roman, we're at peace with them. After the Margot situation, we're already on rocky grounds. We need to keep the alliance," he commands.

"I only go after the ones in our territory," I complain.

"Be more lenient. And don't kill any more. That's an order." With that, he hangs up.

I finish snooping and check my watch. I have a few hours before I need to get back to Cecilia-watching.

I want to learn everything I can about her.

And she'll be none the wiser.

# Chapter 12
## *Cecilia*

I walk out of the clinic with a smile on my face. Not only was Dr. Sanders not in today, but also, I teach my six p.m. class.

It's a beginner's session, but that doesn't matter. I love teaching yoga no matter who the student is. And I love when someone tries something new, especially if it's good for them. I'll always support that.

I feel eyes on me as I walk to the studio and glance around, but no one's watching me. After a few more minutes, I look over my shoulder again. There still isn't anyone looking at me. I'm acting crazy. I really need the class today to calm myself.

I reach the studio, but chance one more glance behind me. There's still no one.

I take a few calming breaths and focus on my mantra of the day. *'Be open to new beginnings, and trust in yourself.'*

With that, I open the door and head inside.

I wave at Courtney, the receptionist. She's a tall blonde always sporting a smile. When she sees me, she comes around the desk and greets me with a hug.

"How was your day, Cecilia?" Her tone shows genuine interest.

"It's been a great day. One of my favorite patients came to the clinic, and now I get to teach this class," I respond with a smile.

"We're so lucky to have you here. The attendees always praise your sessions."

"Thank you, Courtney. I'm always glad to be here." It's the truth. I feel lighter every time I enter the studio. "I need to get ready, but it was great seeing you."

I make my way to the locker room and change into a pair of yoga pants and a matching pale-yellow sports bra. I dress in colors that speak to what the session will be about. Today's session is about finding our inner happiness, so yellow it is.

...

After an excellent class full of happy faces, I'm back on the street heading home.

I feel lighter, more at peace. Yoga and meditation always help me center myself. I'm grateful for every opportunity I have to share it with others.

Once I get to my apartment, I head to my bedroom to drop off my bag. I grab my pajamas and go to the bathroom.

I stop mid-undressing when a strong whiff of my perfume hits me. It lingers in the air, mixed with an unfamiliar musky scent.

I check my bottle, but it's right where I left it, the lid fully on. There aren't any leaks or spills. *How odd.*

I shake off the confusion and finish undressing.

Once I'm out of the shower, I let my hair air dry and go to the kitchen to cook dinner.

Gracie is already in here, sitting at the counter with her computer.

"Grading or homework tonight?" I ask her. Since she's a student and a graduate assistant, she has a mix of her own homework and studying as well as grading work of the students in her classes.

"Both. I have an exam in two days that I need to study for, but I also have fifty-four more papers to grade by the end of the week. There simply isn't enough time in the day," she grumbles.

"I'm sorry. I'd help if I knew anything about your studies. How about I make dinner?" I offer in hopes of lifting her spirits.

"Yes, please. What's on the menu?" she all but begs.

"I have some frozen fish we can bake, or would you prefer I get some chicken from the store?"

"No, don't leave. You're already in your pjs. Let's do fish tonight." I can't tell if she wants me to stay to keep her company or to not inconvenience me. Probably both.

"Perfect!"

I take out the cod, season it, and place it on a sheet pan. Then I chop up a medley of vegetables. Once the oven is preheated and the veggies are also seasoned, I put them and the fish in the oven.

I sit down next to her and look at my phone indecisively.

I open it and stare at his contact.

*Hero.*

It's been a few days since I last saw him, and despite it being unreasonable, I miss him. I know he gave me his number and instructed me to reach out when I was better, but I also know it was an empty offer. He doesn't want to hear from the girl he saved.

Gracie grunts next to me. Next to my ear to be exact.

"Have you seriously not texted him yet?" She sighs from over my shoulder. She's hovering next to me, staring at my screen displaying his number.

"He doesn't actually want me to reach out. He was just being nice," I explain.

"You don't actually believe that, right?" When I shrug, she rolls her eyes. "Girl, he wouldn't have helped you then come by to check on you then demanded you text him when you're better if he wasn't interested. That was not an empty offer."

"But why would he want me to reach out to him?"

"Don't be dense. He wants you. He's so interested, it's not even funny. Give him a chance. Text him," she pushes, and I know I need her to.

"What do I even say?" I need help. I have no idea how to talk to men. But I also don't think Gracie does either. I've never seen her interact in a non-hostile manner to one.

"Start with 'Hi! This is Cecilia. The damsel in distress that you saved. Let's get together and roll around in the sheets all night. Oh, and I'm a virgin, so teach me your wicked ways, my sexy God of Darkness.'" Her tone switches to an airy, high-pitched voice when she speaks as me, and I'm almost offended.

"I am not saying that!" I gasp in horror. "I'm not going to sleep with him! I don't even know him!"

"Semantics," she defends. "Fine, just reach out and see if he's busy tomorrow night."

"But I'm busy tomorrow night," I say, confused. "We're going to that club, remember? For Leo's birthday."

"Exactly. Invite him to come with us. That way it isn't exactly a date, but if he comes, that means he's interested. And it's a controlled environment. And I'll be there to protect you."

"Oh... That actually makes sense. Maybe–" I'm cut off by the oven timer going off.

I take dinner out of the oven and plate everything. When I sit back down, I try to change the subject.

"So, what class is the exam in?"

"Nope. Take out your phone and text him now," she orders, leaving no room for argument.

"Okay. But what do I say?" I ask sheepishly. I've never done this before.

"Just text him 'Hey, it's Cecilia. I'm no longer concussed and wanted to thank you for helping me.'"

"Yes! That's great!" I type it up and just stare at the words.

"Now press send," she instructs slowly.

I take a deep breath and hit send.

*Me: Hey, it's Cecilia. I'm no longer concussed and wanted to thank you for helping me.*

I turn off my phone and start to place it face-down on the counter, but it buzzes, signaling a call.

*Hero.*

My heart skips a beat then starts racing.

"Answer it!" Gracie says. "Cecilia, answer the phone right now, or I'll answer it for you."

But I can't move. I just stay frozen. Gracie shakes me, snapping me out of my stupor.

I pick up my phone.

I push my finger on the green button.

And I hold my breath.

# Chapter 13
## *Cecilia*

"Hey, sunshine," Roman's smooth voice flows through my phone.

"Hey, héroe," I shoot back. It comes out breathless.

"I'm so glad you reached out. I was afraid I was going to have to stop by again, and you'd think I was a crazy stalker," he teases lightly.

"Oh no! I know you're not like that at all. You're too kind and caring. You could never be accused of being crazy."

He lets out a sharp, unexpected chuckle, and my heart stutters. The sound shoots through me, sending a shiver down my spine.

"Oh, sunshine. You have no idea." He sighs wistfully. "So, you wanted to thank me for helping you?"

"Yes! I don't know how I would've made it home if it weren't for you. I'm so grateful."

Gracie nudges me, then mouths, *'put it on speaker.'*

I roll my eyes but do as she says.

"To show your thanks, why don't you let me take you out to dinner," he offers as though *him* taking *me* to dinner would show *my* thanks to *him*.

"Shouldn't it be the other way around? To show you my thanks, shouldn't *I* be taking *you* to dinner?" I suggest teasingly.

"Sunshine, I'll never let you take me out. I'll always be the one spoiling you." It comes out a smooth promise.

I giggle and redden.

"But then how will I be expressing my gratitude to you in this situation?"

"By gracing me with your presence," he says it like it's the most obvious thing in the world.

I blush further and glance at Gracie for help, lost at what to say.

*'Say yes to dinner,'* she mouths to me.

"I'd love to go to dinner with you." It comes out shakily. I'm shaking. I'm nervous I read into this wrong, and he's not actually asking me out.

"Perfect. I look forward to our date." He says *date* like it's his favorite treat. "How about tomorrow evening?"

"Ye–" I started but Gracie nudges me again. "Oof!"

"You okay?" he asks, concerned.

"Yes. But no, tomorrow doesn't work for me. I'm sorry."

"That's okay. What about the next night?" he asks resiliently.

*'Invite him!'* she mouths.

"Yes, that works!" I agree, then continue. "Tomorrow some friends of mine are going to a club. Would you want to join us?" I cringe as I say it, bracing for the rejection.

There's a long pause, then, "Which club?"

"The Syn Den. It's downtown," I offer, in case he doesn't know.

He exhales. "Perfect. What time? And can I pick you up or should I meet you there?" he sounds eager at the opportunity to pick me up, but Gracie's eyes narrow and she shakes her head.

"Let's meet there. Gracie and I have a getting ready routine."

"Great. I'm looking forward to it."

"Me too! I have to go. I enjoyed talking to you."

"Me too. We'll talk again soon." It comes out so assuredly that I almost believe he can see the future.

"Okay," I agree hopefully.

"Goodnight, Celia," he says in a low voice.

"Goodnight, mi héroe," I whisper back.

I stare at my phone on the counter, not wanting to end the call. He doesn't end it on his end either.

Then, a finger clicks the red end call button. Gracie's finger.

"You did so well! Tomorrow's going to be amazing!" she says giddily. Well, as giddy as Gracie gets.

"I hope so."

# Chapter 14
## *Roman*

I park my black Porsche in the back lot of The Syn Den reserved for employees.

I use my key to enter through the employee entrance and make my way into the club. A few workers spot me and throw a 'hey, boss' my way, and I give them a nod of acknowledgement.

I don't need my employees to be my friends. I don't want them to be. They need to fear and respect me, so I won't sit around gossiping with them. But I also won't be rude.

As I make my way through the empty club, I make note of who on my team is working security tonight. I find my head of security, Drew, and pull him to the side.

"What's up, boss? Didn't know you'd be observing tonight."

"I'm not here to work. I'm bringing my woman. I want everyone to know she isn't to be touched. I won't be leaving her side, so no need for extra security on her, but keep all entrances safe. I don't want anyone *uninvited* here." He knows what uninvited means.

No one who shouldn't be on our territory can be here tonight. Despite being at peace with everyone, the Bratva, Mafia, Irish Mobs, Cartels... I won't take any chances.

"Got it, boss. Can I get a name and picture to pass around? And should we get her on the VIP list?" He doesn't question the unusual request.

I've never marked a woman as mine before. But that changes now.

"No VIP treatment for her nor me tonight." She doesn't know who I am, and I intend to keep it that way.

He starts to open his mouth, but the glare I shoot him shuts him up.

"Yes, sir."

"Her name is Cecilia Álvarez Rivera. Five foot seven inches. Latina. Long, dark wavy hair. Lean build. Brown eyes. *Soft features. Breathtaking smile. Beautiful goddess. Sexy–*"

Drew's cough brings me out of my trance. I internally curse myself out for getting carried away.

"Here's a picture of her." I show him one I took when I was watching her through the yoga studio window. I cropped it so he could only see her face and not the skintight, sinful outfit she's wearing or her flexible pose. "I'll text it to you. Make sure the bouncers and security know she's mine. And make sure they know no VIP treatment for us. Tonight, I'm just a customer."

He nods gruffly then turns to inform the men.

I survey the room one last time to ensure everything is how it should be.

I go back to my car and head to my penthouse. I need to get ready before I go to her place. I plan on following the girls to make sure they get here safely.

# Chapter 15
*Cecilia*

I sigh as I throw another dress on my bed. I look at the pile forming and want to pull my hair out.

Half my closet sits on my bed, but nothing is speaking to me.

I can't decide on what to wear tonight.

Clubs aren't really my scene. They don't play music I like, and I don't typically drink. Drunk people put Gracie on edge, and where there's one of us, there's typically the other.

But Leo wanted to celebrate his twenty-fourth birthday at the club, so that's what we're doing.

He wanted to go to one on the other side of town, near an amazing Italian restaurant, but Gracie demanded we go to one within walking distance from the T. It made sense, so Leo went with it.

He tries to avoid fighting with Gracie. She, on the other hand, does not. She'll glare at him and rile him anytime he gets on her nerves. Which is every time she sees him.

I've never been able to figure out why she dislikes him so much. He's a nice guy, always kind to me. All she's ever said is she has a gut feeling about him, and that she always trusts her gut.

Gracie has been wary of men as long as I've known her. She struggles to trust in general, but even more with men. She never shared her story with me, but I know it must be the effect of trauma. I respect her enough to never pry and to go along with what she wants. If she ever wants to leave somewhere or doesn't want to be around someone, I trust her. Even if it doesn't make sense to me.

I know I can be gullible and naïve, but I like being this way. I like seeing the world in a positive light. I like believing the good in people.

It breaks my heart that Gracie doesn't see the world how I do, but maybe it's for the best. One of us needs to be on the lookout for danger.

The only person I've fought her on is Leo. I'd known him for months before I'd met Gracie. We were already close by the time Gracie and I became friends. She only confided in me that she wasn't comfortable around Leo when she asked if he couldn't spend the night at the apartment.

We already had a No Men Overnight Rule, but Leo thought he was the exception. Gracie pulled me aside one night when he got too drunk and started setting up a pillow on the couch to ask if it was okay if he didn't stay the night. She even offered to take the blame and be the one to kick him out.

I agreed, and the next morning she told me she's always had a bad feeling about him. She hasn't tried to hide it since.

I told her she didn't have to come tonight, but she insisted. She doesn't love me being around him alone, especially not when drinking is involved.

"Oh my God! Is your entire wardrobe on your bed?" Gracie screeches from my doorway.

I look at her hopelessly. "I don't have anything to wear."

"You can borrow something from my closet," she offers.

I look at her all-black clubbing outfit. The same black as her entire closet. As opposed to my earth toned closet which doesn't consist of a single article of black.

A black mock neck, sleeveless shirt tucked into a black mini skirt with a chunky black belt. Ripped tights span from the hem of the skirt into her glossy black Doc Martin boots. Her black, leather bomber jacket hangs off her shoulders, even though it'll be hot in the club.

"No, thank you. You know black isn't my thing. Would you mind helping me pick something?" I refuse her offer gently, even though I know I won't offend her.

"Already on it. Where's that wrap skirt you have? The long cream one?" she asks, already heading to my closet.

"It's still in there. It's practically see-through," I explain why it's not a contender. My leg silhouettes show through the bottom.

"Exactly," she says with a wicked grin. "Now get your fitted, green lace blouse with the flare sleeves."

"Okay, that one is actually see through. I need to wear my green tank top under it." I counter.

"No. Wear your green bra under it," she counters.

"Absolutely not!" I'm horrified by even the suggestion.

"Fine. What about your green bandeau?" she compromises.

"If you insist," I concede. Mainly because I don't want to fight, but partly because I know it'll look good.

"On to jewelry. Wear your long, green tagua necklace, your gold filigree earrings, your gold metal cuff, and your regular stack of rings. Keep your seconds, thirds, conch hoop, and helix hoop the same."

I'm a jewelry lover. I'm a gold girl; it brings out my natural tan and is common in my heritage. A lot of my jewelry is from Mamá and Abuela. The rest is from thrift stores and estate sales, one of Gracie and my favorite activities.

I put on the outfit and do a twirl for Gracie.

"What do you think?" I ask nervously.

"Sexy and gorgeous, but still totally you." She grins.

"So... do you think he'll like it?" I turn to the mirror hanging on my closet door but make eye contact through it.

"If you're talking about Roman, then yes. He's going to be tripping over himself when he sees you," she assures me. "But if you're talking about Leo, I'm going to lock you up in this apartment and order a therapist until you get some sense."

"Gracie, be nice to him. He's a good guy. I've known him for years, and he's never given me any indication otherwise," I reprimand her. "Also, it's his birthday."

"Fine." She rolls her eyes. "I'll be on my best behavior."

"Just, please don't spill a drink on him this time."

"It was an accident!" she grunts out.

"Okay, I believe you. Just, no more accidents. Please," I beg her.

"It's going to be okay. I'll be fine. Now let's get there so you can be with your God of Darkness."

"Gentle giant or hero," I correct her.

"Yeah. Sure. Whatever you say." She rolls her eyes.

Well, this is going to be an interesting night.

# Chapter 16
## *Cecilia*

We're sitting on the T, but I have that same feeling of eyes on me as yesterday. I glance over my shoulder, but there's no one in this car watching me. I shake my head and turn to face Gracie.

"What're you looking at?" she asks, glancing over my shoulder.

"Nothing. Just nervous." Mentioning to Gracie that I feel like I'm being watched is a first-class ticket back to our apartment.

"Hmmm... okay. Don't be nervous. Roman's going to swallow his tongue when he sees you."

I laugh at the absurdity despite willing it to be true.

When we finally get to our exit, we get off the car and head to the bar. It's only two blocks from here.

A figure waves at us, and we make our way over.

"Hey, Leo!" I give him a side hug, but he turns at the last minute, making it a full-frontal hug. Knowing it was an accident, I silently pull myself from it but don't make a comment.

"My girl. How are you, Cecilia?" I wince at the use of 'my girl,' and realize I should've warned Leo that Roman was coming. And maybe even have warned Roman about Leo.

"I'm great! Happy birthday!" I squeal, excited to celebrate my friend.

"Thanks, Cecilia." He wraps his arm around my shoulder and pulls me in again, but I brush it off. "Hello, Gracie. I'm glad you could join us." He sounds anything but glad to see her.

Gracie just glares at him.

"If Cecilia's here, then I'm here." It comes out as a warning. *This might not have been the best idea.*

"Where's everyone else?" I ask, looking around for his friends.

"They're inside. I was waiting for you guys."

He places his hand on the small of my back and leads us to the bouncer. Leo very obviously sneaks him a hundred-dollar bill, which the bouncer stares at unimpressed. I hear Gracie snort at it.

"Hey, big guy. Can you let us in?" She bats her eyelashes at him, and he eyes her up and down. His stoney expression warps into a wicked grin. He's about to flirt with her when his gaze lands on me. His eyes widen and he takes a step back.

"IDs," he grunts out.

Gracie looks impressed that her tactic of asking semi-nicely worked. Leo just grumbles.

I hand him my ID first. He looks at it for a full minute before handing it back, then barely glances at Gracie and Leo's. I guess if one of us is of age, he assumes all of us are.

As we walk through the door, Leo's expression becomes almost... sinister.

"Cecilia, baby, tonight's the night! I finally get everything I want," he whispers in my ear.

"I'm glad, birthday boy. I'm sure it'll be a great night." I force a smile on my face. I've never felt uncomfortable around Leo before, but for some reason, right now, I don't want to be near him.

We stop at a table full of guys who must be Leo's friends. He slaps some on the back and makes introductions. I don't recognize these men. They feel dangerous.

Leo leads Gracie and me to another table nearby since theirs is full. He opens his mouth to say something, but his attention drifts behind me. He straightens and his expression darkens.

"Can I help you?" Leo grits out as a smooth voice whispers in my ear, "Hey, sunshine. I've missed you."

I can't help the grin that breaks out. I turn to face Roman who wears a matching grin.

"Hey, héroe. Thanks for coming." I blush as he looks me over.

"You look beautiful," he says with a wistful sigh.

He opens his arms in an offer but doesn't force a hug. I giddily step into his embrace and wrap my arms around his neck. He squeezes me tightly against him and I feel safe. I hear an inhale and... *Did he just sniff me?*

"Who are you?" Leo's tenor voice snaps, breaking us apart.

I step out of the embrace, and Roman flashes him a smile. I take in Roman's outfit. Tonight, he's in black slacks, a black button-up, and dress shoes. The business look works really well for him.

"I'm Roman. Celia invited me. You are?" He holds out his hand in an offer to shake and after a few seconds of hesitation, Leo takes it. Leo flinches at what must be a tight grip from Roman. My hero just doesn't know his strength.

"Leo. This is my birthday night out. And her name is Cecilia," Leo mutters through a tight smile.

"Well then, happy birthday, Leo. Is it your twenty-first?" Roman asks, genuinely interested. It warms my heart to see him make an effort with my friends.

Leo, however, scoffs offendedly, not realizing Roman wasn't insulting him. "I'm twenty-four today, man."

"I remember twenty-four even though it was a decade ago. It's a fun one," Roman compliments.

I make a mental note. He's thirty-four. Only a decade older than me. That's not too old, *right?*

"What are you doing hanging with us then, old man?" Leo seethes.

"Celia invited me out. I couldn't turn down a chance to see my sunshine." Roman puts an arm around me, and I instinctively lean into him.

Roman nods at Gracie, "Hey, Gracie. How've you been?"

I'm surprised to see her grinning. She fist-bumps Roman and tells him, "It's nice to have some good company around." I almost think I imagine the way she quickly glances at Leo, and how Roman tenses at the implication.

"Let's get drinks," Leo suggests, already pushing away from the table, and storming towards the bar.

Gracie, Roman, and I approach the bar at the other end and almost immediately there's a bartender in front of us taking our order.

Our unusual order of three waters.

"Are you sure you don't want something to drink?" I ask Roman. "It's on me tonight."

"It's never on you, sunshine. I'll always spoil you." Roman shakes his head. "And I'm sticking with water tonight. I want to keep my wits about me and remember every detail. It's our first time together fully coherent." He flashes me a smile, clearly referring to my concussed state at our previous two encounters.

"Here you go, boss." The bartender says as he passes Roman the three, closed bottled waters. Roman's eyes tighten for a second before he thanks him and grabs the waters.

With a hand on the small of my back, he guides me back to our table.

Leo's already there, a line of shots in front of him.

"I got one for each of us. Everyone take one." His grin diminishes at the sight of our waters. "Are you guys not drinking?"

"Sorry, man. I drove, so just water for me." Roman explains, keeping his other reason between us.

"I don't drink in places like these," Gracie says harshly, glaring at Leo. He knows this. Every time we've gone out with Leo, Gracie has refused to drink alcohol. I know she doesn't feel comfortable around him, so I understand.

"Guess it's just you and me, Cecilia," Leo says, offering me a shot of clear liquid.

"No, thank you. I'm sticking to water too." I don't give him a reason. Gracie's teaching me that I don't owe anyone an explanation.

"Come on, baby," he whines, circling the table and hovering too closely. He yanks me to him and brings a shot to my mouth.

I turn my head, and understanding my discomfort, Roman gently pulls me into him and steps between us.

"She said no," Roman growls at him, eyes dark. Roman turns to me, and his expression morphs into one of adoration. "Why don't we hit the dance floor, sunshine?"

He offers me his hand, and I eagerly accept.

Maybe tonight will be great after all.

# Chapter 17

## *Roman*

As I lead her onto the dance floor, I can't help but glare at Leo.

This motherfucker has been hitting on her and making her uncomfortable since the moment he saw her. That move to get a full hug was no accident. He keeps pulling her into him and throwing his arm around her as if he has the right, something she's run away from each time. He's not taking the hint. And I'm not the only one who's noticed.

Gracie rotates between glaring at him and rolling her eyes. I can tell she doesn't like him. I don't like him either.

I don't trust him.

When he called *my* sunshine, his girl' and 'baby,' I almost lost control. It took every ounce of restraint to keep from bashing his head in.

It's my bar. I'm Roman Montclair. I could get away with it.

But Cecilia thinks I'm her hero. And beating her friend to death might change her view of me.

And I can't let that happen.

"You look handsome tonight," she says with a beautiful smile.

I can't contain the grin that spread across my face. This beautiful goddess thinks *I* look good tonight. It's ridiculous when coming from her. She's breathtaking.

When I saw her leave her apartment in that skirt, I almost marched over and demanded she change. On anyone else, it'd be beyond modest for a night club. But on her, on my sunshine... it's downright scandalous. No man should get to see her like this.

Her skirt, while floor length, ties at the top so when she walks, her leg slips out. That long, tan, toned leg. And it's thin enough that you can see the outline of her legs through it in the light. It's dangerous.

Then her top. Her lacy, see through top. Yes, she's wearing some tight top under it that covers her tits, but it doesn't stop the images coursing through my mind.

The final piece that makes her entirely irresistible is the blinding smile she wears.

Her beautiful lips upturned, displaying her happiness. She's radiating. I can't seem to look away.

Once we're far enough that I no longer feel Leo's presence, I stop. I turn to where I'm facing the main entrance, just so I can stay aware. With my looming height, I can see over the heads of most people on the dance floor.

Cecilia starts to move, swaying her hips hypnotically in tune with the music. I place my hands on her tiny waist and move with her.

I'm not known to dance. I don't think I've ever been on a dance floor. But I had to get us away from Leo. And I can't resist an excuse to get close to her. To touch her.

As we move, the distance between us closes. She lifts her hair off her neck and lets it fall. I'm entranced in the way it bounces. She brings her arms around my neck, having to step closer to reach. So close, her chest is pressed against mine.

And then I feel it.

I feel her peaked nipples brushing against my dress shirt.

My cock, which has been sporting a semi since I saw her in this damn skirt, hardens fully. I inch closer to her, closing the space between us, and I know she feels it when she lets out a gasp.

A beautiful, soft gasp. It's music in my ears. Drowning out the loud beat of the song thrumming through the speakers.

I start rocking into her belly. Not fully thrusting, but enough to where I feel each brush. My heart is thumping. Her breathing is ragged. All I can see is her.

Then I lean down so our eyes are level. She moves her head ever so slightly to meet my gaze, and it lets off a whiff of her perfume.

I'm like Pavlov's dogs trained to respond to her scent. Precum leaks from my cock. I wonder which panties she's wearing, and if I can get them from her. I don't know how I'll get them, but I know I want them. And I always find a way to get what I want.

"Sunshine, you're torturing me," I groan.

Her big, innocent eyes bear into mine. "I'm sorry," she whispers.

"No, Cecilia. It's the best kind of torture. I never want it to end."

"Neither do I."

Then she raises onto her toes and seals her lips to mine.

The kiss is nothing more than a peck. It's over quicker than I can blink. She pulls back too soon.

*That won't do.*

She just gave me permission. And I'm going to take what's mine.

I move my right hand from her waist and cup the back of her head. I weave my fingers into her soft locks and pull her into me.

Then I capture her lips.

The moan she lets out reverberates through my mouth.

I seek entrance with my tongue by licking the seam of her lips and, like the good girl she is, she parts them for me. I explore the inside of her mouth and battle with her tongue.

Only when she pulls back for air do we separate. Or at least she leans back. I keep her close, not giving her an inch of space. Instead, I bend lower, trailing my mouth down her neck, licking, biting, and sucking. I know I'm marring her tan skin. And it only fuels me. She'll be wearing my mark. The world will know she's taken.

I look up and lock eyes with Leo. He's gripping his glass, glaring at us. Good, let him see who she wants. I shift us just enough to where only her back is facing him. He doesn't get to see any of her pleasure.

She's panting, and one hand travels to my hair. She's holding me close while also raking her nails through the cropped tendrils. It's euphoric.

"Roman," she moans.

And I break.

# Chapter 18
## *Cecilia*

The growl he lets out at hearing his name sends a shockwave down my spine, joining the butterflies in my belly and the tingling in my core.

He pushes a leg between mine where my skirt opens and pulls my left leg from the ground and over his. This position leaves my weight on his thigh right at my center.

The contact makes me moan again.

"Héroe, I... I feel..." I can't finish the sentence, not able to push the words out. Too flustered, too new to the sensation.

"I know, sunshine. Rub yourself on me. Chase that pleasure." It's a command. A demand. One I'm unable to stop myself from following.

I rock myself against him in rhythm with the music. Each brush against my clit has me panting.

"Roman, I'm close," I moan in his ear.

"Fuck, Celia. Keep going," he groans, but I can't. It's too much.

"Don't you dare stop," he grits out, sounding on the verge of exploding.

But I can't move. Can't breathe.

His left hand grips my waist, and his right hand grips my thigh thrown over his leg. Then he starts lifting me, sliding me on him.

His hardness digs into my stomach, grinding into me.

"Rome... I'm close... Please, héroe," I beg. He can't stop now. I'll never recover.

"Are you going to come for me?" he asks in a dark, low voice.

"Yes," I whimper through heavy pants.

And he growls. It's so animalistic, so barbaric, so sexy.

I feel myself flood. My panties were already soaked, but now, now they're drenched.

"Fuck, sunshine. I can feel your arousal through your panties. Through my pants. On my thigh. You've soaked through both layers and are now soaking me."

I whine and close my eyes in embarrassment. I tuck my head and let my hair fall over my face as a curtain. I can feel my cheeks, already flushed from arousal, now burning with mortification.

But Roman doesn't let me hide. He brushes my hair behind my ears and cups my cheeks, lifting my head to his.

"None of that. This is the hottest thing I've ever experienced. Don't you dare shy away."

I nod my head, forced to believe him. His words can't be anything but true. He can't fake the desperation seeping through them.

"Now open those beautiful brown eyes. I want to see you when you come on my thigh. I want to see you tip over the edge. Because of me."

I open them and he's right there. Mere inches from me.

"Are you close, Cecilia?" he asks darkly.

"Yes, héroe... I... I..." I can't speak. Can't think. I've never been so turned on.

"Then comes for me, sunshine. Come on my thigh. Soak me," he demands. He growls it as he pulls me down harder on his thigh.

I tip over the edge. My vision blacks out. I open my mouth, unable to hold back my scream, but it never comes out.

His mouth is on mine, stifling my voice. Reminding me we're in public. It only makes this hotter. I keep coming and coming. He groans into my mouth, and I feel him twitching.

I feel weightless, unable to hold myself up. I sag against him.

But he takes my weight, holding me to him as if it's nothing.

"No one gets to hear your cries of pleasure," he says it so darkly, I have to look up. He doesn't sound like my jovial hero. He sounds like a man possessed. When I look up, his eyes are dark, but when he meets mine, they melt into softness.

After who knows how long, something to our right draws his attention. I go to look, but he captures my lips in a kiss. A sweet, soft kiss.

"Let's get you back to our table. I need to go to the restroom, and I don't want you stranded out here." He places his hand on the small of my back and leads the way.

When we get back to our table, he pulls out a seat for me and lifts me into it. I'd blush further if my entire being wasn't already red.

I look up and meet Gracie's eyes. She's grinning from ear to ear.

*Oh no. I think she saw.*

I chance a look at Leo, and he's fuming. His nostrils are flaring and he's gripping his drink so hard, his knuckles are white. And his glare... If looks could kill, Roman would be on the ground.

*Oh no. I think he might've seen too.*

Roman tosses them an easy smile, then looks at Gracie. "I'm going to the restroom. Watch out for her."

Surprisingly, she nods to him in agreement instead of chewing him out for telling her what to do. I'm surprised she's putting up with him.

He kisses the top of my head then leaves.

"Guess the old man has a small bladder," Leo mutters, clearly drunk. "I bet he's not even coming back now that you've whored yourself out to him."

His glare is now directed at me.

Tears well in my eyes.

His words splash over me like cold water, breaking me from my trance.

*I didn't whore myself out to him, right?*

But I did. I was intimate with him on our first date. If this is even a date.

I look down, blinking away.

I hear a slapping sound and look up to see Gracie shaking her hand, and Leo gripping his cheek.

"Don't ever fucking talk about her like that," she grits out. "Go take five. You're drunk."

He looks at me apologetically. "I'm so sorry, Cecilia. I didn't mean it."

I don't accept his apology. I can't yet. I'm too hurt to forgive him. But we both know by the time he returns, I will have.

Gracie pushes his shoulder, and he walks away from the table.

"Fuck Leo! I hate him, Cecilia! I fucking hate him!" Gracie growls.

"We don't hate. It's bad for the soul," I remind her gently.

"You don't hate. But I sure as hell do. I hope he doesn't come back."

"He will. And we'll pretend it didn't happen. It's his birthday, and I invited another guy and bailed on him to dance with Roman. It's my fault too," I explain.

"Fuck that. Leo being jealous is not your fault. But forget him." She shakes her head, then grins at me. "So, what was that on the dance floor? Seemed like a lot more than dancing."

I groan and lay my head on my hands, unable to make eye contact.

"Did everyone see?" I murmur, too embarrassed to face the world.

"No, just us, and only because we were watching." We see Leo making his way to the table, three bottles of water in hand. "We'll talk about this later. I want every detail."

"I'm sorry. I come bearing apology waters. Time for me to sober up." Leo dips his head in remorse.

I reach for the one closest to me, but he gives it to Gracie. Instead, he hands me the one in his left hand.

I open it and am surprised it doesn't crack like an unopened bottle typically does, but I'm too thirsty to care.

I gulp half the water down and see Leo staring at me with hard eyes and a grin that makes me uneasy.

This grin isn't his usual one. It isn't jovial and friendly.

After a few minutes, the room tilts, then spins. A terrible headache comes on. I lean against the table, still seated, needing help to balance. And suddenly, I'm so tired.

"I'm going to... find... Roman." The words come out slurred.

I let my eyes drift shut, just for a moment.

# Chapter 19
## *Roman*

Once I situate Cecilia in her seat, I beeline to Drew, pissed he cut our dance session short.

"What is it? I said no distractions tonight. I'm off duty," I spit out.

"Mafia's here. Only a few low-level guys, but I figured you'd want to know," he explains.

"Fuck. Fine. Lead me to them. They can't be here tonight."

We haven't had any issues with the Mafia in years, but I'm not willing to risk anything with Cecilia here. Although we have territory lines, the Mafia, Irish Mob, and Cartels don't have the same rigidity as we do with the Bratva. We won't typically kick them out or torture them for coming into one of our clubs. But not tonight.

He leads me to a group of guys in their twenties. They're all pretty drunk. Their Italian heritage is obvious, and their tattoos are clearly Mafia. But they're low-level.

"You need to leave," Drew tells them.

"Why?" one of the older ones counters.

"No Mafia here tonight," Drew explains monotone.

"Come on, man. It's our friend's birthday. We're not causing any trouble," he whines.

"Sorry, guys. Not tonight. It's time for you to leave." Drew's voice is stern, leaving no room for argument.

"Or what?" one of the other guys, a younger one, counters. The rest of his crew whoops and cheers.

"You won't fucking like finding out," I tell them, stepping forward, done with the pleasantries.

"And who the fuck are you?" the younger spits out, snorting.

"I'm Roman Montclair. Now get the fuck out of my club before I lose my patience. Lorenzo will have to come collect your bodies," I growl, name dropping their Capo to convey know how serious I am.

They all raise their hands in peace. "Sorry, man. We didn't realize. We don't want any trouble. We'll go now," the first one says.

He rounds up the others, and Drew leads them out.

Without another word, I make my way back to my sunshine.

As I near their table, my heart pounds at the sight I take in.

Gracie is yelling at Leo from one side of Cecilia, holding onto her arm, keeping her in her chair.

Leo is yelling back, pulling at Cecilia, trying to get her in his arms.

And Cecilia, my beautiful Cecilia, is passed out at the table. I run.

I push my way through the crowd, desperate to get to her.

"Stand back, bitch. I'm bringing her home," Leo spits out, yanking at my Cecilia.

"Let her go. Get the fuck away from us," Gracie yells back, not letting go of her best friend.

"Or what? You think you can stop me?" he seethes.

"Maybe not. But I sure as fuck will," I growl into his ear. "Now fucking drop her."

Leo turns around to face me, letting go of Cecilia. She starts to tilt, muttering incoherently, and Gracie catches her.

Good, she's not passed out... yet.

"What's going on?" I ask, trapping Leo against the table with my body.

"Nothing. Mind your fucking busi–" Leo starts. He doesn't get far into the sentence, because my hands shoots out and grabs his neck, cutting off his air supply.

"I'm not asking you." I get in his face. "Gracie, what happened?" I ask again, even though I can deduce it from the scene. But I pray I'm wrong.

"Leo called Cecilia a whore for dancing with you," she starts off strong, sounding like she's tattling. I tighten my grip on his neck. "He left to get us drinks to cool off. He returned and gave Cecilia a water. Minutes later, she was dizzy and could barely sit up. Stuttering and mumbling. Leo was trying to get her to come home with him. I wouldn't let him."

*Fuck.*

Fuck, fuck, fuck.

This motherfucker drugged Cecilia. He drugged my sunshine.

"She... drank... too... much... Helping... her..." he gasps out.

"She hasn't had anything to drink. What the fuck did you slip her?" I growl.

He sputters, turning red. I loosen my grip so he can answer.

"Nothing," he rasps.

I throw him against the table and punch his face. I feel the satisfying crunch of bone, breaking his nose. Blood spurts, and I ask him again. "What the fuck did you give her? Don't make me ask you again."

"You're fucking crazy," he spits out. "You won't get away with this."

"Try me. What the fuck did you drug her with?" I reel back to hit him again but freeze when he glances over my shoulder with hope in his eyes.

"Help me! He's crazy! He's killing me!"

I turn and see Drew along with a few other security personnel behind him.

"Need help, boss?" Drew asks, cracking his knuckles.

"He drugged my girl. I need to know with what," I say without breaking eye contact with Leo. I punch him again.

"Boss? What the fuck? Who the fuck are you?" he asks in disbelief.

"I'm Roman Montclair. Now tell me what you slipped in her drink if you want to walk out of here alive," I grit out.

He pales, and his eyes widen. *Interesting. He knows my name.*

"It was just a little roofie. GHB. She'll be fine," he defends himself.

I roar and hit him again. Twice more.

Then I throw the filth at Drew.

"Take him to a warehouse. Text me which one. I'll be there in a few hours."

I turn away, knowing if I look at him again, I'll kill him. I face the girls and note that Cecilia's almost completely passed out and didn't witness any of the confrontation.

I look at Gracie, scared she'll be terrified of me. That she won't want me helping her with Cecilia. Which isn't going to fucking happen. Nothing's standing in my way of helping her. But it'd be a lot easier if Gracie accepts me.

But instead of facing me with horror, Gracie holds respect for me in her eyes.

"I can't carry her. I need your help," she mutters, strained from holding Cecilia's weight for this long.

I gently lift Cecilia into my arms, cradling her to my chest. I start walking, careful of the fragile, precious goods in my arms.

"Come with me," I instruct.

Gracie follows without question.

We walk down a hallway in the back and into the main office. I don't use it often, but it's here for when we need it. I head to the adjoining bathroom and sit down on the floor with Cecilia in my lap.

I stick my fingers down her throat until she gags. Thankfully, her reflex is weak, and she starts heaving quickly. I lean her over the toilet as she empties her stomach. I hold her hair and rub her back.

She starts to gain consciousness during the process and tears fall from her eyes. She begs me to stop, and it breaks my heart, but I can't.

"I'm sorry, sunshine. We have to get it out of you," I beg her to understand.

Gracie grabs a washcloth, runs it under cool water, and places it on Cecilia's neck. She then looks away but stays in the bathroom. Clearly the situation is hurting her, but she won't abandon her friend. I find myself respecting this woman more and more with each passing moment.

I repeat the process until nothing comes up at all. By the end, she's crying and more conscious.

Gracie appears with a glass of water and brings it to her lips.

"Rinse, sunshine. Then you can swallow," I instruct her.

She does as she's told.

When that's over, I cradle her back in my arms and carry her to the employee exit. Gracie follows wordlessly.

When we reach my SUV, I open the back door and place Cecilia gently on the bench seat. Gracie climbs in after her.

I get behind the wheel and start driving towards their place.

"Where are you taking us?" Gracie finally speaks up.

"To your apartment. I figured waking up at home would be the best thing for her."

"Thank you. For everything. I don't want to think about what would've happened if you weren't there," she mumbles.

"No. If I was there, if I never left her side, he never would've gotten the chance to drug her," I grit out, anger consuming me.

Anger at Leo.

Anger at the Mafia men.

Anger at myself.

We continue the drive in silence, stewing in the what ifs.

When we get to the apartment, I carry Cecilia up the stairs and into the bathroom. Gracie either doesn't notice or doesn't care that I know the way.

I place Cecilia on the floor and look at her. She has vomit in her hair, what I'm hoping isn't toilet water on her clothes, and blood on her body. I know the blood is from my hands. From attacking Leo. It's his blood. But seeing it on her, seeing her bloody, has me filled with fear and anger.

She can never get hurt. I have to protect her.

"Do you need help showering her, or should I step out?" I offer regretfully. I want to stay. I want to help clean her up. But I know she'd be more comfortable if Gracie does it. And I don't want to take advantage of her in the state she's in.

"I can handle it. Just grab some clothes for her to change into," Gracie responds.

I turn on the water and wait until it's warm enough before leaving.

I sort through her drawers and find a soft t-shirt, panties, and a pair of pajama pants. I see a pile of clothes on her bed and wonder what the hell happened in here. Half her closet is on her bed.

I hand the pajamas to Gracie through the cracked bathroom door and go back to her bedroom. I start hanging up her clothes and clearing the bed.

Once it's clean, I turn down her bed and hunt down some Ibuprofen and a large water bottle. I can tell it's Cecilia's because of the light colors.

I knock on the bathroom door, "Gracie, how is everything in there?"

"You can come in. She's dressed, teeth brushed, and ready for bed," she responds.

I open the door and find a sleeping Cecilia resting on an exhausted Gracie. I gently lift her into my arms and carry her to bed.

I wake her up and get her to take the pain relievers. Gracie sits on the edge of the bed, telling an incoherent Cecilia that she'll be okay.

Gracie and I shut her door, leaving her to sleep and go to the living room.

"Are you okay?" I ask her.

"I'll be fine," she says determinedly. She straightens her back and stares into my eyes, letting me see the fierce truth. This woman has been through some hell. She'll be okay.

"I need to go, but I'll be back before she wakes up. You should get some sleep," I tell her.

"You'll handle him?" she asks.

"He won't be a problem anymore," I promise her cooly.

She nods, "Good. Make him pay."

"Don't worry about him. He's out of your lives forever."

"Thank you." She doesn't look fearful of me. She looks relieved and vengeful.

"Lock the door behind me," I tell her on my way out.

She doesn't question how I'll get back in. She just nods and follows me to the door.

I leave to carry out my promise.

He's going to pay.

# Chapter 20
## *Roman*

I splash cold water over the fucker dangling from the ceiling by the chains on his hands. Leo sputters and coughs, waking up. When his eyes land on me, he recoils.

"What the fuck? What's going on?" he groans out in pain, the beating he took obvious. But the dried blood and crooked nose barely satisfy me.

I need him to feel my wrath.

"We're going to have a little chat," I tell him.

He pales, then gets a spark in his eyes.

"I know who you are, Roman Montclair. I hear things. You're a bad man. You kill people. Torture them. Cecilia will hate you when she finds out," he threatens me.

"*If* she finds out. And if she does, it'll only be on my terms," I correct him.

"I'll tell her. As soon as I get out, I'll go to her," he continues.

"*If* I let you out. And even if I do, you're never speaking to her again," I growl, and the memory of her passed out, drugged resurfaces.

"You can't stop me," he taunts, but there's tremble in his voice.

"I can kill you. Then you can't speak to anyone ever again. Then you can't drug and rape any more women," I spit out, then throw my fist. The crunch as it collides with his ribs soothes me just barely.

I need to make him pay.

He howls in pain, but it's not enough.

"I didn't drug anyone. She had too much to drink," he cries out.

"You're a fucking liar and a rapist. She only drank water." I slap his face, knowing how much more demeaning it is than a punch. And how painful it'll be on his broken nose. "Be a man and own it."

"So, what if I did? It was my birthday. She's been leading me on for years. She just needed a little encouragement. If you hadn't been there, she'd be mine by now." The evil gleam in his eyes steels my heart.

I've had many men in this room, some more deserving than others, but their eyes always give away their worth. And this scum, this filth, is worthless.

I growl as I hit him. My anger overcomes me.

Hit after hit, I break his ribs. His sternum. His clavicle. I keep going until he's nothing but a bloody, bruised bag of bones.

He's howling, sobbing, begging for mercy.

"I don't allow rapists to live. Especially not when they're drugging women in my territory." I grind my teeth, pissed at what I have to do. "But you were Cecilia's friend. And she'd be upset if I killed you. So, I'll let you live."

He spits on me, pure hatred in his eyes. "I'm not going to thank you for sparing me. You're more evil than I could ever be.

I may have slipped a little something in her drink, but you're the one torturing her friend."

"I'm leaving you alive in honor of her. Because she's too good of a woman. But you will remember your lesson."

I grab my knife and a lemon from the table. I cut the lemon in half and swipe the knife through its juices.

I rip up the side of his shirt until his broken ribs are accessible.

Then I get to carving.

*RFM*

My initials forever engraved into his side. Very largely. He will bear his mark of shame, and if I ever capture him again, I will kill him. I tag him as I do all my interrogees even though there's no way I could ever forget the man who tried to rape my girl.

Once the wound is bleeding, I grab half of the lemon and press it into his carving. I twist it and squeeze, letting the acidic juices burn into him.

His screams, his tears, are the only thing calming me.

"You... sick... fuck..." he gasps out. "She'll... never... choose... you."

I growl and unhook his wrists.

"She doesn't have a choice," I mutter, knowing it's the truth. She's choosing me now, but if she ever changes her mind, I'm taking her. Keeping her. And no one, not even she, can stop me. "Now, you need a daily reminder of what you did."

I drag him by his collar to the metal table but keep him on the end away from the weapons. He can barely hold himself up, but even healthy and with a weapon, he'd be no match for me.

I grab a hatchet and lay his left hand down.

When he realizes what I'm about to do he tries to fight me off, but to no avail.

I swing it down, chopping through the bone, dismembering his left ring finger. Now he'll never be able to wear a ring claiming a wife. He doesn't deserve that. And no woman should have to be stuck with him.

I throw a rag at him and tell him to keep pressure on it if he wants to live. No way am I helping this fucker not bleed to death. His life is in his own hands.

"Oh, and one more thing. If you ever go near Cecilia, try to contact her, or even think of her, I'll know. And I will kill you in a more painful way than you can imagine. Then, I'll go after those you care about. Or maybe I'll get to them first. Make you watch. Have your last moments on this earth be watching what you did to the ones you love," I promise. "Do you understand?"

He glares at me. *Good enough.*

I grab his phone and block Cecilia's number. I also delete her and Gracie's contacts and remove all evidence of her from his phone. He'll never touch her again.

I leave the room and call one of my men to keep an eye on him. He can be set free when his finger stops bleeding.

If it doesn't stop, my man will cauterize the wound. And as much as I'd love to be here for that, I have my sunshine waiting for me at her place.

...

In clothes identical to the ones I wore at the club, I stand in the corner of her room and watch her sleep.

The slow rise and fall of her chest are the only indication that she's well. That she's restful and healthy. That I saved her in time.

It calms me.

Only when I can barely stand from exhaustion do I move from my position. I lay on the other side of her bed, and drag her to me, curling her onto my chest.

The feeling of her pressed against me, soothes the fire raging within. She's safe here with me, in my arms. No one can get to her.

No one can get through me.

I'll protect her with my life.

# Chapter 21
## *Cecilia*

I wake up with a pounding headache. Opening my eyes makes me nauseous and dizzy. I groan in response.

As soon as the sound leaves my mouth, movement from the ground has me prying them open again.

Roman sits up from where he's lying on the ground next to my bed and looks up at me.

"Sunshine, you're awake." He sighs in relief.

I try to remember what happened last night that led to Roman sleeping on my bedroom floor, but it's blank. I can't remember anything.

"Roman, what happened? I wasn't planning on drinking, but did I blackout? I can't remember a thing."

I try to sit up but groan again. He's by my side in an instant, helping me up.

"How are you feeling?" he asks, genuine concern in his voice.

"Terrible. Nauseous. Dizzy," I whimper.

"Here, take these and drink this." He hands me some Ibuprofen and a glass of water. I take them and chug the whole thing.

"Why do I feel like this? I've never been this hungover."

"What do you remember?" he asks cautiously.

"I remember getting ready with Gracie. The T ride over. Getting into the club. Ordering a water. Dancing with you..." I blush at the last statement because I remember more than just dancing. "After that, it's pretty blurry. I think I threw up at some point. And showered." I look down and see I'm in pajamas. "Did you... did you undress me?" I blush at the question, but I've never been naked in front of a man before, and I would've rather my first time not have been blacked out and covered in vomit.

"No, sunshine. Gracie undressed, showered, and redressed you. I cleaned up your room and prepped it for bed while that was happening. I would never take advantage of you like that," I can see the honesty in his eyes. He really means it.

"I believe you, hero. Thank you for taking care of me. I didn't mean to get drunk. I'm so sorry," I can barely look at him, I'm so overcome with shame.

"Sunshine, no. You weren't drunk," he sighs and sits on the edge of my bed. He grabs my hands before looking me in the eyes. A look of pain crosses his face. "I left you for five minutes to go to the restroom after we were on the dance floor. I swear it was only five minutes. When I came back, you were hunched over. Gracie was trying to take care of you..." he sighs again. Swallows hard. Squeezes my hand. "You were drugged. Roofied." His eyes are hard, and anger clouds them. He exhales and goes back to normal.

I take a moment to breathe. I call up a mantra and repeat it to myself until I'm calm. *Forgive those who hurt you and the world will heal you.* I do a few breathing exercises until my heart slows to a normal pace. I open my eyes and grip his hand with both of mine.

"Thank you for telling me," I say sincerely.

"Nothing happened. Listen to me, Cecilia, nothing happened to you. I found you before the scum could. Gracie was with us the whole time. We took you to the bathroom, and I made you throw up the drugs. I'm sorry, but we needed to get it out of your system. Then I drove you guys home. She showered you. I wasn't in the room when you were undressed. Then I put you to bed and slept on the floor next to you to watch over you. Yes, you were drugged. And I know that's horrible. Physically and mentally. I can't imagine what you're feeling after such trauma. But listen to me. No one touched you. You were not physically violated in any way. I promise you."

I nod, knowing he's telling the truth. I can feel it in my bones.

"I believe you, mi héroe. You wouldn't let anyone hurt me. You saved me. Once again, you're my hero." I move one hand to cup his cheek, and his eyes close with the contact. "Thank you, Roman. Thank you for taking care of me."

"Always, Cecilia. I will always take care of you," he promises fiercely.

He leans forward pressing his forehead against mine. We just breathe each other in. Then he pulls back just enough to lift me into his arms and crush me to his chest.

"I'm so sorry I left you, Celia. I'm so sorry. None of this would've happened if I'd been by your side," his voice is pure anguish.

"No, Roman. You're not to blame. The stranger that did this is. The lost soul who made this poor decision is. You saved me. You kept me safe. You took care of me. That's all that matters."

I breathe him in again, and the scent of *him* and lemons enters my nose.

"Mmmm, you smell like lemons. It's making me want a cup of tea."

He tenses, then pulls back a little. There's a strange gleam in his eyes, but he shakes it away.

"I'll make you some tea right now." He starts to get up, but I stop him.

"I can do it."

"Absolutely not. Stay in bed."

"I need to get up. My body is protesting being still for this long."

He sighs but nods, and cradles me to him as he stands, carrying me out of my room.

"I can walk, silly goose."

He lets out an unexpected chuckle. "I can't remember the last time someone called me a 'silly goose.'"

"Well, you're being one. But it's okay. I appreciate it," I tell him as I snuggle into his arms.

When we get to the kitchen, Gracie is already in there, working on her laptop. She closes it when she hears us and races to my side.

"How are you feeling? Are you okay? Do you remember what happened?" she rushes out.

"I'm okay. I feel a little sick, but some tea will help. Roman told me what happened. How some guy roofied me. I'm not angry. I'm hurt and feel violated. But I forgive him. He's a lost soul." Gracie gapes at me, even though she should be used to my forgiving nature.

"You can't be serious!" she gasps.

"Gracie, it's not healthy to hold on to grudges. It's bad for the soul," I remind her. I've told her dozens of times, but she chooses not to listen.

"You've got to be kidding me," she huffs then sits at the counter.

"Thank you, both of you, for taking care of me. I appreciate it so much."

"You know I love you, girl. I'm always going to take care of you. Especially if you're in a state where you can't take care of yourself. Let's just be more aware in the future," Gracie tells me.

"I love you too." I tell her.

Then I realize how awkward this exchange must be seeing as I'm still in Roman's arms.

"Erm, you can put me down now, héroe?" I ask softly.

He doesn't move for a beat, then places me on the couch. He heads to the kitchen, reaches into the pantry, and pulls out my tea stash.

Gracie plugs in the electric kettle, and they work seamlessly together.

It's odd to see her comfortable around a man, but I guess the shared trauma and seeing what a good man he is won her over.

Roman sets the tea in front of me and sits in the chair across from me.

"You can have some tea too if you'd like," I offer.

"I'm okay for now. I need to get going but wanted to wait until you were awake and situated."

"Oh." I try to hide my disappointment. "Can we see each other again soon?" I try to mask the want in my voice. I want him to say yes more than I want my next breath.

"Of course, sunshine." A smile crosses his face. "As soon as you're up to it, let me know. I'll take you to dinner. On a proper date. But only once you're ready. We're doing this on your terms."

I blush and nod. "I'll text you later."

With a final kiss to the top of my head, he's out the front door, and Gracie's locking it behind him.

"Well, what do you think of him?" I ask her, needing her insight.

"He's perfect for you. He took such great care of you. That man is already falling for you. You need to give him a chance. A real chance. Don't push him away... I don't think he'd let you even if you tried," she mutters the last bit under her breath.

"Do you really think so? That he likes me?" I ask, full of hope.

"Definitely. I think that man would do just about anything for you."

# Chapter 22
## *Roman*



I stare at the message for the millionth time since she sent it this morning.

I'm waiting to respond because I don't want to seem too eager. I'm too fucking old to be playing these games, but I don't want her to know the power she has over me. That I'd drop everything for her. That I have dropped everything for her.



I don't want to wait until the end of the week, but I also don't want to have to cut our dinner short because she has work in the morning. My schedule isn't exactly a nine-to-five, so I can work around hers.

Her answer is immediate.



I deliberate for a full minute before deciding I'm not playing texting games.

The line rings twice before she answers.

"Hey, Roman. What can I do for you?" her sweet voice flows through the phone speaker.

*You could let me ravish you.*

I picture her on her back, legs spread, in only those sexy panties of hers I've been collecting. I picture tasting from her core, breathing in her scent. I picture thrusting into her tight pussy. How she'd moan. How she'd feel. What she'd look like coming apart from my cock instead of my thigh.

"Umm... Roman?" she asks, breaking me from my fantasy.

"Sorry, sunshine. I just wanted to call and check in. See how your day's going?"

"Oh! Thank you!" Her surprise is palpable and adorable. "My day's going well. My favorite patient, Mrs. Orla, came in today. She baked me a French silk pie. I'm so excited to try it. She's an excellent baker."

"You like pie?" I ask, wanting to know her likes, dislikes, favorites... I want to know everything about her, so I can treat her and give her the perfect life.

"Yes! I have such a sweet tooth. Especially for chocolate." *Noted.* "What about you? What do you like?"

I'm stunned silent for a minute.

I don't remember the last time someone asked me something so personal. Even if it's just as trivial as *do I like chocolate.* No one's cared. I've never let anyone get close enough to care. But Cecilia... she cares. She asks because she wants to know.

I have to swallow past the lump in my throat to answer.

"I love chocolate too. I have a hidden sweet tooth. I don't let myself eat it too often though."

"Why not?" she asks, again, genuinely curious.

"I'm conscientious of my health. I don't want to get Alzheimer's or cancer when I'm older. I always want to be healthy enough to take care of my family."

"Family? Do you have kids?" she sounds hesitant.

"No, sunshine. No kids yet," I pause before adding. "But I'd like some someday." *With you. I'd like some with you someday.*

"Me too. All I've ever wanted is a family of my own. I wouldn't mind having half a dozen kids. A home full of love and laughter and happiness," she says it so wistfully.

I close my eyes, and I can see it.

Our home. Full of our children. Children that are half me, half her. Sons and daughters running around. Visible proof of our love in the family we create.

It's a newfound dream. I've never thought much about kids, but now that I see our future together, I know it's all I want.

And I'll stop at nothing to get it.

# Chapter 23
## *Cecilia*


I stare at my reflection in the mirror, repeating my mantra of the day.

*Kindness brings in goodness.*

"You look great!" Gracie exclaims as she walks into the bathroom.

I'm in a burnt orange, flowy maxi dress. It has a lowcut V neckline. The flowy top cinches at the waist then flows to my ankles. The sleeves are so flared, they're practically drapes. I have beaded green and orange bracelets on my wrists, my normal gold stack of rings, a pair of gold filigree earrings, my other normal ear accessories, and a long jade elephant necklace.

I left my hair down in its natural waves and kept my makeup light. I wanted to stay true to myself.

It's so easy to want to become someone else who you think will impress others. Or wear a mask to protect yourself. But then you aren't true to yourself.

There's bravery in being your raw self, and I'm tapping into that courage now.

I want Roman to see the real me and stay because he likes it. Because he likes me. And the only way to do so is to stay true to myself.

"Are you excited?" Gracie asks with a grin. I think she's almost as excited as I am.

"Yes. I'm really looking forward to seeing him... but I'm also nervous. I've never been on a date with a guy I'm actually interested in," I confess.

The few dates I've been on have all been first dates, and the guys didn't interest me afterwards. Roman already interests me, so I'm nervous.

"Don't be. He's already obsessed with you. Look at all the lengths he's gone through to take care of you," she counters.

"That's just because he's a decent guy. I'm worried I don't know how to do this," I sigh. "He's also a decade older than me. I've never done more than kiss a guy until Roman. What if I'm not experienced enough for him?"

Gracie scoffs. "Seriously? Come on, Cecilia. Men love an inexperienced woman. He'll probably come in his pants when he finds out you're a virgin."

I wrinkle my nose at her crudeness.

"Do they actually? Wouldn't they want a woman who knows what she's doing?"

"Babe, I can assure you, men like teaching you about sex," she promises. "Plus, he knows what he's doing. He's not going to need you to show him. Wasn't the dance floor orgasm the hottest thing ever?" She fans herself as if she's the one who had the blinding orgasm, and for a second, I regret telling her. But I couldn't have kept it from her.

"Yes," I mumble. "But how do I tell him that's the furthest I've ever gone with a man? When would I even tell him that?"

I seriously don't know how to do any of this. I'm regretting waiting on intimacy until I find my soulmate. I should've explored and experienced more in college. Now I'm in my twenties and haven't even seen a man naked.

"You don't have to tell him, but I think you should. But wait until you start getting physical. Don't just blurt out, 'I'm a virgin' at dinner. That'd be oof."

"Okay, thanks."

A knock at the door interrupts my train of thought.

I take a deep breath. "I guess this is it."

"It's going to be great. Don't worry about it," Gracie says as she heads to her room to give us some privacy.

I open the apartment door, and there he is in all his glory.

He's wearing a black button up with the top buttons undone, showing a tasteful amount of tattooed skin. The sleeves are folded below his elbow, exposing more tattooed, veiny flesh. His corded forearms are on display. His black slacks have to be custom made to fit his huge build. His facial hair has grown out a little longer than a five o'clock shadow. The dark stubble looks sexy. All of him looks sexy. And tempting.

My thighs clench as a wave of arousal tears through me.

His eyes are on me, gliding from my head to toes and back up again.

"Fuck, sunshine. You look enchanting. Bewitching. Ethereal." The awe in his voice catches me off guard. "You're a goddess."

I've been called pretty, beautiful, even gorgeous, but I've never been called those. I've never been told I don't look of this earth. My cheeks flush at the compliment, and my heart soars.

"Thank you, héroe. You look dashing," I say, returning the compliment with one just as true.

His cheeks tinge red a little, and he smiles so cutely.

He offers me his hand, "Come on, Cecilia. It's time for our date."

I take his offered hand, and we exit my apartment as a happy couple.

# Chapter 24
## *Roman*

We finished eating a while ago. So long ago, our dishes have already been bussed. But we're not in a rush to leave.

I don't think she's even noticed how long we've been here or even the disappearance of our plates, because she's been so caught up in the conversation.

I've been enthralled too, but not so much that I forget my basic instincts to always be vigilant and aware. She's too oblivious, she has no caution. But that's okay. I'll watch over her.

"So, what do you do?" she asks curiously.

"I work in security. My brothers and I own and run Syndicate Enterprise. It's a private security and defense company." The lie rolls off my tongue effortlessly even though it's not one I have to use often. I'm not typically in a position where I'm giving my job title. The people I deal with already know who I am and what I do.

"Oh wow! That's really impressive. It explains your build." She blushes as though she didn't mean for it to slip out. "I'm sorry. The wine is getting to my head. I just mean you're strong. You can carry me around easily. You have a nice, strong build."

*So, she likes my build. That'll be my motivation at the gym this week.*

I chuckle at her. She's adorable trying to backpedal, but I heard the compliment, and I'm not forgetting it.

"I keep in shape to do my job. I'm more hands-on than my brothers." It's not a lie, more of a misdirection.

"I can't believe you really are a hero in real life!" she fawns, and I try not to choke on my wine.

I can't believe this naïve woman thinks I'm a hero. She's so wrong, it's absurd. But I won't correct her. Because to her, I'll be her hero. While for her, I'll be a villain. I think of Leo and tighten my grip. To everyone else, I'll be a monster. The monster all the monsters fear.

"It's what I do," I say grimly, then change the topic. "What do you do?" I ask despite knowing the answer.

"I'm a PT tech at a physical therapy clinic." The way she draws it out and takes a sip of wine tells me something I didn't know.

"But you don't like it?" I confirm.

"It's not that I don't like it. It's just not my dream. It's not fulfilling," she says it with such conviction.

"You say it so decisively. What is your dream?" I tense, needing to know now.

She blushes and looks down, unsure. After a moment, she murmurs something under her breath, straightens her spine, and tells me something that changes me forever.

"My dream is being a mother. It's my life's purpose. I know I brushed up on it. And I know not everyone finds the honor in it. It's outdated to some. But all I want is to be a mom. I want to have a house full of kids, full of love. I'd leave whatever job I have and focus on raising them while my husband works," she says it softly, but I hear the truth in her words.

I can't breathe. All I can see is a house full of children that look like her... and me. Our children. Running around. Her at home, waiting for me, love and adoration in her eyes.

It's a future I want so badly, I vow to have it... no matter the cost.

"You'll be an amazing mother. There's so much honor in being a stay-at-home mom. They sacrifice so much for their children. I would never expect it of my wife, but I'd be grateful if that's what she chooses to do," I explain.

"You do? You really think it's honorable and not lazy or outdated?" Her eyes fill with hope that I'm telling the truth, so I confide in her.

"My mom was a stay-at-home mom. She took care of us while my dad worked. She sacrificed so much to do so. I'm forever grateful to her for it," I reveal.

"She sounds like an amazing woman," Cecilia says with awe, and I'm pleased.

"She is. She'll love you." It comes out before I can think better. Bringing her home to Mom isn't really a first date topic, even if I know it'll happen eventually.

"I'd love to meet her," she says with a smile. "Mamá had to work. She immigrated here from Ecuador when she was eighteen. She was all on her own when she moved. Her parents didn't come. She worked to survive. Papá moved here when he was two. His mom, my Abuela, brought him over. When he met Mamá, he was instantly in love. They married young and worked hard to provide for my sisters and me."

"That's a beautiful love story. The sacrifices they made to ensure a good future for you guys is inspiring," I say truthfully.

She gets her strength from her parents. "How many sisters do you have?"

"I have an older sister, Carmen, and a younger sister, Valentina. Carmen is married to an amazing man, and they have a daughter. My parents and Abuela live with them in Worcester. I'm here, doing my thing. Val wanders around. She's in Worcester too but moved out. She's the wild one," she smiles fondly. "What about you? Any siblings?"

"We're the opposite. All boys, four of us. We all live in Boston. My eldest brother is Dominic, then Matthias, then me, then the baby is Sebastian. We all work for the Syndicate… Enterprise." I catch myself just in time. "My parents also live in Boston. We're close. We even have family dinner every Sunday. Oh, and there's Margot. She's Matthias's fiancée. She's like a sister to me."

"That sounds lovely. I'm sure having them close by is nice. I miss my family sometimes, and without a car, I can't see them as often as I'd like," she sighs.

I vow to bring her to my family. They'll love her. And they'll be her family too soon enough.

Although, I'm going to have to find a way to convince this sweet, naïve girl that we're all legal businessmen.

I open my mouth to answer but am cut off by a cough.

I turn and see the restaurant manager at our table.

"Excuse me, but I wanted to let you know, the restaurant is closing for the evening. Would you mind paying and letting us close, sir? I'm sorry for the inconvenience." He gulps and trembles, not making eye contact.

I look up and see the rest of the wait staff off to the side, eyeing us cautiously. It's obvious I intimidate them.

I also make note that the restaurant is empty of customers. I check my watch and see they closed twenty minutes ago.

"The apology is ours. We lost track of time." I pull out a few hundreds from my wallet and leave them on the table. "Keep the tip as an apology."

I pull out Cecilia's chair and help her up. When I look down, I see her staring at the wad of cash on the table with her mouth agape, and I realize my mistake.

Most businessmen don't carry hundreds around and tip more than two hundred percent.

*Shit.*

Well, nothing I can do about it now.

We continue chatting on the drive to her apartment. Once we park, I make my way around the car and open the door for her, as I've done all night. My mother did raise me to be a gentleman, even if I haven't ever used those manners. Cecilia deserves the best.

I open her apartment door and follow her up.

"Oh, you don't have to walk me in," she says when she realizes what I'm doing.

"Sunshine, in this apartment on this side of town, I'm always making sure you make it into your unit. For safety, and because I was raised right." It comes out teasingly, but little does she know how serious I am. I will always protect her.

When we get to her door, she invites me in. She's timid about it, and not for the first time, I wonder how experienced she is with men.

A woman who looks like her, who is her, an absolute goddess of a woman, has to have had hundreds of men lining up for her.

But not anymore. No other man will ever have her again.

"No, sunshine. I'm just walking you to your door." I turn down her offer, because if I enter that apartment, I'm not going to be able to hold myself back. And I want to take this slowly. I want to win her over before I get the prize that is her body. I need her trust first.

I lean down to kiss her cheek, but she turns at the last minute and captures my lips with hers.

The unexpected contact has me warring with my resolve. *Would it really be so bad to be with her?*

I kiss her back gently, despite every fiber of my being screaming to take control. She's a delicate flower, and I won't ruin her.

When I'm on the verge of coming in my pants... again... I pull back.

It's mortifying enough that I did so at the club for the first time since I was a teenager. I can't make it a habit.

We separate, and she opens her door.

"Buenas noches, mi héroe," she says dazed.

Her blown pupils, flushed skin, and rapid breathing give away her arousal. I have to take a step back, needing the space to restrain myself.

"Buenas noches, sunshine," I repeat back, competent enough to know it means goodnight.

She giggles as I butcher her parent's language.

She shuts the door, but I stare at it a little longer, wondering if I could break in to watch her sleep again.

Realizing I don't know her or Gracie's sleep schedule, I sigh and leave.

But it doesn't matter.

Soon enough, we'll be going to sleep in the same bed every night. In my bed. In my secure penthouse.

# Chapter 25
## *Cecilia*

I close the apartment door behind me and lean against it. I close my eyes and just relive the events of tonight.

"That good, huh?" Gracie's voice pulls me from my thoughts.

She's sitting on the couch, watching a true crime documentary, spoon-eating a jar of peanut butter. So, she's having a her normal Friday evening.

I sit on the other end of the couch and throw my hands up in defeat.

"Is it too early to say he's perfect?" When what I really want to ask is, '*Is it too early to know he's the one?*'

"Oh, wow. I didn't expect it this soon," she says wide-eyed.

"Am I being crazy? Delusional? Naïve?" I groan in exasperation. "There's no way he feels the same this early."

"Feels how?"

"In love." I'm sure I look just as shocked as she does at the words. I didn't expect them. Didn't realize I was feeling this way. But now that I've said it, I know it's true.

I'm falling in love with Roman... *what's his last name?*

Oh my goodness!

I'm falling in love with a man whose last name I don't even know!

"Calm down. You look like you've seen a ghost. It's not a bad thing. I think some studies show that you know if you're going to marry that person by the third time you meet... or something like that, right?" She sounds less sure by the end.

"You're asking me? Why are you asking me? I don't know these studies!" I cry out hysterically.

"It's fine. The premise is some people just know early on. That's not a bad thing."

"You don't think it's just because he's the first guy I've cared about?"

I'm scared that's the truth. That this isn't love, but infatuation. That I'm confused because he's the only guy I've ever engaged with.

"I think that's a great reason. Many guys have thrown themselves at you. He's the first guy because he's the only one you've returned feelings for. You've finally found someone worth giving a chance."

"Oh. That... that actually makes sense," I concede, not having an argument for it.

"Duh!" she grumbles, as if she always makes sense.

"Do you think he could like me back?" I ask, praying she says yes. Praying he likes me. Loves me.

"Babe, look at him. How many times has he saved you? And he's never once demanded anything in return. Hell, he even respects your boundaries. He slept on the floor next to you because you were drugged. He had me undress and shower you because he didn't want to take advantage of you in that state. He asked you nicely to take you out to dinner. He came to a club full of people over a decade younger than him just to see you."

I see the point she's trying to make, but I also see another point.

"What if he just sees me as a friend? He's had ample opportunities to make a move, and he hasn't. What if I've been friend-zoned?"

"Girl, I saw the dance floor. He had to physically pull himself back. And his concern over you and anger at the guy, that's not friend feelings," she counters, so sure of herself that I start to believe her. "And let's not pretend that your lips aren't red and swollen."

I flush at the reminder of our kiss.

It was so sweet, full of restrained need.

I unconsciously run my fingers across my lips, feeling his phantom kiss.

"Yeah, he's so not friend-zoning you." She snorts and grabs the remote. "As much as I love hearing about your love life, I need to finish this episode and find out who murdered this woman."

On that disturbing note, I take my leave. I have no interest in finding out who killed that woman.

"Those shows only make you crazier! How are you ever going to trust someone when you suspect every man is capable of murder?" I sigh as I leave.

"Every man is capable of murder," she counters obstinately.

"Not Roman. My hero could never!"

She doesn't respond, too engrossed in her show, so I leave.

And as I fall asleep, all I can think about is him.

# Chapter 26
## *Cecilia*

The weeks are passing in a blur. There's a new ray of light in my life. A new constant.

*Roman.*

We see each other at least three times a week. And the nights we don't get together, we make it up by calling. Even if they're nights he's busy working security, he'll still make time for a five-minute phone call.

Everything has been perfect.

He's been perfect.

He's everything I could want in a man.

He brings me flowers and chocolates. Always walks me to the door. Is the perfect gentleman. He's so respectful.

*Too respectful.*

He's taking it at my pace, but ugh, my pace is too slow. We haven't done anything more than kiss since the club.

I appreciate him respecting me. I really do.

But I want him to make a move.

I want to feel that magic with him again.

So, on our next date, I'm making a move.

# Chapter 27
## *Roman*

I can see it working.

I can see her falling.

Falling for me.

Falling for her hero.

I've been the perfect gentleman. Wooing her with gifts. Treating her with respect. Taking things slowly.

*So damn slowly.*

It's taking everything in me to hold back. I'm tapping into self-control I didn't know I possess to not make a move. To pull back after every goodnight kiss. To turn and leave, instead of taking her inside and ravaging her.

I will admit to breaking in and replacing her panties once they no longer smell like her sweet pussy but instead like my release a time or two. Or three times. Maybe more.

Knowing those lacy panties that smell of her sweet cunt and perfume wait for me at home are the only things that give me enough self-control to pull away from her. To end our kisses. To not throw her against the wall and take her in the hallway.

But I have to stay strong.
I have to earn her trust.
I have to be her hero.
Until hero is all she sees.
Until she's so blinded by hero, she can't make out the villain.

# Chapter 28
## *Cecilia*

I unlock my front door like I do after every date, but instead of turning around and kissing him before opening the door, I open the door first, then face him.

"Do you want to come in?" I force myself to maintain eye contact. I need him to see how much I want this. I suspect he's been holding back physically because he doesn't want to rush me, but I am done with waiting.

"I'd love to," he says with a wolfish grin. It's not wolfish in a scary sense, more predatorial. He's ready to pounce.

With his palm on the small of my back, he leads me in.

"Is Gracie home?" His voice is low, matching his hooded eyes.

"She's not here. She won't be back until late." *Because I asked her not to be. Because I planned this.*

I continue to my bedroom, but he redirects me to the couch.

"Why not my bedroom?" I ask, suddenly self-conscious. Have I read this wrong? Does he not want me like that? We go on dates and kiss, but he's never tried to make a move. I start to redden with embarrassment.

"Sunshine, if we go to your room, to your bed, I won't be able to resist you. And I want to do this right. To be a gentleman. I'm not going to sleep with you yet, despite every fiber of my being begging to." He pleads with me to understand. His voice raw with need and restraint. "Your bed would be too much of a temptation. I'm trying to be a better man."

"Oh," I whisper, stunned silent for a moment. "So, we're not going to kiss on the couch? I can turn on a movie or somethi–"

I'm cut off by his mouth viciously attacking mine. He's relentless. His tongue parts my lips and duels with mine. Every nerve in my body lights up. I'm on fire.

I wrap my arms around his neck and scrape my fingers through the buzzed hair, loving the feeling of the poky strands. He groans into my mouth and continues his assault.

He lifts my butt, and I take the hint, wrapping my legs around him. He walks to the couch with me hanging on him like a monkey. He sits down, and I'm sitting on top of him. Still kissing him. I lift my skirt enough to allow me to move my knees so I'm straddling him.

I pull back, desperate for oxygen, despite not wanting to break the contact.

He takes the opportunity to trail his lips down my neck. Licking, sucking, *biting.* I can't stop the moans from escaping me. Can't stop the trembles rolling through my body.

My hips move of their own accord. Grinding into the hardness between my thighs. Pressing my core onto him.

Just like at the club, he uses one hand to move my hips, controlling the pace. Controlling the friction. I'm blinded with every pass.

His other hand runs through my loose waves then grips them at the base of my skull, pulling my head back, causing me to arch my back.

He licks around my right nipple though my top. Despite the fabric barrier, I can feel him scorching my skin.

He continues guiding my hips on his, continues meeting my movement, grinding into me.

Then, he bites my nipple. And it's euphoric. I groan uncontrollably.

He growls in response, and tightens his grip, pulling me closer.

I reach to take off his shirt, needing to see him. Needing to feel his skin on mine.

When I pull at the neckline, he separates just enough to whip it off.

And reveals his tattoos.

His entire torso is covered in intricate ink. It's mesmerizing. I want to trace every pattern, every shape, every word etched into his skin. I want to trace them with my tongue.

"Fuck, sunshine. Look away. Another second of you eye fucking me, then being on the couch won't stop me from taking you." His plead comes out a demand. Instead of begging me, he's commanding me.

I look down and lift the bottom of my blouse, ready to shed it, when he grabs my wrists, stilling me.

"Please," he begs. "You can't undress. Seeing you will kill me. Destroy every last ounce of restraint. Please, keep it on this time."

Instead of answering, I lean in again and capture his mouth with my own.

He doubles his efforts, thrusting against me, maximizing the contact and the pleasure. His hand leaves my hip and lands on my thigh.

He slowly starts trailing it up.

Under my skirt.

Up my hips.

Stopping at the lacy strap of my thong.

He pulls against it lightly, then traces his fingers along the seam, until he's at the front.

"Is this sweet pussy wet for me?" It comes out so quietly, I'm not even sure he meant to say it.

When I don't answer, he lifts his gaze to mine.

"Cecilia, I asked you a question. Is your sweet cunt wet for me? Wet because of me?" His voice comes out sternly.

"Yes," I say after a gulp.

"Are you sure?"

"It is, I swear. You can check," I gasp out, needing him to believe the effect he has on me.

The grin that breaks out across his face is beautiful. It lights him up. He looks alive in a way I've never seen.

"That's all I needed to hear," he says in a low voice.

Then, his fingers trail down, over my thong, until they're covering my opening. My wet opening. So wet, I've soaked through my thong.

He growls when he finds what I promised would be there.

He pulls the panties aside and runs his fingers along my core. He does it a few more times, soaking his fingers.

Then, he pulls his fingers from my panties and lifts them to his mouth.

He sucks off my arousal while maintaining eye contact. The loud sucking is positively sinful. I can't help the flush that stains my skin.

He drags his fingers from his mouth, and they crawl back up my thigh. He stops at the strap of my thong *and tears it.* He moved to the other side and does the same.

He pulls my thong off and brings it up to his nose, inhaling my scent.

He places it to the side and brings his fingers back to my exposed core.

He runs his fingers through the wetness again, collecting it, then brings them up to my clit. He rubs circles around the swollen bud, and I throw my head back in pleasure.

He stills immediately.

"Cecilia, eyes on me when I'm touching you. When I'm playing this perfect body like an instrument I've mastered. When I make you feel this good, you watch me and know who's doing this to you." It's a promise of pleasure and the threat of denial rolled up in wicked words.

"Okay," I whisper.

"Good girl," he says after a growl.

He trails his fingers back down, until they hover over my opening. Then he dips one in me.

Even lubricated by my own arousal, there's a pinch of pain. My body not familiar with the intrusion.

"So... fucking... tight," he groans, gasping and panting. "You're going to be the death of me."

"I'm sorry," I mumble, embarrassed by my lack of experience.

"Fuck no, sunshine. You're fucking perfect. This tight pussy is going to kill me. Choke me to death. And I'll die the happiest man."

He pumps into me a few more times, and once I'm well adjusted, he adds a second finger. It takes a few more strokes for me to relax, but then he changes his angle and starts brushing against a spot inside me that has me seconds from my release.

"You like that, sunshine?" he asks.

It takes everything in me to answer, but I know how much he needs to hear it.

"Yes! I love it," it comes out a breathy moan.

He continues thrusting his fingers in me but adjusts his palm so that it's brushing against my clit, and I explode.

His name comes out a prayer on my lips, and I fall over the edge. My pussy spasms arounds his fingers, and I hear him groan. His entire body tenses, and I feel his member twitch. I'm too far gone to think about it.

He pulls his fingers from me and licks them clean.

"Let's get you cleaned up," he says.

He grabs my discarded, ruined panties and rubs them through my slick folds, collecting my arousal, effectively cleaning me dry.

He's the perfect gentleman.

# Chapter 29
## *Roman*

I lift Cecilia off my lap and stand, ready to clean myself up in the bathroom.

I came in my pants.

*Again.*

But it can't be held against me when a goddess is coming apart in my lap. On my fingers, choking them to death.

Only two fit inside her. She was so damn tight. It has to have been a while since she's been with a man.

My vision reddens at the thought of her with another man. I have to take a deep breath and turn my back to her so I don't scare her with my fury.

"OH MY GOODNESS! What is that?" Cecilia screams, jumping to the other end of the couch. To the end away from me.

I whirl around, scanning the surroundings, looking for the threat, ready to neutralize anything that has my woman so scared.

"Cecilia, what is it?" I demand.

I take a step towards her, and she scurries further away from me, cowering in fear. Cowering from me.

What the fuck?

"Why... why do you have a gun?" she whispers, her eyes reflecting the terror in her voice.

*Fuck.*

I forgot about the gun that's always in the waistband of my pants on my back. And since I'm shirtless, it's exposed.

"Sunshine, I work in security. I have to be armed to protect myself and others," I exhale in relief as the lie comes quickly. "Plus, with my training, it's only right I remain armed at all times in case there's ever a situation where I need to step in. I'd hate for something to happen that I could've prevented if I were armed. I owe it to the world." I lie so easily to her, but it's for her own good.

And it is true. To some degree. I am armed to protect. Maybe not every stranger on the street, but definitely her.

"Oh. That makes sense." She nods as she lets it soak in. Then smiles. "I'm sorry I freaked out. I just wasn't expecting it. I've never seen a gun in real life." Then my naïve, gullible girl shoots me a blinding smile. "See, you truly are a hero. Thank you!"

*Fuck, that was almost bad.*

I need a contingency plan. I need a plan in place if she ever finds out.

With that settled, I clean myself in her bathroom and come back to the couch. She's falling asleep, so I lie down and cuddle her, holding her tightly against me.

When her breathing evens out, I wait a few more minutes, basking in her peace, then carry her to bed.

I tuck her in and stand in the corner watching her.

Only when my midnight alarm goes off, signaling it's time for me to patrol our territory, do I leave. And I leave with a heavy heart.

On my way out the door, I collect her panties from the couch.

I inhale her release and groan at the scent.

These will last me a while.

With a smile, I shove them in my pocket and leave her door. I lock it with the extra key I made, and head down the hallway.

See you soon, sunshine.

# Chapter 30
## *Cecilia*

"It was a good day at work. Everything is going well. Bash is making progress on a new product..." Roman's smooth voice carries through my phone speaker during our routine goodnight call.

I love hearing from him at the end of the day.

Most of the time he doesn't talk about work, but it's interesting when he does. He's a hero, saving people's lives every day. It's so admirable.

"Sunshine, will you join me for family dinner this Sunday? I'd love to introduce you to them. We've been dating for months, and I know they'll love to meet you." The way he says it, so slowly, I can hear the trepidation in his voice. But I can also hear his hope and excitement.

My heart stops.

Me? Meet his family?

It's such an honor. I didn't realize he's as serious about us as I am. Meeting the family is important, right? That's a big step, right? I'll have to ask Gracie.

All I know is, I want to. I want this with him.

"I'd love to, héroe. Thank you." I try to contain the excitement in my voice.

He exhales in relief.

Did he really think I'd say no?

"Thank you, sunshine. I'm so excited for you to meet everyone. They're going to love you."

"I just know I'll love them too. Anyone who raised such an amazing hero is an automatic yes to me. If they're anything like you, it'll be great," I assure him.

"Alright, sunshine. Time to end the call. You have work in the morning," he says it so dreadfully, as if hanging up is painful for him.

"All right, silly goose. I'll talk to you tomorrow. Goodnight, héroe," I whisper into the phone.

"Goodnight, Celia. Sweet dreams," he whispers back.

Then the call is over.

And instead of turning off the lights and going to sleep like he said, I jump out of my bed and fly down the hallway.

I knock on Gracie's door once, then four more times until she answers.

"What in the hell is wrong with you?" she grumbles, looking disheveled.

"I am so sorry. I didn't realize you already went to sleep." I feel terrible waking her up.

"It's past eleven. Of course I'm asleep. I have an eight a.m. in the morning," she says just as sleepily then yawns.

I didn't realize I'd spoken to Roman for over an hour tonight.

"I can just let you go back to sleep. I'm so sorry."

"No, you already woke me up. Tell me what's wrong," she demands, stubborn as always.

"Roman invited me to family dinner on Sunday. This is a good thing, right? I mean, if he wasn't serious about me, then he wouldn't introduce me to them, right? I just don't know what I'm doing!" I throw my hands up.

"Take a deep breath. Get in here, let's talk this out." She opens her door further and goes to her bed. I sit on it with her ready to delve into this new development.

"So, what do you think?" I beg for her advice.

"I think this is great news. He wants his family to meet you. He has brothers, right?" she asks.

"Yes, three. And one of them is engaged. His parents will be there too. I haven't heard about anyone else, but I can't be sure there aren't more." I give her the rundown.

"Okay. You'll win over the mom and dad easily. There's no way parents won't like you. Now, we know nothing about the brothers or the fiancée. I'd say work on getting the fiancée to like you, then her soon-to-be-hubby will follow suit. That's the majority which should sway the other two brothers," she masterminds like a general preparing for battle.

"Or I could just be myself and hope that's enough for them. Not come in with some battle plan to win people over," I suggest the much more realistic option.

"Ugh, you're no fun. But you'll be fine either way. They'll love you. You're a bundle of joy and optimism. You and unlikeable are oxymorons," she says it almost insultingly, but I think that's just the grumpiness from being woken up. "It's why you attract so many morons," she grumbles.

"Roman's not a moron!" I defend my man.

*My man?*

I guess he is my man.

"I'm not talking about him. Never mind. I'm just cranky." She groans. "If that's all, please go away. I want to sleep."

I give her a hug, which she begrudgingly returns.

"Thank you so much, Gracie. I'm feeling better already! Love you!" I tell her as I prance out.

Okay, I can do this.

I'll just spend the next few days meditating on it.

# Chapter 31
## *Cecilia*

Inhale, one... two... three... four...

Hold, one... two... three... four...

Exhale, one... two... three... four...

Hold, one... two... three... four...

I repeat the box breathing technique until I'm calm enough to see through the nerves and tap into the excitement.

Roman is behind the wheel driving us to his parents. One hand holds mine as he navigates traffic with the other. The pure power and confidence in which he drives, sliding one palm over the wheel smoothly, has me clenching my thighs.

*This is not the time to get turned on, Cecilia.*

Now that I'm calm and ready to go, I'm looking forward to meeting his family. I just know they're going to be amazing, just like Roman.

We pull into the driveway of a beautiful mansion. Despite the incredulous size, it feels homey. There are gardens full of colorful flowers and a fountain in the front. It's gorgeous.

There are already three other nice cars parked in front of the house in the horseshoe, so we pull in behind one. I hope we're not late.

Roman lets us in, despite my protest of not wanting to barge in without knocking. He said it's fine, and he knows his family better than I do, so I follow along.

We go through a few rooms then open a door. He enters first then steps aside, revealing a beautiful dining room where his family is seated.

*Oh no, we are late.*

I take a deep breath and call up my mantra of the day.

*Be your truest self and those meant for you will embrace you.*

I smile awkwardly as the room silences, and I start to get the feeling that Roman forgot to mention that I was coming along.

"Hey, guys. This is Cecilia, my girlfriend," Roman says smoothly.

My heart skips a beat at the introduction. *His girlfriend.* We've never discussed labels, but it makes sense since we're dating.

I smile and wave.

They're silent for a few more beats, then the other young woman speaks up. "Welcome! It's such a pleasure to have you. I'm Margot, and this is my fiancé, Matthias." She shoots me a radiant smile, and I start to warm.

This is going to go well, I just know it.

"It's so nice to meet you. Roman has told me so much about you guys." I turn to the older couple. "Mr. and Mrs. Montclair, your home is absolutely lovely. Thank you for having me."

"Of course, dear. Please, call us Evelyn and Damien," his mother responds sweetly, sending me a warm smile. "We're so glad to finally meet you. Please, sit down." I look and realize there's only one empty seat. I guess Roman did forget to mention I was coming. She stands up when she realizes. "I'm so sorry. We'll have a spot made right away. Please, sit."

I can tell she's upset, so I shoot her another smile and give her an out. "I'm so sorry for intruding. I can leave if this was meant to be just family. Roman must've forgotten to mention it." I turn to him and lean into his comfort. "Héroe, how silly of you." I shoot him a teasing smile, silently letting him know I'm not upset.

The room seems to hold its breath, but I'm not sure why. I go over my words, wondering if I said something wrong.

Roman pulls me into a hug and smiles down at me apologetically. "I'm sorry, sunshine. I thought it'd be a nice surprise. And maybe we'd avoid the interrogation they put Margot through."

I giggle at his reasoning. As always, my hero was just trying to protect me.

"No, dear, you're absolutely welcome. We're so excited to meet you. You'll have to stay late so we can chat more." Mrs. Montclair seems so hopeful when she says it.

My heart immediately warms. She likes me. She's welcoming me.

"We'd love to," I say at the same time Roman says, "We don't have time."

I look up at him and send him my warmest smile while pleading with my eyes. "Hero, please. I want to get to know your family."

He melts instantly, like he always does for me. I'm so lucky. "Of course, Celia."

I blush at the use of the nickname only he calls me.

Once a setting is made, Roman pulls out the chair and lets me sit, ever the gentleman.

Dinner goes smoothly. We talk about Matthias and Margot's wedding. They're getting married soon. They seem like such a happy couple. They complement each other well.

The way he looks at her... There's pure adoration in his gaze.

I used to long for that, but now, sitting next to Roman who grips my hand under the table, around his family, makes me realize I may already have it.

# Chapter 32

## *Roman*

I can see the confusion in their eyes. Their wary gazes. The way they're trying to piece it together.

They want to know more about Cecilia. They've all been welcoming, but they're taken off guard. They didn't expect this. They didn't expect her. But neither did I. I didn't expect her.

But sometimes life has plans for you. And it gave me Cecilia. The best thing to ever happen to me. So, they better get used to it because she's not going anywhere.

"So, Celia, when did this start?" Dom asks bluntly.

*Celia. Not Cecilia.*

I see red. How fucking dare he? That's *my* name for her! Only mine.

"It's Cecilia to you," I say calmly, struggling to keep my voice even for Cecilia's sake. I don't want her to hear the anger I've been able to hide from her for so long. I glare at Dom, who sits on the opposite end away from Cecilia, so she can't see the murderous look in my eyes.

My beautiful sunshine giggles, thinking I'm joking.

I'm not.

But I don't correct her. The ones who need to know now know.

"A few months ago," my Cecilia answers him, her voice drawing me in. I lock eyes with her and return her fond gaze. "He saved me. He's my personal hero. He's rescued me more than once since then." She squeezes my hand, and my heart clenches. "My life has been unexpectedly chaotic these past few months, and he's always there for me when I need him. It's like he just knows."

"Of course. I'll always be there to protect you, Celia. I'll always be here to keep you safe." I keep my voice light and warm, but my insides steel at the promise. "You'll never get rid of me."

"It makes sense. Since his job is saving people. It's amazing that you guys run Syndicate Enterprise. You keep people safe. That's incredible." The pride in her voice amazes me. I preen at how high of a pedestal she has me on.

The room stills.

Margot drops her fork with a clank. Matthias's mouth hangs open. Dom stiffens. Bash pales. Mom and Dad share a sharp glance.

But I glare at them.

I shoot them a silent warning. A threat. If they break this cover, if they expose my lie, if they reveal what I truly do...

I love my family, but I don't care who I have to hurt to keep her.

And I will always keep her.

Even if she doesn't want me to.

She's mine.

"Yes," Matthias replies in a clipped voice, heeding my threat. "It's great to have him on the team."

I nod indiscernibly at him in a silent thanks. I'd have hated to shoot them on my way out and escape with Cecilia thrown over my shoulder. I don't want her to see that side of me.

The conversation carries on, but they're all off kilter.

Cecilia's oblivious to it, my sweet, naïve girl. And that's all that matters.

...

"Brothers, we need to discuss some *business* matters in the office," Dom demands, staring into my soul. "Now."

"We can talk tomorrow at the office," I lie smoothly, knowing there's no damn office. "Mom and Dad want to meet Cecilia properly."

"It's okay, héroe. I can talk to your parents and Margot while you talk to your brothers," Cecilia offers generously, completely misunderstanding the situation.

It's a bad idea for a number of reasons.

The first being, I don't want to discuss my relationship with my brothers. I know there's no *business* we need to discuss. They want to know what's going on. Who she is. Why I'm lying to her. And I don't want to delve into it with them.

The second being, I don't want Cecilia around any members of my family unmonitored. Not because I don't trust her, but because I don't know what they'll tell her. And God forbid one of them exposes my lies.

But Matthias grips my arm as he rounds the table in warning. They're not letting this go. I don't have an option.

I give Cecilia a quick kiss on the cheek and whisper, "I'll be back in a bit, sunshine. I love you." With that I turn and leave.

We enter the office, and I freeze.

*What the fuck did I just do?*

I just told Cecilia I love her.

For the first time.

As I'm being led out of the room by my furious brothers.

*Fuck.*

# Chapter 33
## *Cecilia*

I'm being led to the sitting room by Roman's parents and Margot, but I can't focus on anything they say.

*'I love you.'*

Roman's words echo in my mind.

I'm elated that he said them, that he told me he loved me, but as he's leaving the room, with his family around, not giving me the chance to reply, caught me off guard.

Nevertheless, he said it. And I know he meant it.

We'll discuss it later, and I'll tell him I feel the same way.

"Cecilia, what is it you do?" Mrs. Montclair interrupts my realization once we sit on the couch and chairs.

"I'm a PT tech for a physical therapy clinic in the city. It's a nice job. I get to help people heal, and that's really fulfilling," I say with a smile. Even though my job is hopefully temporary, I do enjoy helping the patients. "I also teach yoga after work some days."

"That all sounds amazing. You seem like a selfless woman," she replies with a smile of her own, and it warms my heart.

"You really do... So, how did you end up with Roman?" Margot asks with what can only be described as a dumbfounded expression on her face.

It takes me a moment to respond as confusion reigns through me.

"Roman saved me. He's one of the most selfless people I know," I explain to his family who I'm sure know this, but I'm met with incredulous faces. "I got knocked into a metal street pole on the way home from work and Roman literally caught me and carried me over a mile to my apartment. He took care of me when I first got the concussion then returned a few days later to check in. He gave me his number, and when I reached out, he asked me out. We've been dating since then." I sigh dreamily at the memories of how my hero and I started our relationship.

"That sounds... very kind of Roman," Mr. Montclair says slowly.

I can't make sense of the long pause or the confusion that remains etched in their features. Maybe I'm reading their scrunched brows and slight frowns wrong.

"He's been nothing but kind since. We went to a club for a friend's birthday, and I got roofied. He took me home and took care of me," I pause. "He's always taking care of me. He's such a great man. I'm sure this isn't a shock to you guys."

Suddenly, all of their expressions shift. Their eyes soften, their brows relax, and sweet smiles take over.

"Of course, dear. We're just surprised he's doing all this for a woman. In his thirty-four years on this planet, I've never been introduced to a girlfriend. I'm just surprised at seeing this new side of him." His mother fidgets with her hands, and I wonder if I'm making her uncomfortable praising her son.

"Oh," I say surprised. "I didn't realize he's never brought a woman home before."

My heart skips a beat at the realization. I'm the only woman he's ever introduced to his family. That means we must be serious in his eyes. I mean he did just profess his love to me, so this shouldn't be too much of a shock.

"I don't think he's even had a girlfriend before. He's never even mentioned a woman," she explains with wide eyes.

"I'm surprised you were able to chip through that tough exterior," Margot chimes in.

"Tough exterior?" I repeat, now the one confused. "He's never been anything but gentle and kind with me." I laugh awkwardly. "I feel like we're talking about different people."

"No, no, no. I'm sure he just shows you a different side than what he shows his family. He has to be tough for his... job," Margot rationalizes.

It calms me because that must be the case.

"I'm sure you're right," I agree. "So, what is it you guys do?"

"We retired a while ago, but Margot here is an audiobook narrator!" Mrs. Montclair says proudly.

I blush at the obvious response that the older, rich couple is retired. My parents still work even at their age, but their circumstances are different.

"That's really cool, Margot. What kind of books do you narrate?" I ask, genuinely curious. I've never met anyone with that career.

Margot blushes, then tells me about the romance novels she records.

As the conversation ebbs and flows, I realize how warm and welcoming Roman's family is. It feels like they've already accepted me, and I couldn't be more honored.

I already feel at home with them.

# Chapter 34
## *Roman*

As soon as the door closes to Dad's study, three sets of eyes glare at me.

"What the fuck is that?" Dom spits out pointing at the door in the general direction of the dining room.

"What is what?" I feign confusion. "You've never met a girlfriend before? Or you've never seen a pretty woman? Or is it you've never experienced a woman being kind to her man?"

It's petty to come after his lack of a dating life, but I don't care. They pulled me away from Cecilia, and I'm pissed about it.

Plus, Matthias laughed at it, so I'm not too far off.

"You little shit! Did you forget I'm not only your older brother, but also your boss? And the head of this family?" Dom glares at me, his nostrils flaring in anger.

"You're really going to try to control me with those things? The Syndicate wouldn't be anything without me doing your dirty work, and you damn well know it!" I seethe.

I'm hoping if we focus on work, the attention will shift from my relationship.

"Speaking of work, I didn't realize you were on Syndicate Enterprise's payroll," Matthias muses.

"I didn't want to expose who we are and what we do to her until I knew we were serious. I also don't want to expose her to the underworld. I have to keep her safe." I glare at Matthias. "You of all people should understand that."

"What I'm seeing isn't just you lying about your job. You're lying about everything. Hell, she doesn't know you at all. You're acting like a complete stranger. We both know you aren't loving and caring. And you sure as fuck aren't a hero!" Matthias throws back at me.

I have him pinned against the wall, my arm against his neck in seconds.

"I am her hero!" I grit out, beyond furious. I won't tolerate anyone saying otherwise.

"Down boy," he croaks out as I'm choking him. "I see I've hit a nerve."

Dom pulls me back before Matthias passes out.

"Why are you hiding who you are?" Dom demands.

"I'm not hiding. Maybe this is who I truly am! Ever thought of that?" I counter.

"Bullshit. We know you better than anyone else. You're a vicious killer. An instrument of pain. You're the best at what you do for a reason. You're not a sweet boyfriend," Dom calls me out.

"Fine... It all spiraled too quickly. And once she realizes that I'm not a good man, she'll leave me. She's too kindhearted to be with a killer. So, for now, she doesn't need to know." I pause, then add. "And if any of you tell her, I'll fucking destroy you."

"You're fucking catfishing her!" Bash accuses.

"I'm doing what to her? What the fuck is catfishing?" The only catfish I've ever heard of is the bottom feeder.

Bash rolls his eyes at me but explains anyways. "You're pretending to be something you're not. You're lying to her and hiding your true identity. It's vile."

"Fine, so what if I am *catfishing* her? What she doesn't know won't kill her!" I argue with my full chest. "Matthias, wouldn't you have rather Margot not have known about the Bratva and anything Syndicate related? She would've been much safer."

Matthias sighs, knowing I'm right.

"Yeah, it would've kept her safer and avoided that whole *situation*. And I'll never involve her in Syndicate affairs again." He sighs. "I'm on Roman's side here. Until he's sure she can trust him and won't run away from him, I think he can keep his darker side hidden."

"What is wrong with you two?" Bash demands incredulously.

"Get off your high horse. When you meet the love of your life, you'll understand the drastic lengths you're willing to go to keep her," I scold him.

Bash looks to the side longingly. His eyes get a faraway look, and I can tell his mind has drifted elsewhere.

"Bash?" I hiss, breaking him from his stupor.

"What? Oh... yeah. Fine, I get it. Whatever it takes to keep her." It's as though he understands the words. As though he's doing whatever it takes.

"Slow down, everyone. How well do you actually know this woman? Are you sure she isn't a spy?" Dom asks, paranoid as ever.

"Cecilia isn't a spy. She's the most peace-oriented, kindhearted human to ever walk this planet. She'd never be involved in something nefarious. Plus, I've gone through her apartment multiple times and tailed her for days. She's just a normal woman," I explain, smiling at how sweet of a woman my sunshine is.

"You've been tailing your woman and breaking into her apartment!" Bash's eyes about fall out of his head. "You're a sick fuck!"

"You would do the same thing if you were in my shoes!" I counter, but I'm not quite sure it's true. Bash has always had the tightest moral compass out of us. He's only just forgiven Matthias for how Matthias got Margot and his unwitting role in it all.

But to my absolute shock, he keeps quiet. He doesn't attack me like he did Matthias when he found out what he'd done to get Margot. He doesn't fight me on this at all. In fact, the more he stews on what I said, the more he relaxes, until he finally nods in agreement.

*What the fuck is going on with him?*

"I'd also perform an extensive background check on my woman... er, I mean, if I had one. Want me to check out Cecilia? I just need her full name," he confesses, not making eye contact.

*Why is he acting so weird?*

"Do it," Dom demands.

"No need," I counter. "Cecilia is an open book. She'll tell me anything I want to know. She's not a threat."

They stare at me slack-jawed. I know it goes against everything we preach, but it's just not needed. Cecilia isn't hiding anything.

"Are you sure? I can get it to you within the day," Bash offers.

"Do it," Dom repeats. "This isn't up for discussion."

"Fine. I can send it to you tomorrow."

"I can just stop by, and you can explain everything to me," I offer, not wanting to inconvenience him more. "Your penthouse isn't far from Cecilia's place." It offers me a great excuse to visit her.

"Oh... umm. I actually moved," Bash reveals.

He's met with three more shocked faces.

"Where'd you move to?" Dom demands.

"Shady Meadows."

"Why the fuck did you move to the middle-class suburbs an hour away from the Syndicate and Syndicate Enterprises? Fuck, it's an hour away from all of us. You have millions in the bank! Why live somewhere so below your paygrade?" Dom asks what we're all thinking.

It doesn't make sense. His penthouse is in a better location and is much nicer. It's also heavily secure with Syndicate Enterprise measures. Why would he move?

"Don't worry about it. I'll send you the update. You've been away from your woman for forty minutes. Don't you want to get back to her?" he counters.

I know he's just trying to switch the subject, but I don't care. I need to get back to Cecilia.

# Chapter 35
## *Cecilia*

When Roman joins us in the sitting room, he seems calm. Happy. Normal.

His family continues to look at us with confused expressions. It's like they're trying to solve a math problem that they just don't understand.

I know they like me, but I wonder if I'm not the kind of woman they thought he'd be with and if that's why they're so taken aback.

When it's time to go, we hug his family and walk to his car hand in hand. He opens my door for me and even buckles me in, checking to make sure it's secure.

We talk about his family and how dinner went on the way home.

And I refrain from bringing up what he said.

*'I love you.'*

I want to wait until I have his full, undivided attention.

When we get to my apartment, he parks, opens my door for me, and leads me into my building with his hand on the small of my back. We bypass the elevator as we always do and climb the stairs.

When we get to my front door, I unlock it and let him in.

"Let's go to my room. I want privacy for this conversation, and I don't know what Gracie's doing tonight," I explain.

I want us to be alone so we can discuss what he said. So, I can tell him I love him without interruption. Without distraction.

"Okay, sunshine," he murmurs and follows behind me.

I look back and see his face guarded. His eyebrows are furrowed, and his lips are thinned. He looks almost scared.

When we get to my room, I sit on the bed next to him, but he pulls me onto his lap, straddling him, so I'm facing him.

"Roman," I say, at the same time as he says, "Cecilia."

We just stare at each other.

"You go first," I tell him.

He looks like he's going to decline but thinks better of it.

"Cecilia, I'm so sorry if meeting my family was too much or too soon. I don't want to lose you. Please don't end things. You're everything I could ever want, and I won't let you go." The last bit comes out fiercely, and I believe him. He'll never let me go, and that warms my heart.

His grip on my tightens as he speaks, and I can feel how serious he is.

"Roman, that's not it at all. I wanted privacy to discuss what you told me earlier." His face freezes, then he sighs.

"I'm sorry if telling you I love you was too soon. It's just how I feel. You don't have to say it back but know that I mean it. I've never brough a woman home to my family. Fuck, I've never even called a woman my girlfriend. I don't know how to do this, but I know how I feel." His eyes shine with truth. I can hear the sincerity in his voice.

"Héroe, that's not it at all." I smile and lean closer. "Yes, you took me by surprise, but only in the best way. I wish I could've told you how I felt when you did, but you were pulled away."

Hope glimmers in his eyes.

"Roman Montclair, I love you. I love you so much. You're my hero in every sense of the word. I know it's only been a few months, but I can't imagine life without you. You've become so important to me. An integral part of my happiness. I love you, and I don't ever want to let you go."

I smile as he beams.

He's perfect.

We're perfect.

# Chapter 36
## *Cecilia*

He captures my lips between his soft ones and kisses me with a fervor he hasn't before. It's all-consuming love. It's uncontrolled and commanding.

His tongue demands entrance, and I gladly oblige, parting my lips for him. With every swipe against mine, electric shocks run down my spine.

His hands roam. Up my sides. Over my back. Through my hair. They control me. Pulling me into him.

His hips roll, grinding into my core. Each movement sending shivers up my spine.

And every few seconds, he pulls back to tell me, "I love you."

And with every whispered word, my decision solidifies.

Tonight's the night.

# Chapter 37
## *Roman*

Cecilia pulls back and looks at me with strong eyes. She steels her back, tapping into her strength.

"I want to have sex with you," she says definitively.

My heart stops, then races.

"I want that too, sunshine," I tell her with a grin, then leans in, ready to attack her neck.

"No, Roman. I want to have sex with you tonight." She looks at me with hopeful eyes.

My already hard cock grows impossibly larger at her words.

My goddess wants me to fuck her, right now.

I take a deep breath, trying to reign in the beast inside. If I come on too strong, if I'm too rough, I could scare her away. And I won't risk that. So, I'll tap into every ounce of self-control I possess and go at her pace.

"Roman... is that okay? I don't want to pressure you to do anything." She looks so nervous that I almost laugh.

*Her* pressuring *me* into sex is absurd.

I've wanted to bury myself in her sweet pussy since the first time I laid eyes on her. It's taken everything in me not to rush it, but I needed this to be her choice. And I don't regret waiting. Not even the months of blue balls, coming in my pants, and panty thieving that the waiting has caused.

"Sunshine, there's nothing I want more than to make love with you. The wait has been hell, but I'd wait twice as long if it meant I'd finally have you." I cup her cheek as I say it.

I keep my crude words to myself. My sweet goddess deserves to be shrouded in love and respect. She's goodness incarnate and deserves to be unadulterated. Even if what I want to do to her is positively sinful. For all her goodness, I'm hell incarnate.

She blushes and lifts her dress over her head, leaving her in a matching nude bra and thong. It's the first time I've seen her naked, and I can't look away.

Her smooth stomach, toned from all her yoga, calls to me. I have to refrain from tracing my hands, or tongue, over it. My eyes trail lower and land on her pretty little lace thong. My cock twitches at the sight. Even her plain beige bra doesn't slow me down. It's just a regular bra, nothing special about it. Except the fact that it's holding up her tits. My Cecilia's tits.

I lean forward and bite the flesh exposed above the bra cup. I groan as she moans.

*Fuck, she's so responsive.*

She starts tugging my shirt up, and I take the hint, whipping it over my head and throwing it to the floor.

She reaches behind her back and unhooks her bra. It hangs loosely on her shoulders, the slightest movement threatening it to slide off.

"Shrug," I command hoarsely.

She obeys, and the bra falls down her arms, revealing her perky breasts.

They're not big by any means of the word. Fuck, they're rather small. But they're perfect. Delicate and dainty, just like the rest of her.

I suction my lips around her left nipple, over her heart. I waste no time sucking, licking, nibbling. She writhes underneath me, grinding onto my cock. I'm thrusting my hips, meeting her movements.

I pull back though, because coming in my pants from dry humping on her bed isn't how tonight's going to end.

My cock will be inside her.

I watch her gaze drop to my cock, straining against my slacks.

"Take my cock out, sunshine," I demand in a low voice.

"Huh? Oh... umm." She stutters as she fumbles with my belt. Her shaky hands hinder her from undoing it.

"Cecilia, stop," I grit out, despite every fiber of my being begging for her touch. I grab her hands, halting her motion, and pull them to my chest. "What's wrong? If you don't want to do this, we don't have to."

*Please don't say stop. Please.*

"It's not that. It's just..." She turns away from me, but I cup her cheek and drag her eyes to mine. "It's just that I've never done this before," she whispers.

And my heart stops while my cock simultaneously leaks precum.

"Never done what before?" I whisper too, unable to believe my ears.

*Could my sweet sunshine possibly be a virgin?*

There's just no way a goddess like her has saved herself for *me.*

"Anything. I mean, I've kissed a few guys before." She pauses when I grunt at the mention of other men. "But besides that, I've never done anything else with a man. What we've done is the farthest I've ever gone, and only with you."

She seems embarrassed about it, but I can't fathom why.

She just gave me the greatest gift.

"Cecilia, you're a virgin?" I ask, needing to hear it.

"Yes," she whispers.

"Fuck, sunshine. Fuuuck." I don't have words. I close my eyes, and focus on taking deep breaths, so close to losing control.

"I'm sorry," she mutters as tears form in her eyes.

"No!" I quickly shout, not wanting her to get the wrong idea. "I'm shocked that a woman as perfect as you has waited so long and is willing to give something so precious to me. Thank you, sunshine. I'm honored."

"You don't mind?" The hope in her voice almost crushes me.

"Fuck no! This is the greatest gift anyone has ever given me. I promise to make it good for you."

And I will. I know it can hurt for women on the first time, but I'll do everything in my power to lessen the pain. I will never hurt Cecilia.

"Thank you, héroe. There's no one I'd rather it be," she tells me with a full smile.

I pick her up, and place her on her back next to me, then start to move. If I want to do this right, I need her ready.

I position myself between her toned tan thighs.

"I'm going to talk you through this. The first thing I'm going to do, is take this sexy thong off you," I tell her as I pull her thong down.

"Then, I'm going to feast. I've wanted a taste from the source since I licked my fingers after they were inside of you the first time. I'm not going to stop until you've come on my mouth, flooding me with your juices. I'm fucking famished for you."

I pounce, slowly stroking my tongue through her folds.

Her wetness coats me, and I moan into her pussy. It's fucking delicious. She's fucking delicious. Floral and fresh. She moans as I circle her clit with my tongue.

"How's this, sunshine?" I ask against her pussy unable to pull back even to talk to her.

"Ugh," she groans in pleasure.

*I'll take that as a good sign.*

I continue my assault, lapping her up like a man dying of thirst. I want to taste this sweet pussy every day for the rest of my life. I've found my happy place.

My thighs are glued to the bed. If I move a muscle, I'll come in my pants.

But then she cries out, grips my hair, shoves my head deeper into her, and starts shaking.

"I'm... I'm... coming," she cries out in a breathy voice.

And it's too fucking late for me.

She floods my mouth, and I flood my pants. I can't stop it. She's irresistible without even trying. But now, coming against my lips, my tongue inside her, her juices drowning me... I can't be blamed.

I let us breathe for a moment, then tease her entrance with my pointer finger.

"Now that you're drenched for me, I'm going to stretch you with my fingers. You're too tight for my cock right now. So, you'll come a second time on my fingers. I want to feel you choke the life out of them. I don't want to be able to hold a gun again, because of your tight pussy."

"I don't know if I can go again," she whimpers.

"Oh, sunshine. You can. There's a lot left in you."

"Okay, I believe you." She gives me the go ahead after a few beats.

I push a finger in easily, her slickness allowing easy entry. I slowly slide in and out of her, watching her cunt suck it in.

I wiggle in a second finger, and she gasps at the tight fit.

"Do you like this? If it hurts, tell me and I'll adjust," I tell her, needing her to understand this is about her pleasure.

"Don't stop! Please, don't stop!" she begs.

And I'm just a man, unable to do anything but please his woman.

So, I pump in with that second finger until her pussy accepts it with ease. Then I wiggle in a third one, all the while, my tongue toying with her clit.

The sight before me will forever be engrained in my mind. Anytime I ever need happiness, I'll picture this.

My goddess laid out on her bed, panting, writhing, begging. Pure perfection.

And when her back arches off the bed, when she lets out a scream of pleasure, I continue finger fucking her exactly the same way, successfully pushing her over the edge.

Miraculously, and only because I came minutes ago, do I not follow her over the edge. Granted, I'm rock hard and ready to go, but the next place I'm coming is in that tight pussy.

"How are you feeling, sunshine?" I ask her as I kiss and lick my way up her body, until we're at eye level.

"Weightless. Happy. Perfect," she says with a dazed smile. "Are we going to have sex now?"

"Yes, sunshine. We're going to have sex now that you're ready," I grumble, barely able to hold conversation with her aroma wafting around the room, her taste tattooed on my tongue, with my cock begging to know what the inside of her feels like.

"I'm going to push my cock into you slowly. It's going to be okay. I'll be gentle. Once you get used to the size, we'll start fucking. Is that okay with you?"

"Yes, please," she mutters.

I undo my pants and pull them and my underwear off and throw them across the room.

Cecilia stares at my straining cock with wide eyes. Her face pales slightly. I know I'm above average in every way, but I also know she's perfectly capable of taking me.

"It's big. Is it too big?" She chews her lip nervously.

"It'll fit. Your tight pussy will make room for me. You were made for me," I assure her.

I position myself at her entrance and look into her eyes.

"Roman, I love you. And I trust you," she says sweetly.

And I have to take a breath to center myself.

# Chapter 38
## *Cecilia*

"I love you too, sunshine."

His eyes gleam with love, and he leans down and kisses me. It's sweet and soft and full of love.

I feel his tip at my entrance and widen my legs hoping to help ease him in. He pushes in, and I feel the stretch. He's big. Much bigger than his three fingers. But he goes slowly, and once his head is in, he stills.

"Good job, sunshine. Good girl. You're taking me so well. This is the widest it'll be. You did such a good job." He kisses me again, and I relax around him.

He starts to gently rock into me. Easing his way in. A little further each time.

He's slow and patient, stopping every time I wince.

Then, I feel him tear through my barrier. I tense up involuntarily at the pain.

He freezes and balancing his weight on one arm, he brings the other hand to my cheek. He brushes away a stray tear and kisses the streak.

"It's okay, sunshine. That's it. It's done. I'm so sorry. I don't ever want to hurt you. I'm so–"

I cut him off with a kiss. He has nothing to be sorry for. After a minute, I pull back, and he continues.

"I'm going to give you time to adjust, but once you're ready, I'll start moving. I love you, Cecilia María." He brushes another kiss against my cheek.

I can tell how hard it is for him. He's tightened every muscle. I know how badly he needs to move, but he's putting himself second to me and my needs, and he's waiting.

*What did I do to deserve this man?*

"I'm ready, héroe. Please, move," I beg him.

He sighs in relief and starts rocking into me.

The pain dissipates, and suddenly, overwhelming pleasure fills me.

"Fuck, sunshine. Your pussy just tightened, choking the life out of me," he groans.

He never speeds up to a quick pace, but the slow lovemaking is perfect for my first time. It's everything and more than I could ever want.

He's everything and more than I could ever want.

He brings his hand from my face down to between us and starts playing with my clit in strong, even circles.

I tighten and suddenly I'm pushed over the edge.

"Roman," I moan out his name.

He covers my mouth in a kiss as he groans, twitching inside me, following me over the edge.

I can feel his release pumping inside me, but in my haze, I don't think anything of it.

This third orgasm isn't like the rest. It's different with him inside me. It's more intimate with his lips on mine. It's everything I could ever want.

He breaks the kiss and lays his head in the crook of my neck.

"How was that, sunshine? Was it as good for you as it was for me?" I nod, and he sighs in relief. "I've never felt love like this, Cecilia. I want your first time, and every time with me, to be great for you. I love you."

"Roman, it was perfect. It was better than anything I could've dreamed of. I love you so much. Thank you for taking care of me." I move slightly, and wince at the soreness. "I may not be able to walk tomorrow."

I can feel his lips turn up in the corner of my neck.

"Bad boy! You can't like that," I tease him.

He twitches inside of me at the words, then slowly pulls out.

He sits up and watches our combined juices pour from me. I watch him collect them with his fingers and push them back into me.

I just stare, confused and mesmerized.

Until a harsh reality shocks me.

"I'm clean, obviously. But I'm also on the pill, to regulate my hormones, so there's no risk here," I assure him, not wanting him to worry about a pregnancy.

He freezes, mid-collection. His brows furrow, his lips turn down, and his shoulders hunch. I can't make sense of this change of behavior.

Before I can dwell on it, he looks at me softly. "I'm clean too. I've never gone bare before. Only with you."

He puts on his pants and walks to the bathroom. He comes back with a wet cloth and cleans me. Then he lays me in bed and pulls me to him.

I fall asleep in his arms, and I know there's no going back.

And I don't want to.

# Chapter 39
## *Cecilia*

It's been weeks of this heaven. The days pass in a blur of pure happiness. Every day has been a great day. Nothing's been able to dampen my mood.

Because of him.

Because of my hero.

He's perfect. Life with him is perfect. We either see each other or call every day. He makes me a priority. Some days he walks me home from work, and I cook dinner for him and Gracie. Others we'll go to the park or out to eat.

On weekends, he'll take me to different spots around town, and show me around. It's been surreal.

Even when we're just hanging out at the apartment, it's great. It's him. Roman is my dream man. There's never been someone more perfect for me. The universe is truly rewarding me.

I'm envisioning our future, and it's one I want so badly.

And I'm starting to think it's less of a dream and more of a promise.

# Chapter 40
## *Roman*

I haven't ever smiled this much in my life. It's my sunshine, she makes me happy. She brings me so much joy. She brightens my life.

The past few weeks have been perfect. I can tell she feels the same way. She just doesn't realize they've been so great because I've carefully cultivated them to be so.

I'm her dream man. Sweet, caring, gentle, kind... It's not all a farce; I do enjoy being those things around her. She brings them out in me. But it's not all honest either. I've kept many things hidden, including my threatening nature and stone-cold killer instincts.

Hell, even the sex has been soft. We've been making love. Which isn't bad at all. I love her, and I love making love to her. It's just different than the hard and rough way I've always fucked. But I can't take her that way because I won't risk scaring her. She's so kind and fragile, I can't tarnish her.

She doesn't suspect anything. She's as naïve as ever. My sunshine has the awareness of a rock, which despite helping me keep her, concerns me. I've reserved every morning and every afternoon to following her to and from work, even if it's out of my way. I just have to make sure she's safe. She doesn't suspect a thing, which again, is concerning.

Anyway, she can keep being oblivious and optimistic. I'll keep her out of harm's way. She'll never be hurt again. She'll never be alone again.

Just as I never will.

We'll be by each other's sides for the rest of our lives.

No matter what it takes.

# Chapter 41
## *Cecilia*

As I walk into my apartment from work, the smile vanishes from my face.

A large duffel bag, huge suitcase, and stuffed backpack sit by the door.

My heart drops at the realization.

Today's the last day.

Gracie's sitting on the couch and when she sees me, her eyes well up, matching my teary ones.

"It's already time?" I whisper around the lump in my throat.

"Yeah. Off to London I go." She walks over and gives me a hug. "I'm going to miss you."

"Stop!" I choke out, knowing if she becomes any more emotional, it'll break me. "It's only for the summer semester. You'll be back in three months, and I'll be here waiting."

"Three months feels like eternity," she grumbles.

I feel the exact same way, but I won't let her know that. She's been so excited to study abroad. For as long as I've known her, it's been her dream to go to London. I'm so happy she's finally able to do it.

"It's going to be a great experience. Time's going to fly by so quickly. Enjoy it. You've wanted this for so long." I pull her into another hug, and we hold on to each other.

Gracie's not big on physical touch, so this long hug speaks volumes.

"I will. I'm really excited," she tells me. "And you'll be great here. Roman will keep you company. Just, be careful."

"I'll be fine. Nothing bad ever happens in Boston."

"You're an idiot." She rolls her eyes at me. "Just don't leave Roman. He'll take care of you."

"I have no intentions of letting him go," I say with a blush.

"Good. Don't forget, if anything happens, call me. Time difference be damned, I'm always here for you. I love you, girl."

"I love you too! And the same goes for me. I'm only a call away. Now, I'm going to cook us dinner. Anything you want," I tell her, wanting to do one last thing for her.

"You don't have to. But if you do, can you make the Ecuadorian steak and eggs?" she asks with a grin, knowing that of course I'll make churrasco Ecuatoriano for her.

While we eat, I double check her plan for tomorrow and make sure she's checked in for her flight. She insists on taking the T to the airport, so tonight is our last time seeing each other.

We stay up way too late. I insist she goes to bed before her early flight. She insists she's sleeping on the plane, so it's fine.

At three a.m., we part ways with a final hug.

I fall asleep with a heavy heart. I know this is for the best, but I'm going to miss my best friend.

At least Roman is here for me. I don't think he has any intention of leaving.

And neither do I.

# Chapter 42
## *Roman*

"Are you sure there isn't anything I can do to help? I hate sitting around while you do all the cooking," I offer.

I don't ever want her to feel like she's waiting on me. She's my equal, not my servant.

"After the onion incident, I think it's safest if you stay out of the kitchen. I'll have to teach you how to properly dice one soon, though." She flashes me a bright smile of encouragement. "It's really not as difficult as you made it look, I promise."

I laugh at the memory. Turns out vegetables are harder to cut than humans. Who would've known?

I walk behind her, wrap my arms around her waist as she stirs the delicious smelling dish and rest my head on hers.

"Anything you say, sunshine," I tell her as I rock us to the music playing throughout her kitchen.

"It's weird being here alone. I mean when you're not here. With Gracie gone, the place feels so empty. So lonely. I don't like it," Cecilia confesses with a soft sigh.

*You won't be alone for long.*

...

I get to my apartment a little past three in the morning. After we watched a movie, she was tired, so I left.

I made a pit stop at one of the clubs. There was a Mafia member causing some issues, bothering some customers. It's unusual for the Mafia to cause us trouble, but new, young members can be difficult to control.

By the time I got there though, he had left. My men didn't even get a name. A fight had broken out on the dance floor, demanding their attention. A jealous boyfriend or something. My men left the Mafia guy to break the fight, and he snuck off.

Since enough time had passed for Cecilia to fall asleep, I went back to her apartment for a few hours just to watch her. She's so beautiful when she sleeps peacefully. It took all I had to leave.

And I needed to leave.

Because I have some cleaning to do.

I look around my penthouse and make note of what needs changing before she moves in.

I start with my weapons. Since I was the only one living here, I left guns, knives, and other unsavory tools lying around. The penthouse is heavily secured with an alarm system Bash built for Syndicate Enterprise, so I'm not worried about people breaking in.

I collect the weapons and put some in a large safe in the closet of a guest room that goes unused. I leave a few hidden throughout the apartment in areas I don't think she'll check. In my desk drawer. Behind a picture on the wall. On the back of the top shelf in the pantry. Above the fridge. In my nightstand's bottom drawer...

Although my place is locked down tighter than Fort Knox, I won't risk not being able to protect my Cecilia on a moment's notice.

Once that's settled, I look around my apartment. The living room houses a charcoal couch, a glass coffee table, glass side tables, black leather chairs, and black walls. The kitchen is full of stainless-steel appliances, black marble countertops, and charcoal cabinets. My bedroom contains my California king on a black leather headboard, with black bedding, a charcoal grey rug, and about as much personality as the rest of the house.

Room after room, my eyes are opened to how bleak my apartment is.

*Oh my God. Am I goth?*

I shudder at the appalling thought and look up interior designers. I need a place that Cecilia will love and feel at home in… and this dungeon is not going to cut it.

Once I've found a few I like, I send emails asking how soon they can decorate my entire penthouse. I'm thinking earth tones, dark woods, maybe some greens. The perfect mix of my sunshine and me.

As I get ready for bed, I look forward to a future with her by my side every night.

# Chapter 43
## *Cecilia*

*CRASH!*

I jolt out of my downward dog pose as my front door swings open.

My heart pounds. My hands shake. My breathing comes in quick pants.

None of it from the yoga, but because there's a masked man entering my apartment with a gun in his hand.

I lay flat on the ground, hidden from view behind the couch. The man makes his way to my kitchen and opens my fridge. As he hums to himself, I make my escape.

I grab my phone and army crawl to my bedroom quiet as a mouse. I can still hear him going through the kitchen, not a care in the world. With trembling hands, I dial the only person I know will protect me.

Roman answers on the first ring.

"Hey, sunshine! What are you up to?" he asks cheerfully.

I choke back a sob while trying to form words.

"Roman," I croak out. "Help me."

"Cecilia, what's wrong?" His tone shifts instantly. He's on high alert.

"There's a man... in my apartment... with a gun." A tear slips down my cheek as the reality of the situation hits me.

I may not make it out alive.

"Cecilia, where are you?" he rushes out. I can hear his steps pick up, like he's running.

"I'm in my bedroom. He doesn't know I'm here." I continue whispering to keep it that way.

"Can you get to Gracie's room?"

Thank you, Universe, for not having Gracie be here. I'd rather die alone than have my friend die with me.

"Cecilia! Can you get to her room?" he asks again, this time more urgent.

I quiet to hear where he is, then I hear a *SMASH* in the bathroom.

In the bathroom between Gracie's room and my room.

"No, he's in the bathroom," I tell him and Roman curses. "What if he comes in here next?" I start hyperventilating.

"Cecilia, focus. I need you to listen to me. Shut your bedroom door then go into your closet. Hide behind your clothes. Don't make a sound." He pauses, as if listening to my lack of movement. "Now, Cecilia!"

I do as he says, shutting myself in the closet. All the while, the robber destroys my apartment.

I hear him breaking things. The precious items Gracie and I have collected over the years. With each shatter and crash, my heart cracks.

"I'm in the closet," I whisper to him.

"Good girl," he says. "How many are there?"

"Just the one." I whimper, because even though it's just one man, it's one man with a gun, and I know my chances are low.

"Okay. That's fine. Just stay quiet," he instructs.

I can hear his fear. A door opens on his end, then an engine starts. I can practically feel the rumble of the car as he accelerates too quickly.

"Be safe, hero. You can't get into a wreck–" I pause when realization hits me. "Roman, you can't come here! He has a gun! You could get shot!" I need him to understand the danger.

"Cecilia, you're hiding in your fucking closet while a man with a gun robs you. I'm going to be at your place in eight minutes. Have you called the cops?"

I know I can't reason with him. Heck, I'm not even being reasonable. I'm being robbed at gunpoint, and my first instinct was to call my boyfriend not the police.

"No. I'm sorry. I thought of you first," I explain, knowing how stupid it sounds.

"No, sunshine. You did the right thing. I'll get to you before they do," he promises. "Now, on another line, call 9-1-1. Tell them your address and what's going on. I'm seven minutes away. Just don't get caught. I'm almost to you, Celia." His desperation bleeds into his words, and I hear the engine speed up.

"Roman, I love you. If I don't make it–"

"Cecilia, no! No talking like that. I'm six minutes away. Call the cops," he grinds out.

I put him on hold and dial 9-1-1.

I pray the cops get here before Roman does.

I know his love for me is clouding his judgement, because he's no match for a man with a gun.

I just pray he doesn't hurt himself being my hero.

# Chapter 44
## *Roman*

This fucking motherfucker. Robbing my sunshine at gun point. Breaking in while she's there. Terrifying her. Traumatizing her.

I'm going to fucking kill him!

"FUCK!" I yell, slamming my palms against my steering wheel as I weave through traffic.

This isn't what was supposed to happen.

She shouldn't ever be in harm's way. And now she's at risk of being shot.

Fear shoots through me at the thought, but fury tramples it away.

This fucking bastard signed his death certificate the moment he strode into her apartment with a gun while she was there.

I make a phone call.

# Chapter 45
## *Cecilia*


"Miss, are you still there?" the 9-1-1 operator asks, grabbing my attention.

"Yes. Sorry. I'm just trying to listen," I murmur under my breath, not really caring if she hears me.

A ringtone sounds, and I almost pass out from the shock. I check my phone frantically trying to turn off the sound.

But it's not coming from my phone.

It's coming from the hallway.

Right outside my door.

My heart stops. He's right there. Right outside my door. Mere feet away from discovering me. I hold my breath, scared he can sense me breathing.

I hear a male voice curse, then pick up the call. I can't make out what he says, but he's off the phone in less than a minute. I hear his heavy footsteps trailing down the hallway, through the living room... and out the front door.

The apartment door slams shut, and silence falls.

"Miss? Did you hear me? Officers will arrive on scene in twelve minutes," she says kindly.

"Oh, uh... They don't need to come anymore. I think... I think he just left?" The end sounds more like a question since I'm still confused by his retreat.

Did he really leave?

Just like that?

Could the universe really be looking out for me that well?

"No, miss. We're still coming to the scene. Do not leave the closet until an officer finds you. He could still be there. And we don't know the state of your apartment," she explains, and it makes sense.

So, I stay put.

I sit in silence, still on the line with the operator, waiting for the cops to save me when the front door creaks open.

I hold my breath as icy tendrils shoot down my spine.

*He's back.*

*He's here to finish what he started.*

I hear lighter footsteps beeline straight to my bedroom. There's no hesitation in them. He knows exactly what he wants.

My bedroom door breaks open, and I stifle a whimper, slapping my palm over my mouth.

I shrink back further into my clothes, even as those light steps walk right up to my closet door.

Tears well in my eyes, and one slowly slides down my cheek.

My closet door opens, but I don't move. I don't open my eyes. I don't think. I don't breathe.

I know he's here. I know he's found me. I know this isn't a fight I'll win.

But I can't open my eyes and look at him, knowing the fate that awaits me.

Warm, calloused hands grab me, scooping me from the floor, and more tears drip down my cheeks.

"Shhh, sunshine. It's okay. It's just me. I've got you," Roman's smooth voice consoles me.

I open my eyes to see his brown ones staring right into mine.

"Hero! Oh, my hero! You've saved me!" I cry out hysterically.

I bury my head into his shoulder and finally allow myself to break. I sob into his neck. Even knowing that I'm drenching his shirt, I can't stop. I can't care in this moment.

Because he's here.

Roman is here.

To save me.

As he always does.

As he always will.

# Chapter 46
## *Cecilia*

Roman holds me to his chest while sitting on my bed. He rocks me in his arms while whispering soothing words until I finally collect myself.

"I'm sorry for being such a mess. I know it could've been worse. I was just really scared," I tell him, my voice rough from the crying.

"No, sunshine. This was a traumatic experience. You have every right to react how you are. I should've announced myself when I entered. I'm sorry I didn't. I'm sorry I didn't get here sooner." His grip on me tightens as he says it.

"Roman, it's not your fault someone broke in," I tell him. His breathing halts for a second before he leans down and kisses the top of my head. "I'm just ready to put this behind me."

He coughs awkwardly. "Umm, about that..." He sighs. "He messed up your apartment pretty badly. The place is trashed. I'm really sorry, sunshine. I know how much you love it here."

My heart breaks further. All the things Gracie and I spent years collecting, using our last pennies to buy, the memories spent together... all of them are gone. Broken. Destroyed.

"How... how bad is it?" I hesitate, hoping beyond belief everything is salvageable.

"He must've been high. The place is destroyed. I don't think you'll be able to live here. Hell, I don't even think you'll get your security deposit back."

Tears well in my eyes again. I don't know how it's even possible with how much I've cried.

The front door opens again, and I feel nauseous. *What now? Who could it possibly be?*

Roman stands and gently sets me on the bed.

"No! Please don't go!" I beg him, not wanting to risk him.

"I'll be okay, Cecilia. I promise. Lock the door behind me." He kisses the top of my head, pushes some hair behind my ears, and approaches my bedroom door.

We hear two sets of footsteps throughout the apartment.

Roman pulls a gun from under his jacket and holds it at eye level, as I've seen them do in Gracie's crime documentaries.

Roman opens the door silently, shuts it behind him, and takes off.

"POLICE! DROP THE GUN!" a woman shouts from the living room.

"I'm Cecilia's boyfriend, not the robber. I got here about eight minutes ago, and he was already gone. Cecilia is in her room on her bed. She can confirm. I'm lowering my weapon now, but you're not going to be putting handcuffs on me." Roman's voice bleeds through the walls. It's strong and firm. He knows what he's doing.

But what is he doing? You can't just tell officers not to arrest you. I'm pretty sure that's not how it works.

"Cecilia, it's just the cops. Come out of your room, please, sunshine," Roman instructs carefully.

I rush out, not wanting to find him detained because he's bossing the officers around.

"I'm Cecilia. I'm the one who called. This is my apartment. That's my boyfriend, Roman. He just got here. The robber is gone. It's okay–" I halt abruptly as I take in my surroundings.

Our coffee table is broken. Our couch is ripped up along with the armchairs, the ones Gracie and I brought from an estate sale. Our TV is shattered. I turn to the kitchen. Our cabinets hang off the wall. Our ceramic dish set that we thrifted is broken, shards sprinkle around the kitchen like diamonds.

Everywhere I look, remnants of my once homey apartment lay destroyed and unsalvageable.

My whole life, everything I own, is wrecked.

"Miss? We need to get your statement," the woman officer who must be in charge tells me. But I can't move.

Roman crosses the room in three strides and pulls me to his chest, crushing me into him.

"She'll talk when she's ready," he growls at them.

"Miss, we need a statement now. We have other places to be, and since there is no longer an active threat, we can get going once a statement is made." She flashes me a tight smile, and I can tell she means well.

"Okay. I'll tell you what happened."

And I do.

I tell them everything. And they ask questions along the way. I'm not much help since I didn't see his face or anything distinguishing, but they don't make me feel bad. Well, except for the other officer's scowl.

"How do we know there was even a robber?" he hisses out, his hard eyes bearing into mine.

"Oh... Uhh... I'm not sure what you're asking." My faces pinches in confusion, because... *what?*

"He's implying that you trashed your own place for insurance money," Roman seethes. "Listen here, fucker. If Cecilia says there was an armed man that broke in, then there was an armed man. She's the sweetest soul. She would never break her own things. She wouldn't break anyone's things. And she wouldn't lie."

"I'm sure your girlfriend is the greatest woman around." He rolls his eyes. "But we have to be the ones to determine it."

"Officer Evans!" the woman officer hisses.

"I'm just doing the job, Officer Nguyen," he responds, his voice dripping in condescension.

"And you'll do your job without blaming the victim," Officer Nguyen orders him.

"I don't understand. Why would I break my things, just to ask for money? I don't even have insurance on this place," I explain, still confused. "Unless my health insurance covers the cost?" I glance up at Roman for the answer.

He sighs and drops a kiss on my hair.

"No, sunshine. Health insurance is different than renter's insurance. How did you rent this place without insurance? I'm pretty sure it's illegal not to have renter's insurance."

"I don't know. I think we opted out." I try to recall the lease Gracie and I signed over a year ago.

Officer Nguyen comes to me and hands me her business card.

"Call me if you need anything or remember anything. We have another call to get to." She starts to walk away, then turns back to me. "Cecilia, I would advise against staying here. Not only is the building itself not safe, but also, with the condition this unit is in, I wouldn't recommend it. And while in my professional opinion I don't think the robber will return, we can never be sure."

With those caring yet troubling words, she and her partner leave.

"Roman, I don't have anywhere to go. I only have enough money saved to stay in a hotel for a few nights. But I... I don't think I can stay here. It's just, every time I close my eyes, I'm back in that closet, fearing for my life." I look up at him, tears welling once again. "I don't know what to do."

"Sunshine, you can stay with me as long as you need. Don't worry about it for even a second. In fact, I'd love for you to move in permanently. Not only so I can always keep you safe, but also because I love you, and I hate going days without seeing you." His voice shines with hope.

He pulls me in for another hug, and new tears form. Tears of gratitude.

I think about it and realize it's the perfect solution. We're happy together. And while I never saw myself living with a man until marriage, this is an extenuating circumstance. And I can't deny that around Roman is the only place I'll feel safe.

"Thank you so much, héroe. I can't tell you what this means to me. You really are my hero. Saving me every time." I lean up and kiss him on the lips.

He leans down to meet mine and pulls me in. The kiss is sweet and comforting. It feels like home.

"Let's pack up your things and bring them to my place. You don't need to be here any longer," he kindly suggests.

We do just that, then head downstairs to his car.

The entire drive home, he wears a victorious grin, and I can't help but smile at it.

Maybe something beautiful did come out of this.

Now I don't have to live alone.

And now, I'll be with my hero always.

# Chapter 47
## *Roman*


I glance at Cecilia's sleeping form as I slip out of our bedroom.

*Our bedroom.*

*In our penthouse.*

I finally have her here. With me. It's everything I could want. If only it hadn't gone down the way that it did.

It takes me less than an hour to find him.

I follow him as he stumbles out the back alley behind the bar. These fuckers make it too easy for me.

I silently approach, until I'm behind him. I perform my normal dance, knocking him out, carrying him to my car, and driving him to a warehouse.

He wakes up by the time I have him hanging by his wrists from the ceiling.

"What the fuck, Mr. Montclair? I did as you said! I broke into the apartment and trashed the place. You still have to pay me for it," he mutters, confusion evident in his voice.

He's desperate for his money, but I'm desperate for his blood.

"You didn't follow my orders. You went too early. She was there! She saw you with a gun. She was terrified, hiding in her closet, while you destroyed her apartment. For that, you're going to suffer," I spit in his direction as fury rolls through me.

It's all the warning I give before swinging my fist into his stomach. He howls in pain, but it's not enough.

All I can hear is Cecilia's trembling, whispered voice, as she called me from her closet scared for her life.

All I can see is Cecilia curled in a ball in her closet, white as a ghost, shaking and crying because this fucker doesn't know how to follow instructions.

As he begs for his life, I continue hitting him. Making him bleed. Breaking bones. Basking in the pain I inflict.

Only when he's finally passed out from pain, do I stop.

I carve into him, branding him with my initials. Not that I could forget the man who took my money then scared my woman with his gun.

I throw a few hundreds on the table. Even though he fucked up, I'm a man of my word. I pay what I owe him and leave without a sound.

I get back to the penthouse an hour later, smelling of soap and lemons. When I get into bed, I pull my sunshine to me and cradle her in my arms.

Finally feeling at peace, I drift to sleep.

# Chapter 48
## *Cecilia*

I wake up in an unfamiliar room. As I look around, I remember where I am, in Roman's penthouse. I remember the events of yesterday that led me here.

Here, to this warm, homey bedroom.

Yesterday, when I got here, Roman gave me a tour. I wasn't surprised by how welcoming and comforting the place feels. It's just like him. There's warm wooden furniture all throughout with accents of olive green and rustic orange. There are even plants here. I couldn't have designed a better home.

A chest rises under me as Roman inhales. I'm draped over him, my head resting on his chest, my arm thrown over his shoulder, and my leg thrown over his. His arm curls over my back, keeping me glued to him.

It's not the first time we've shared a bed, but it's never felt like this. It's never felt so complete. So... homey. I could see us waking up like this every morning.

I feel his hardness press into my thigh, and when I put weight on it, a low groan emerges from his throat.

He's just waking up, and something comes over me. A mix of gratitude and lust. A desire to do something special for my hero.

I kiss his chest lightly, once, then twice. I start kissing my way up his neck, until I reach his chin. He's letting out sounds of pleasure, and when I reach his lips, he beats me to it, closing the distance between us, trapping me to him.

We kiss slowly as I try to convey my gratitude towards him.

This time it's my tongue slipping into his mouth. He allows me to take control, letting me lead the kiss.

When we finally pull back, desperate for oxygen, he grumbles.

"What a way to wake up," he sighs, with a sleepy grin.

"I wanted to thank you for saving me. For always being my hero. Well, I still want to thank you," I explain in a sultry voice.

His brows furrow in confusion, only to shoot up when my palm makes contact with his hardness over his boxers.

"Sunshine, what are you doing?" he groans.

"I want to thank you in a special way. I want to make you feel good. I want... I want to take you in my mouth," I explain, trying to not make it sound crude.

"Fuuuck, sunshine. You don't have to do that." The struggle in his voice is evident.

"Please, héroe. I want to do this for you," I beg. "And I'm curious. I've never done this before."

"If you're sure, then I'll guide you through it. But know you don't have to." His voice is strained.

I get off of him and crawl down the bed until I'm situated between his legs. I go to pull down his boxer briefs, and he helps me by lifting his hips. When his length springs forward, I gulp through my anxiety and grip it with my hand.

*I can do this.*

He slides up the bed until he's sitting against the headboard.

I try to rub up and down, but despite my inexperience, I know it's too dry.

"It needs to be wet, right?" I ask him, blushing at my greenness.

"Yes, sunshine. You can spit on it, or I can spit on my hand," he offers.

"No, not you. I want to be the one to do it," I say fiercely.

I need to be the one. I want to do this for him. On my own.

I look up and see his eyes widen.

"Okay, sunshine. That'd be great." He swallows hard and stares at me.

I move until I hover over him. I look down at his large size, open my mouth, and spit.

I watch as it drips onto him and see him tighten.

"Fuck, Cecilia. You're going to be the death of me," he says through gritted teeth.

I look up and smile, knowing I feel the same.

# Chapter 49
## *Roman*

I watch as her spit lands on my cock, and I can't hold back my groan.

It's the most beautiful sight, aside from her pussy swallowing me.

She moves her hand up, collects the saliva, and moves it down my hardness, spreading it. Soaking me.

I already feel close to the edge just from her touch, but I won't let myself come too soon. I know she wouldn't think less of me, but fuck, it'd be too embarrassing.

"How... how do I do it?" she asks, flustered.

Fuck she's so innocent. So pure. The fact that I'm the first man, her first experience in everything, fills me with a pride I can't begin to explain. I'm forever her man. The only man who will ever touch this goddess.

Except for kissing. And it's taking everything in me not to hunt down the men who've had the privilege of feeling those soft, pillowy lips of hers.

"Like this," I instruct as I wrap my fist around her hand and stroke myself to show her how I like it. I squeeze her hand tighter, needing more of a grip.

"I don't want to hurt you," she tells me as she tries to loosen her grip.

"You won't, sunshine. You could never hurt me." It's not the truth though. Although she could never physically hurt me, she has so much power over me. If she were to reject me or try to leave, it'd be like no pain I've ever experienced.

But nonetheless, her grip won't hurt my cock. It'll be the opposite.

She tightens her grip, and I pump her fist up and down. The feeling of her tiny hand, wrapped around me, jerking me off, has me almost blinded.

My eyes start to fall closed as I'm overcome by pleasure, but then they fly open at an unbelievable feeling.

Cecilia's tongue licks the precum off my tip, and I can't hold back my groan.

But it's nothing compared to her lips wrapping around my head, sucking me in.

I have to press my fingernails into my sides, letting the pricks of pain pull me from the edge.

"Sunshine... you don't... have to..." I try to grit out, desperation shining through.

She can't stop. It'll kill me if she does. But she also needs to know she doesn't have to blow me.

She locks eyes with mine and sinks lower onto me. Her tongue flattens against my underside, and my eyes rolls back.

"Yes, sunshine. Just like that. Use your tongue, and suck," I growl out.

Keeping my hips pinned against the mattress is a trial all on its own. Every fiber of my being is screaming to thrust up, to choke her with my dick, but I know I can't do that to her. This is her first time. I need to be gentle.

She looks at me with questioning eyes, then without releasing my cock, she grabs my hand and places it on her head. I instinctively weave my fingers into her waves.

"Do you want me to guide you?" I ask, wondering how I got so lucky.

She nods slightly, and I get to it.

Despite wanting to take her deeply, I know she can't handle that today, and I don't want to scare her.

I bob her head up in down at the perfect speed, not too slow, but not too fast.

She takes me so well.

"You're doing such a good job. My good girl. So perfect at sucking my cock. Making me feel so good," I praise her, knowing how much she loves it, and needing her to be validated in what she's doing.

She moans around me at the words, and the vibration shoots up my spine.

She bobs up and down a few more times, then I feel a brush of fingers against my balls.

"Oh fuck, Cecilia. Hold them, just like that," I moan out.

She listens perfectly, and fuck if I've felt anything better.

She goes extra low, taking me deeper than before, dragging her tongue down with her, and squeezes my balls. I know I'm seconds away from exploding.

I try to pull her head off me, but she fights me, staying attached.

"Cecilia, I'm about to come. Get off," I tell her, not wanting her to be stuck with a mouthful of my release.

But instead of listening, she grunts her refusal and takes me further down.

It's the last straw.

I try one last time to drag her away but it's no use.

I come, my release shooting from me, and down her throat. She takes me so well, swallowing the entire time. The feeling of it, of her milking me fully, is euphoric.

It's unreal. The image will forever be engrained in my mind. I'll never be able to look at her sweet throat and not picture her swallowing my release over and over again.

Only when my cock starts to deflate does she pull back and drop me from her mouth.

"Was that okay?" she asks shyly, and I almost laugh at the absurdity.

This goddess just gave me the best experience of my life and she's doubting herself. That won't do.

I pull her onto my lap, straddling me, so she can see the truth in my eyes.

"That was perfect. I've never felt so good. You can't be of this earth because nothing from here could ever feel like this. Thank you, sunshine."

I need her to understand that although I'm not inexperienced like her, she makes me feel things I've never felt before. It's different with her. And I don't ever want to go back.

"Promise?" she asks with more confidence.

"I promise. You did such a good job, you deserve a reward," I tell her with a wicked grin.

I place her against the headboard, sink between her thighs, lift her sexy nightgown, and pull down her lacy thong. I inhale her sweet scent before leaning forward, ready for my sweet breakfast.

"Oh no, Roman. You don't need to do this. That was just for you," she tells me.

"Absolutely not. You're soaked from getting me off. You deserve your turn." I lick through her wetness and groan and the taste. "And don't ever think eating you out isn't a treat for me."

I go to town, having my way with her. It's not just me on cloud nine. Her wiggling, writhing moans, and groans all show how much she loves this. Needs this.

And when she finally comes, I follow suit, ruining my sheets.

*So much for not embarrassing myself.*

"Thank you, héroe. I don't know what I'd do without you. You're perfect, and I love you," she tells me, her eyes shining with love.

I preen.

I don't care how I got her. I don't care what I've had to do to be her hero. I don't care what I've hidden from her. Being her hero is everything.

And nothing will get in my way.

# Chapter 50
## *Cecilia*

I've been staying at Roman's penthouse for a few weeks now. Honestly, I've been here long enough to admit what this is.

I'm living with him.

My parents are very traditional, and they've passed that on to me. I never thought I'd move in with a man I wasn't married to, but I guess we had some extenuating circumstances. It's not our fault that my apartment was broken into and most of my belongings were destroyed. And I can't be blamed for only feeling safe around my hero.

Speaking of my family, I look back down at the text from Mamá.

*Mamá: Por favor, ven a visitarnos el próxima fin de semana para el cumple de tu hermana. Te extrañamos mucho. Con amor, Mamá.*

I stare at the message, debating how to respond. She wants me to come visit next weekend for my sister's birthday. Of course I'm going, but I hesitate before asking if Roman can come with me. I've mentioned my boyfriend on a few of our calls, and I've already met his family, so it's time for him to meet mine.

I know he won't care that my family has less than his, that we're immigrants, that there are four generations living in one house. That's not why I'm hesitating.

And my family won't care that he's not Latino. They'll be welcoming and happy to meet him. I'm not hesitating because of them.

I actually don't know why I'm hesitating.

I pick up the phone and respond.

*Me: Obvio que voy. ¿Puedo llevar a mi novio también?*

The response is immediate.

*Mamá: ¡Sí! Todos son bienvenidos. ¡Estamos ansiosos por conocerlo!*

I smile at her excitement to meet him. Our house has always been welcome to all. My parents love hosting, often having friends over for dinner.

Now, all I have to do is ask Roman.

...

Roman enters the kitchen after working all day and going to the gym, and groans.

"Sunshine, what smells so good?" I can hear the excitement in his voice.

"I made empanadas and ají sauce," I explain, excited to share more of my culture with him.

He moans, holding his stomach.

"I was going to shower and change before dinner but change of plans. If they're ready, let's eat now," he says, already grabbing two plates from the wooden cabinet.

"Alright, héroe. We can eat now, even though it's only five-thirty in the afternoon," I tease him.

He makes himself a plate, placing twelve empanadas on it. The pile he makes with them is ridiculous. I try to stifle a laugh at his large appetite, but I knew this about him. It's why I made four dozen. He's a big boy, I know he needs a lot to fuel him.

By the time we sit down, he's wolfed down two.

"Fuck, sunshine. These are amazing. One of my favorite things you've made so far," he tells me after swallowing his fourth. "But please know, you don't ever have to cook for me. Don't get me wrong, no one can cook like you. I could live off your food. But you're not my servant. You're my girlfriend. And I don't ever want you to feel like you have to do things for me," he tells me.

His words fill my heart to the brim. He's perfect.

"I love cooking. Especially for you. Truly, I do. Cooking is something that brings me great joy. It reminds me of cooking with Mamá and Abuela as a little girl. I love sharing that with you," I explain.

"Okay," he says then shoves another one in his mouth whole. "Did your Abuela or your Mamá teach you how to make these? I need to know who to write my thank you card to," he tells me with a smirk.

And it's the perfect segway.

"Abuela showed me. These are the Colombian way to make them. They're a popular dish all over Latin America. I think the Spaniards taught us how to make them. But each country differs a little. We use cornmeal instead of wheat flour. Also, they're typically a snack or appetizer, but I made them a little bigger so we could have them as a meal. I thought you'd like them."

"Thank you, Abuela," he mutters then shoves another one in his mouth.

"Speaking of my family, I'm going to visit them next weekend for Carmen's birthday. I was wondering if you wanted to come with me? You're invited. Full disclosure, we'd be there for the whole weekend. And it's in Worcester, so it's about an hour and a half away by train. Don't feel like you have to come, but I'd love if you did. They'd love for you to come too. They're excited to meet you." I glance down, not wanting to meet his eyes when he turns me down.

"Sunshine, that sound amazing. I'd love to come." He reaches out and holds my hand. "And don't worry about the train. I'll drive us."

I'm so excited, I jump from my seat, round the table, and launch into his arms. He catches me in the hug and pulls me in.

"Thank you! Thank you! Thank you!" I chant.

"Of course, Cecilia. I can't wait to meet them." He kisses my hair as he says it.

In this moment, I know what pure happiness feels like.

I'm about to introduce the perfect man to my family.

A man who I'm sure will be my family.

And I couldn't be happier.

# Chapter 51
## *Cecilia*

The car ride to Worcester took almost two hours after work today. Friday traffic was crazy. I texted Carmen during the drive, letting her know we'd be late.

Roman holds my hand the entire drive. The love radiating from him only strengthens my excitement at introducing him to my family.

"A few tips. Eat everything offered. Turning down food is considered extremely disrespectful. I'm sure they made a ton, so I'm sorry if you get full," I wince as I tell him.

"Sunshine, I've tasted what they taught you to make. Nothing could ever make me turn down that food. It's delicious," he tells me with a sure smile.

"Okay. So, my abuela's name is Luz Marina. You should call her Doña Luz Marina. My papá's name is Hernando. You should call him Señor Hernando. And my mamá's name is Ana Lucía. You can call her Señora Ana Lucía. My older sister's name is Carmen. It's her birthday. Her husband is Felipe, and their daughter is Rosa. My younger sister is Valentina. And that's everyone."

"Umm, sounds good," he says nervously.

"Oh no! That's a lot. I should've written it down," I start to get nervous. It's all formalities, and they'll forgive him if he messes up, but I don't want him to mess up. I want him to do well. "I'm sorry. I feel like I didn't prepare you enough."

I want to cry. I should've done better.

"It's okay, sunshine. They're your family. I'm sure it'll be fine," he calms me.

We pull up to the two-story, four-bedroom house. Our penthouse is bigger than the house and a third of people live there. For a few beats, I feel guilty for how lavishly I've been living. But I snap out of it quickly. My family is happy, even if they aren't wealthy. Money won't change that. Plus, I still only make a PT tech's salary.

We park on the street in front of the house, and Roman walks around the car to open my door. Instead of walking up the path, he goes to the rear door of the car, opens it, and emerges with four bouquets, a potted orchid, a bottle of wine, and a bottle of rum. I stare at him, mouth agape.

I didn't tell him it was customary to bring gifts. I'd honestly forgotten. But here he is, surprising me in the best way, as always.

"Oh, Roman. Thank you. They're going to love it."

I kiss him on the cheek, and he leads me up the path to the door.

We knock, and it immediately swings open.

"¡Cecita! ¡Mi hijita! Me alegra tanto que estés aquí." Mamá hovers then pulls me in for a hug. She kisses my right cheek, and I return the greeting.

"I'm really happy to be here." I step aside, presenting Roman. "Mamá, this is my boyfriend, Roman. Roman, this is my mamá."

He steps forward and kisses her right cheek as she does his.

"Señora Ana Lucía, thank you for hosting me. I'm grateful to be here." He hands her the potted orchid. "This is for you. Cecilia told me she gets her love for gardening from you."

Mamá swoons. She takes the plant and fusses over it.

"Roman, this is gorgeous. Thank you so much. I'll take care of it and grow it into a beautiful flower," she promises him. She opens the door and welcomes us in.

Abuela comes down the hallway, practically running. I swear her cane has trouble keeping up with her.

"¡Hola, Ceci María! Ven, dame un abrazo," Abuela orders.

I comply and give her a warm hug, kissing her right cheek. She squeezes me tighter then pulls back.

"Now, step aside. I want to meet the man who's stolen my granddaughter's heart," she demands and pushes me aside. I laugh at her wild excitement.

"Hola, Doña Luz Marina. Thank you for welcoming me into your home." He leans down a foot and a half to meet her barely five-foot frame and gives her a kiss on the cheek like he did Mamá. "I got these for you." He hands her a big bouquet of pink carnations.

He can't know this, but Abuela loves carnations. They were all around her village growing up.

She preens as she snatches the bouquet from his hands, as if afraid he'll change his mind.

"Please, come in. Would you like some tinto, joven?" Abuela offers, and I can tell by her grin that she already likes him.

"Yes, please," Roman answers with a warm smile, even though he has no idea what he just agreed to.

"Don't worry. It's just Colombian coffee," I tell him under my breath. He squeezes my hand in response.

Mamá brings us to the living room. We sit on the worn couches, but before I can talk, I hear the familiar giggle of a four-year-old girl.

"¡Tía Ceci!" Rosa squeals, before launching herself into my lap.

I laugh along with her before pulling her in for a hug.

"Rosa, you've gotten so big! I almost didn't recognize you," I tell her as I wrap my arms around her.

"Tía Ceci, I'm four years old. I'm a big girl now!" she tells me proudly as she holds up four fingers. A chuckle next to us draws her attention and she frowns. "Who are you?" she snaps at Roman.

"Rosa, be nice. This is my friend, Roman," I scold her.

"Roman, are you Tía Ceci's boyfriend? Do you kiss her? In the movies, the boy always kisses the girl!" she says, and I redden impossibly.

"Nice to meet you, Rosa. I am your tía's boyfriend. But it's not polite to kiss and tell, so I won't answer the second question." I smile at his nonanswer. "I have a gift for you," he tells her.

He pulls out a small bouquet of daisies, and my heart melts.

Rosa grins and grabs them. Her little fingers smoosh the stems as she beams.

"Tía, I like him. I want to be his girlfriend next!" Little Rosa tells me confidently.

Roman, who I don't think has much experience with four-year-old girls, pales at the comment and shrinks back.

"Rosita, stop harassing Tía Ceci's boyfriend. You're turning into my Abuela!" my sister yells as she rounds the corner.

I jump up and rush over, giving Carmen a big hug.

"Happy birthday, hermanita! It's so good to see you!" I squeal.

She squeezes me so tightly.

"Thank God you're here. Val, Rosa, and Abuela are driving me crazy. Maybe you can help calm them down," she whispers desperately.

I just laugh.

"Now introduce me to that sexy hunk on the couch! You definitely failed to mention he looks like a god," she says loud enough for Roman to hear.

"That's the truth! Back in my prime, I would've tied him up and taken him," Abuela says even louder as she walks in with small clay mugs of tinto.

I almost keel over in mortification.

And to my absolute horror, Roman is blushing.

I've never seen that man blush.

"Erm... Thank you, Doña Luz Marina," Roman chokes out.

It's the most awkward I've ever seen him.

I guess four generations of Rivera women hitting on you can throw you off. Well, three women. Mamá would never do such a thing.

She hands him his tinto, and watches as he sips it, studying his reaction. I don't think she'd kick him out if he doesn't like the tinto, but I can't be sure.

His eyes light up when he tastes it, and he grins.

"This is amazing! I don't know how I've lived this long without ever having it!" he tells her.

And she nods in approval.

As introductions are made, Roman continues to impress my family. He gives both my sisters bouquets of roses, pink for Val and yellow for Carmen. Abuela, Rosa, and Carmen are mild compared to Val. She teases him to no avail. I think Roman started avoiding her.

When he finally meets Papá, he shakes his hand and hands him the bottles of Malbec and an expensive rum I've never heard of. To say he was won over is an understatement.

Felipe is also given the alcohol, since Roman didn't know who would prefer what. Felipe seems more than glad to have another man around. With this crew, Papá and he are greatly outnumbered.

My heart explodes at the possibility that my family accepts Roman.

And that maybe one day, he'll be a part of it.

# Chapter 52
## *Roman*

I think everything is going well. I did extensive research into Colombian and Ecuadorian cultures, traditions, and customs wanting to be able to show them respect. And gain their approval. I know how much Cecilia values her family. If they don't approve of me, I don't know how she'd react. That's not a risk I'm willing to take.

I also want my future in-laws to like me. It'll make my life easier as their daughter's husband and their grandchildren's father.

But now that I've met them, my motivation has changed. I want to impress them because they're great people. I want them to accept me into the family because it's a family I want to be a part of.

After several rounds of appetizers, all traditional Colombian and Ecuadorian dishes, I'm almost full. I know they prepared a lot in honor of me coming, so I refuse to turn any away.

Cecilia hasn't eaten nearly as much as me, only taking a few bites of each. But doing the same wasn't an option for me. Anytime my plate was empty, someone would serve me more. If the weekend continues this way, I'll have gained significant weight by the time we leave.

Everything has been beyond delicious. If I had my way, we'd never leave. Or we'd bring her mom, Abuela, and sisters with us. But now that I think about it, Cecilia can probably make all of this. But if she doesn't want to, I'll learn. I'm not great in the kitchen, but if it yields this, then I can learn.

I look around the house. It's decorated brightly, with warm orange and yellow accent walls. There's pottery and art all over the walls. All beautiful and handmade. Herbs and leafy plants take up most corners and many shelves. There are woven blankets over the couches. Framed family pictures hang on the walls. I'm looking forward to looking at them and seeing a smiling Cecilia over the years. The whole place smells of spices, herbs, and coffee. I think I'm in heaven. Cecilia growing up here makes so much sense. Even though there's a lot going on, it isn't messy. It's homey and warm.

"Alright, let's eat dinner," Cecilia's father says.

His accent is thick, just like his wife's and mother's. But they've all been speaking English. I know it's for my sake, and I appreciate it. The Spanish language learning app I downloaded and have been using everyday the past week and a half has been useful, but the few times I've heard them talk in the language, I've been completely lost. They speak so quickly.

We walk into the kitchen, and my stomach drops at the countless dishes laid out. I just pray I'm not sick by the end of the night. I've never eaten so much that I've thrown up, but I've also never eaten this much.

But there are definitely worse problems to have when meeting your in-laws than overeating delicious South American food.

"Roman, serve yourself first," Señor Hernando instructs.

I start to decline, knowing ladies should be served first, but Cecilia shakes her head slightly, silently telling me to go along with it. It must be customary for the guest to start.

I load up my plate until you can't even see the clay. I sit down at one of the seats on the side of the table, knowing not to take the head, and wait. I'm not eating until everyone is seated.

Once everyone is at the table, Cecilia to one side of me and her mother to the other, we say a prayer. It's in Spanish, so I understand none of it, but I still bow my head reverently.

Conversation is flowing. Food is eaten. Alcohol is drunk. And I'm sporting the most genuine smile I've had in a while that isn't directly caused by Cecilia. It makes sense that her family are the only other ones who can bring out this jovial side of me.

Cecilia and her sisters clear the table. I was physically pushed back into my seat by Cecilia when I stood up to help.

"I've never had more delicious food. This was incredible," I tell her family.

"I'm glad to hear, joven. Is Cecilia not cooking for you?" her abuela asks.

"She cooks for me. I try to help, but I'm not great in the kitchen," I explain, not wanting them to think I make her cook. "She doesn't have to though. She's my girlfriend, not my servant. We're equals. I'm grateful for all she does for me, and not just in the kitchen."

The room falls silent, and I realize I might've offended her family. I noticed that only the women cooked tonight. I look at Cecilia apologetically, but she's staring at the table.

All I can hear is my heart pounding.

"I like this one, Ceci María. You should keep him. He has a good head on his shoulders," her abuela says, and I deflate in relief.

"I intend to," Cecilia tells her and squeezes my hand under the table.

She's going to keep me. She doesn't have a choice. She's mine, and I'm hers. Forever. But it's nice to hear she feels the same.

When I look up, Carmen is grinning across from me and winks at me. I wonder if she has the capability to read my mind. Or if it's obvious how much I want, *no*, need her.

When Val comes in with dessert, my eyes almost well up. I don't know how I have any more room in me, but I find a way. I will not turn down any food.

Once I've eaten enough to keep me hibernated for months, I stand up.

"Thank you so much for hosting me tonight. I should probably get to the hotel. What time would you like me over tomorrow?" I say, only for Cecilia's grandmother to scoff at me.

"Roman, you will stay here. We will make room. We could never let you get a hotel," Cecilia's mom tells me.

I glance at Cecilia, and she nods.

"Alright. Thank you."

I'm not surprised when Cecilia and I are separated for the night. I end up on the couch, while Cecilia shares a room with her niece.

As I lay there, I feel more at home than I did in the cold penthouse I lived in for a decade before Cecilia came into my life. I didn't realize how empty my life was before her.

Now I have a sense of home in her.

# Chapter 53
## *Cecilia*

It's been a great weekend. My family loves Roman, and he loves them too. He seems happy, and he's always engaged in conversation. It feels natural having him here.

It's Saturday evening, and Roman is showering. Mamá is helping Abuela take a shower. Carmen and Felipe are putting Rosa to bed. Val went home. So, it's just me and Papá.

"Venga, mijita," Papá leads me to the backyard.

We sit in the rocking chairs near the garden.

"¿Estás feliz con este hombre?" he asks me.

*Are you happy with this man?*

I don't even have to think about it.

"Sí, Papá. Nunca he sido tan feliz," I tell him.

*Yes, Papá. I've never been this happy.*

"Me alegra, Cecita María." He puts a hand on my arm. "Yo veo cómo te mira."

*I'm glad, Cecita María. I see how he looks at you.*

"¿Cómo me mira?" I ask him, desperate for his thoughts. My papá is the wisest man I know. I need his insight.

*How does he look at me?*

"Como si fueras el sol, y todo su mundo girara alrededor de ti," he tells me softly, and a tear drops down my cheek.

*Like you're the sun, and his whole world revolves around you.*

# Chapter 54
## *Roman*

The women work in the kitchen preparing Sunday lunch, much to my dismay. I know whatever they create will be delicious, but I don't love the precedent of the women cooking for me. I think it's because I was raised only with brothers. We did all the chores.

I corner Señor Hernando on the patio. He's outside watering the garden.

I'm more nervous for this conversation that I've ever been. And I'm in dangerous situations daily. I've been shot and tortured, but it's never been like this.

"This is my wife's garden," he says softly with his back to me. "But when she's busy cooking for our family, or taking care of my mother, or watching our granddaughter, she'll forget about it. This garden brings her so much joy, so when she accidentally neglects it, I tend to it." He turns off the hose and turns to look at me. "Anita es mi vida. She's my world. I'd do anything for her. So, I do for her what she doesn't do for herself. I may be the patriarch of this family, but she's the glue that holds us together. We couldn't function without her. I will always take care of my wife." His eyes harden, and he straightens in a way that makes his look younger and more formidable. "Would you do the same for my daughter?"

I soak in his words and realize I've been looking at this wrong. Yes, his wife does the cooking and cleaning, taking care of the family. But her husband takes care of her. It's different from how I was raised, but it doesn't make it wrong. And if that's how Cecilia wants us to operate, I can adjust. Because I'll always take care of her.

"Cecilia, your daughter, she's my priority. Her happiness, health, and safety go before my own. She's my sunshine, and my day can only shine brightly if hers does. All I want is to take care of her for the rest of our lives. That's actually what I want to talk to you about," I stand taller, needing him to see me as worthy. "I'd like to marry your daughter. And I want your approval. I know how much her family means to her, so without it, Cecilia would be conflicted."

I hold my breath, praying he doesn't shut me down.

"Ah, I see," he tells me, then motions with his hand for me to continue.

"Sir, I love your daughter. And I'll spend every day making her the happiest woman on this planet. She walks around with my heart in her hands. She is my heart. I won't, can't, spend a day without her. She'll never want for anything. I want a house full of our children running around happy and free, and I know she wants it too. I love her and would do anything for her." I'm begging him to understand. He needs to know what Cecilia means to me.

"Would you sacrifice your own happiness for hers? Your success and fortune? Your life?" he asks calmly. His eyes never leave mine, and I can tell he'll know if I lie. But I don't have to.

"Yes. I'd give anything up for her, even my life. I'll protect her, provide for her, keep her safe and happy and warm. She'll never know struggle or pain." My voice is strong as I promise him promises I've already made to myself.

"Good. Roman, you're a good man to my daughter. I see it in the way you treat her, the way you look at her. We will be honored to have you as a part of the family. Yes, you have my approval. I look forward to calling you mi hijo." He looks so deeply into my eyes when he says it, that I suspect he can see into my soul.

"Thank you, sir," I promise him. Relief floods through me. This went better than expected.

He shakes my hand but doesn't let go. Instead, he pulls me in, and his features shift from formidable to dangerous.

"Cecita is my little girl. Even though she's grown, she'll always be mijita. If you harm a hair on her body, I don't care who you are and what you're capable of, Roman Montclair, I will destroy you," he tells me in a low voice. It's calm, and that makes it all the more terrifying.

I thought I knew threats. I thought I knew danger.

But I realize, I've never come across the love a father has for his daughter, and what he's capable of doing to those who hurt her.

And I know if we ever have a daughter, I'll go to just as many lengths to keep her safe.

I didn't think I'd ever find respect, or fear, in a threat. Especially not coming from a man old enough to be my father, but I do. I respect this man all the more. And fear him a little.

"Yes, sir. If she's ever hurt because of me, I'll let you," I dip my head in acknowledgement.

He squeezes my hand once more, then drops it and steps back.

"I know there's more to you than she's aware of. Cecilia's optimism can blind her. I don't care who you are or what you do, as long as you take care of her," he pauses. "A word of advice from a man who's been a husband for over three decades: A sturdy foundation cannot be built on lies. One gust of truth, and the house will fall."

With those ominous and foreboding words, he turns back to his garden whistling once again.

And I'm left standing there, contemplating how much of my life I've hidden from Cecilia.

And how long before a gust of truth ruins it all.

# Chapter 55
## *Cecilia*


I'm watering the plants around the penthouse wondering how Roman kept them alive before I got here. I'm pretty sure he doesn't know the care routine for a single one. I've never seen him tend to them.

"Hey, sunshine," a sweet voice whispers from behind me, and I jump in surprise.

"Héroe, you scared me!" I tell him as I lightly swat his chest.

He grabs my hand quicker than I can track and presses it against his heart.

"Thank you for taking such great care of these plants. I was wondering if you wanted to pick out some for the balcony?" he offers.

"I'd love that!" I perk up at the idea.

This penthouse is beautiful. Practically my dream home. But I haven't picked anything out or decorated it at all. I'd love to get some plants that I choose to decorate with. And when Gracie gets back, we'll have to go thrifting and to some estate sales to get things to decorate with.

I told her about the apartment, and even though she was upset, she was happy I was okay.

Roman's been fixing up the apartment. I refused his offer to pay someone to do it, so now on weekends or when he's free, he'll work on it. Sometimes I go with him. He's banned me from using power tools after an *incident,* but I still make myself useful.

We haven't made plans for what we're doing when she comes back. I think she knows that as much as I love living with her, I don't want to move out of Roman's place. I love living with him. But I also don't want to abandon her.

We'll just have to see what happens.

"Why don't you get dressed, sunshine, then we'll go to the greenhouse," he tells me as he wraps his arms around me from behind and pulls me into him.

I bask in his warmth for a beat, then make my way to our bedroom.

I stare at my closet, unsure what to wear. I'm fingering through my outfits when a hand stops on one and pulls it out.

"Why don't you wear this one?" Roman whispers in my ear.

I look at the white maxi dress perfect for the summer with its breathable sleeves, empire waist, and loose bottom that falls to the ground. It even has small flower decals on it.

"Sure," I tell him, giddy that he cares what I wear.

...

An hour later, I look out of the car window, unsure as to where we are.

Roman turns down a gravel road and continues on to what must be private property. We finally find a driveway that leads up to the most beautiful house I've ever seen. No, not a house. A mansion.

It's Tudor revival style. The outside is stone with many windows. The two chimneys give it a warm, homey feeling. There's a balcony above the patio full of plants. The gray roofing somehow perfectly matches the warm stone walls. There are lanterns all over, and to the side, a pond. It's beyond beautiful.

"I don't understand. I thought we were shopping for plants," I tell him while staring out of the window, still mesmerized by the mansion.

"We are... sort of. There's a greenhouse in the back."

Roman gets out of the car, walks around, opens my door for me, and helps me out.

"Thank you." I flash him a sweet smile.

When his hand meets mine, it's damp with sweat. I've never known Roman to sweat.

He takes a shaky breath as he leads me on a path around the house. I'm too caught up in wondering what has him worried to take in the view.

Until we get to the 'greenhouse.'

It's not a greenhouse at all. It's an outdoor courtyard garden. Every beautiful flower, herb, bush, and tree that can be grown in Boston is here. And they meld together so perfectly.

In the middle of the ground is a mosaic, but I can't make out what it is with the brown blanket strewn over half of it. On the blanket is a picnic basket, the one we use when we go to the park.

And all around the courtyard, there are hundreds of candles. All lit, casting a warm glow.

It's ethereal. I feel like I'm standing in a garden from a Greek mythology tale. I certainly don't feel like I'm in Boston.

I turn in circles trying to take it in. Roman gently leads me by the small of my back through the garden. I slowly walk taking in every plant. They're gorgeous.

"Pick out the ones you like, and we'll get them." His soft voice flows in my ear.

I look at him and notice he's not taking in the beautiful sight, no, he's taking in the sight of me.

I blush and let him guide me to the picnic blanket.

"Before we start dinner, there's something I need to ask you," he says.

Then he coughs, clearing his throat. He shifts his weight from each leg, and I can feel the nerves radiating off of him.

I grab his hands in mine to stop the trembling.

"Deep breaths with me. We're going to do a box breathing technique. In, one... two... three... four. Hold, one... two... three... four. Out, one... two... three... four. Hold, one... two... three... four," I talk him through the meditation sequence.

We do it four more times until he's back to a normal shade and isn't trembling. Then he steps back.

He gets down on one knee.

Grabs my hands.

And my heart freezes.

"Cecilia María, sabía que te quería desde el primer momento en que te vi," he starts, then pinches his face in concentration, reaches into his back pocket, and pulls out a sheet of paper.

*Cecilia María, I knew I wanted you from the first moment I laid eyes on you.*

"No me distraigo ni paro mi trabajo para ayudar a desconocidos. Pero me llamaste tu héroe, y nada pudo detenerme," he continues, butchering every beautiful Spanish word that falls from his lips.

*I don't get distracted or stop work to help strangers. But you called me your hero, and nothing could stop me.*

"Seguiste diciéndome héroe, y cuanto más lo escuchaba, más quería ser eso para ti."

*You continued calling me hero, and the more I heard it, the more I wanted to be that for you.*

Tears well in my eyes.

"Nadie me ha visto nunca como tú. Nadie me ha hecho querer ser mejor hombre."

*No one's ever seen me the way you do. No one's ever made me want to be a better man.*

He clears his throat.

"Estaba tan perdido hasta que te conocí. No me di cuenta de lo frío y vacío que era mi vida. No me di cuenta de qué no sabía lo qué era el amor. Hasta tú."

*I was so lost until I met you. I didn't realize how cold and empty my life was. I didn't realize I didn't know what love was. Until you.*

"Chocaste conmigo y todo mi mundo se puso patas arriba."

*You knocked into me, and my whole world flipped.*

"Me diste mi sol. No conozco la felicidad verdadera si no es contigo."

*You've given me my sunshine. I don't know true happiness if it's not with you.*

"Tu sonrisa ilumina mi día, tu risa es música para mis oídos. Eres mi corazón, viviendo fuera de mi cuerpo."

*Your smile lights up my day, your laugh is music to my ears. You are my heart, living outside my body.*

"Eres todo lo que puedo desear en una pareja. Eres todo lo que siempre voy a necesitar."

*You're everything I could ever want in a partner. You're everything I could ever need.*

"Tu optimismo me salva de mi pesimismo. Eres la calma de mi ansiedad. El color de mi oscuridad. El bien de mi mal."

*Your optimism saves me from my pessimism. You're the calm to my anxiety. The color to my darkness. The good to my bad.*

I open my mouth to contradict him. To tell him he's not bad. But he shushes me and continues.

"Por favor, déjame ser tu héroe por el resto de nuestras vidas."

*Please, let me be your hero for the rest of our lives.*

He pauses.

"Por favor, pasa el resto de tu vida conmigo."

*Please, spend the rest of your life with me.*

His voice cracks.

"Sé mi esposa," he all but begs.

*Be my wife.*

# Chapter 56
## *Roman*

My heart stops, sweat drips down my forehead, and all I can hear is a loop of me butchering her parent's language.

What if she says no?

What if she hated the speech?

What if she doesn't like the ring?

*The ring!*

I fumble into my pocket and pull out the black box.

I open it and display the engagement ring I selected for her.

It's a gold ring with a large marquise diamond in the center. Surrounding the main diamond are baguettes and round diamonds.

Gracie helped me pick it. It took us forever to choose the perfect one.

But if she doesn't like it, I'll get her another one.

I look up from the ring and see tears streaming down her cheeks. She's nodding, staring at me not the ring.

"Is that a yes, sunshine?" I ask this time, not acknowledging the fact that I told her to be my wife, not asked.

She doesn't get to say no. But I'd rather she choose to say yes.

"Yes, Roman. Yes!" she chokes out between tears.

I put the ring on her finger, but she still has yet to look at it.

She launches herself into my arms, shaking with sobs.

"I love you, Cecilia. And I'll love you all the more as my wife," I tell her, squeezing her to me.

"I love you too, my soon-to-be husband," she says with a bright smile.

My world shifts at the word. *Husband.* I'm going to be her husband. She's going to be my wife. *My wife.*

She pulls back just enough to kiss me. I lean down, meeting her lips.

It starts as a sweet, loving kiss. It's slow as we explore each other. As we taste each other. As we feel the love between us.

But what starts out innocently, quickly turns heated.

She pushes at my shirt, and I pull it over my head, not bothering to unbutton it. I start gathering her dress, ready to rid her of it, but she glances behind us at the windows of the mansions.

"What if someone sees?" she asks timidly, even as she unbuckles my belt.

"No one's here. I rented the whole property for the night," I assure her.

She's out of her damn mind if she thinks I'd ever risk someone seeing her naked. Seeing her pleasure. Seeing her at all, damn it.

We quickly undress each other, then I crawl down her body to get her ready. I'm greeted with wetness.

I pull down her panties and lap her up. I keep going until her back bows off the ground. Until she's screaming my name. Until she's begging for my cock.

We take it slowly, savoring every thrust. Memorizing each moment.

When she squeezes around me, falling over the edge, I follow suit, unable to resist my goddess. I lean down and capture her lips with mine, feeling her screams of pleasure reverberate through my mouth.

And when we part, I clean her with her panties, and put them to the side, saving them. I don't need to use my stock of panties that often now that we live together, but old habits die hard.

I hear a gasp and look over to see her staring at her ring.

Her eyes are wide, her right hand covers her mouth, and more tears well.

"Roman, I have no words. It's beautiful. Oh, it's perfect," she whispers. "It's fit for a princess."

"No, it's fit for a goddess. My goddess of sunshine. It's fit for you," I tell her as I kiss her gently.

Everything in the world feels perfect.

# Chapter 57
## *Cecilia*

We eat the picnic that he packed as we talk about the future.

"I see us moving out of the penthouse. What do you think?" Roman asks after he swallows a bite of his caprese salad.

"I've always seen myself living in a cottage on the outskirts of town. With a big garden. But it'd have to be big enough for all the kids. I don't even know if they make cottages that big." I explain dreamily.

"If they don't, we'll build one," he assures me as he pulls me onto his lap. "How many kids do you want?"

"I've always wanted a big family. At least five kids. But I'll welcome as many as the universe gives me," I tell him, praying that's not a deal breaker.

"The more, the better. We can have as many as you'd like. It's your body that carries them. I'm grateful for anything you provide," he tells me.

His words warm my heart.

"Thank you, héroe. Plan on a huge house full of loud, messy children," I tease him.

"I wouldn't want my home any other way. As long as you're standing by my side through it all."

He presses a kiss on my hair, and I snuggle deeper into him.

"When do you want to get started? You're still young, so I don't want to rush you, but I'm almost thirty-five though, and I'd like to be able to watch our herd grow up," he sounds sad to admit it.

"Any time after we're married. Maybe as soon as we're married. All I've ever wanted is a family of my own. Plus, women have a biological clock for reproduction. If we want a big family, we need to start soon," I tell him.

"You're fucking perfect. You know that, right?" He inhales, and I think he's sniffing my hair. "What about your job? I won't make you quit, but that many pregnancies and kids are a lot on their own. I can't imagine juggling a job along with it. We can always hire help though," he offers.

"No, I want to be the one to raise our kids. If you're okay with it, I'd quit my job and focus on the kids. It was only a placeholder. I've never been too invested in it," I tell him, hoping he doesn't think I'm a freeloader.

"That's perfect. I'd be grateful if you were to stay at home with the kids." He sighs happily.

"I don't want you to feel used though," I tell him nervously.

He chuckles as though it's ridiculous.

"Sunshine, I have to work for the family business. I can't stop. And even if I did, I still have more than enough in the bank for us to be set for life. Bash and Matthias handle my financials, and they do a damn good job."

I knew he has money based off his cars and penthouse, but I didn't realize it was that much.

"Okay. Just know, even if we had nothing, and had to work for every penny, I'd still choose you and that life with you," I tell him.

"I know, sunshine. You're not a gold digger. But that doesn't mean I'm not going to spoil you. It's my privilege now as your husband." His tone reveals his pride, and I can't help but smile.

"What do I offer in the relationship? What can I give you?" I ask him, needing to be an equal.

"You being a mother and giving us children is more than I could ever contribute. No money or job could ever equate to that. I'll forever be grateful to you for it. It's all that I could ever want." The rawness in his voice solidifies what I've always thought.

That he truly is a hero. So selfless and strong.

"I love you, héroe," I whisper to him, as I turn to kiss him.

"I love you too, sunshine," he tells me before pressing his lips to mine.

# Chapter 58
## *Cecilia*

We walk up the driveway of my future in-law's mansion, and excitement waves through me. I'm shaking with eagerness to tell them about the engagement.

I called my family the next day and told them. Everyone was so happy for us. My papá hadn't seemed surprised, and when I mentioned it to Roman, he told me he had asked for his approval. It meant so much to me that Papá accepts my fiancé into the family.

We decided to wait to tell his family in person, since we were visiting soon. We come almost every Sunday for family dinner, and I just know they're going to be happy. I can't wait to call them family.

We enter the sitting room, and Mrs. Montclair sees the ring immediately. While it's not gaudy, it's also certainly isn't small by any means.

She flies out of her chair and wraps her arms around me.

"Welcome to the family, Cecilia! We're so glad to have you," she tells me as her eyes brim with tears.

"Thank you. You've always been so welcoming. I'm honored to call you family." I return her fierce hug.

"Evelyn, let the girl breathe," Mr. Montclair says as he pulls his wife off of me. Then he turns to me, "Cecilia, you've been like family since the first time Roman brought you over. We're glad he's making it official. We'll be honored to have you as a part of the Montclair family." His eyes soften as he talks.

"What's going on?" Matthias's voice echoes from the doorway as he takes in the scene.

Before anyone can answer, Margot leaps forward.

"Oh my God! Welcome to the family! I've always wanted a sister! And Evelyn and I are way outnumbered! This is amazing!" she gleefully says as she pulls me in for a hug.

After exactly three seconds of contact, Matthias pries her from me and glues her to his side. There isn't a breath of space between them. Margot just rolls her eyes at her fiancé's jealousy.

Bash, having witnessed the full transaction from his spot, stands up. He shoots Roman a wary look then brings me in for a hug.

"You're already like a sister to me. I'm excited to have you around." Then he leans in and lowers his voice so only I can hear. "You're good for him. You bring out a better side of him. Just... just don't give up on him when things... change. He's a good man for you, and that's all that matters."

With those confusing words, he pulls back and slaps Roman on the back, congratulating him once Matthias lets go of him. Then Matthias turns to me and hugs me quickly.

"Margot and I love having you around. Give him hell but always have room for forgiveness. Your heart is big enough for it. That's how you're able to look past his... shortcomings," Matthias tells me, and I just stare at him, unable to comprehend either brother's bizarre advice.

We sit down around the room, Roman and I on a loveseat small enough that I'm practically glued to his side. He doesn't seem to mind though, wrapping his arm around me and pulling me in tightly.

Dom walks in and looks around the room skeptically noting the excitement in the air. He's the only one I've had an issue bonding with, but it seems Margot is in a similar position. Roman tells me Dom is just closed off and has a difficult time trusting. I guess working in security and seeing people's terrible actions can do that to you.

His eyes land on me and Roman, and they narrow further.

"What's going on?" he demands.

"Cecilia and I are engaged," Roman tells him in what has to be as few words as possible.

"Engaged?" Dom repeats.

"To be married," Roman says with an eye roll.

"Obviously," Dom grunts, clearly not impressed with Roman's sarcasm. "Are you sure this is a good idea?" he asks, locking eyes with Roman.

Roman's grip on me tightens, as though he's scared I'm going to change my mind and try to flee.

"I don't see why it wouldn't be. Making the love of my life my wife seems like the best idea," Roman responds darkly.

As Roman and Dom have a staring contest, communicating silently, Margot steals my attention.

"So, Cecilia, do you guys have any wedding plans yet? Any idea of when or where you'll get married?" she asks.

"Oh, umm, it's all so new. We haven't had a chance to talk about it. I'd rather have a shorter engagement. We'll of course wait until after your wedding. We don't want to take any attention from you," I say in a light voice, not wanting her to feel like her wedding is being overlooked.

"Don't worry about that. Plus, my wedding is in two months. I don't think even the best wedding planners could get a wedding done before then." She laughs. "If you need any help with anything wedding related, please reach out to me. I'd love to help out and pass on what I've learned," she offers sweetly.

"That would be amazing!"

The rest of the evening goes well. Everything is a normal Montclair Sunday family dinner. Down to Dom's cagey attitude, and Bash and Matthias's curious gazes.

After dinner, as usual, the brothers meet in the office.

His parents, Margot, and I convene in the sitting room and talk weddings.

It's amazing being a part of such a beautiful family. I already feel at home here.

# Chapter 59
## *Roman*

All three of my brothers stare at me incredulously in Dad's office.

"What is wrong with you?" Bash exclaims, throwing his arms up in exasperation.

"What do you mean?" I feign ignorance.

"You can't marry her without telling her who you are and what you do! You're lying to her! She deserves to know the truth!" my little brother lectures me.

"No, she doesn't. What she doesn't know, won't hurt her," I correct him in a sharp voice.

"Not yet, but when she finds out, the betrayal will crush her," Matthias chips in.

"You said you supported keeping her out of our world!" My frustration seeps into my voice.

"I said you should keep it away from your girlfriend. Not hide your identity from your wife," he corrects.

"What's the difference? I mean really, what's the problem with it? I love her, and she loves me."

"She loves the mask you've carefully cultivated for her. Not the real you," Dom cuts in.

I start doing the box breathing Cecilia taught me to calm down.

In, one... two... three... four.

Hold, one... two... three... four.

Out, one... two-

"For fucks sake, look at you! What the fuck are you doing?" Dom grumbles.

"I'm doing box breathing because you guys are pissing me off, and Cecilia will have questions if some of us leave the room with black eyes and broken noses," I glare at them conveying it won't be me leaving injured. I'm even more pissed now that he's interrupted my meditation exercise.

"This isn't you! You're not just lying to her, you're lying to yourself too. You can't keep this up forever. Something's going to break you, and you'll terrify her," Bash, ever the voice of fucking reason, chimes in.

"How would I even tell her? 'Hey, sunshine. Remember how I told you I work for Syndicate Enterprise doing security? Well actually, I lied. I torture and kill people for the crime family the Montclair brothers run. Hope this doesn't change your mind, seeing as you love peace and would never harm a fly,'" I say sarcastically.

"Maybe that's not the best approach, but you'll think of something," Matthias unhelpfully butts in.

"Figure it out." Dom orders. "Now, let's talk about the Bratva. Roman, what've you been seeing on the streets? What I've seen in official capacities is they're abiding by the laws. They haven't been an issue since the Margot situation," Dom says, and Matthias attitude darkens when his wife's misfortune is mentioned.

"Everything's been fine. There haven't even been many in our territory. It's been quiet. Too quiet. They've been too good. It isn't like them. I know they're up to something." I grumble, knowing what their response will be.

"Roman, we've been over this. Until we have something concrete, we need to continue on as normal." Dom sighs, then faces me. "They may not even be doing anything wrong. Or at least not anything worse than what we already know about. You may be trying to find something that isn't there."

"You know damn well that's not true! They're fucking scum, and they're doing something terrible. That's why they're hiding it so well. I fucking know it!" I spit out, pissed that they don't believe me.

They all look down, clearly not wanting to piss me off further. Since being with Cecilia, the anger outbursts have been less frequent, but they're testing me right now.

"I'm fucking leaving. Stay out of my relationship. And if any of you tell Cecilia anything, I'll make you suffer in unimaginable ways. I won't lose her," I threaten then storm out.

Outside the door, I do more breathing exercises, needing to calm down before I'm back with my sunshine. She's never seen me angry, and she's not going to now.

Once I'm back to the calm, complacent Roman she loves, I find her, give her a kiss, and we leave holding hands.

Like a normal couple.

Like a simple man who loves his fiancée.

Like the man she thinks her fiancé is.

And I'll be damned if she ever learns the truth.

# Chapter 60
*Cecilia*

Since the engagement, life has been perfect. Roman and I have been living in perfect harmony. I start off each day with yoga in front of the wall of windows, enjoying the beautiful view. Then we have breakfast together. Mamá sent me tea leaves she grew, so I drink my tea while Roman makes his tinto. Abuela taught him how to make it before we left.

Afterwards, I head to work, and he does the same. He's finished the repairs on my apartment, but we've made no mention of me moving back. It's not customary for us to live together out of wedlock, but I can't bring myself to care.

When I get off work, he meets me outside the clinic and walks me to either the yoga studio or home. Most nights we cook together. Or, well, I cook, and he plays music and helps with the mundane things like shredding and stirring. He's gotten skilled enough to make rice on his own now.

We fall asleep in each other's arms every night. And wake up the same way every morning.

It's more than I ever thought I could have. I didn't realize how much I craved this love, until now. Until I have it. And I know nothing could ever take it away from me.

# Chapter 61
## *Cecilia*

I'm eating some leftover lasagna from last night during my lunch break in the empty break room. Since I'm the last one to leave the clinic today, I'm the only one eating lunch so late.

It's quite peaceful.

I have my earbuds in, and I'm listening to a podcast about meditation and inner peace. I'm trying to find material for the next yoga session I teach. I can't help but smile as I realize everything is perfect in my life. I have found true inner peace. And one man can be credited for a lot of it.

I'm so transfixed in my podcast that I don't hear the door open. I don't realize I'm not alone until two hands land on my shoulders and start rubbing them roughly.

I instinctively tense and glance up despite already knowing who it is.

Dr. Sanders leans over me with a grin that makes me uneasy.

"Cecilia, at the end of your shift, meet me in my office." That smile makes me nauseous. He winks then leaves as though nothing happened.

I push away the rest of the lasagna, my appetite gone.

For some odd reason, I feel like I should let Roman know what's going on. That I'm feeling uncomfortable. Then I roll my eyes at the ridiculous thought. What could he even do?

Dr. Sanders has been almost hostile to me since I appeared with my engagement ring. He makes inappropriate and derogatory comments. It's making it impossible to have a good day at work. But I save the day with Roman every evening.

...

The rest of the day goes by too quickly, and before I know it, the office is cleared except Dr. Sanders and me.

I slowly make my way to his office. There's a ringing in my ears. It's not the first time I've had a doctor ask me to stay late, but it feels different this time. I can't explain where the paranoia is coming from. Maybe Gracie rubbed off on me more than I realized.

I open the door and he's smiling at me.

"Sit, Cecilia. We have some things to discuss," he says, pointing at the chair next to him.

I sit silently, not knowing what to say.

"You're getting married soon. Do you still plan on working for us now that you have a sugar daddy?" he asks, flicking his gaze to my obviously luxurious ring.

"Yes, I'm still going to work," I murmur, looking away.

"He makes his slut work. Interesting. If it's money you're after, you could've come to me. I have a few things you could do on the side to earn a little cash." He grabs his crotch while eyeing me up and down.

Tears well in my eyes, but I won't let them shed. I won't let him see that he's getting to me.

I must stare in silent shock for too long because he just chuckles darkly.

"Well, the offer still stands. Think on it, doll." With that, he waves his hand at me dismissively and turns back to his computer.

I run out of his office, out of the clinic, and onto the sidewalk.

I start hyperventilating.

I can't seem to slow my breathing.

I can't seem to slow my heart.

I can't seem to do anything.

Then hands grip my cheeks, raising my head.

I flinch and jump back, fighting the contact. Not letting him touch me.

"Sunshine, it's me. It's your fiancé," Roman soothes me.

I collapse into his arms, and he crushes me into his chest.

"Breathe with me. In, one... two... three... four. Hold, one... two... three... four. Out, one... two... three... four. Hold, one... two... three... four," he guides me through multiple rounds of box breathing until I can breathe normally.

"Now, tell me what happened, Cecilia. What sent you into a panic attack?" His eyes search mine, begging for an answer.

"Dr. Sanders... he was horrible. He... he... grabbed my shoulders," I collect my breathing as Roman's grip on me tightens. I've never seen him look so upset, so murderous. "He said horrible things. Called me a slut. Offered to pay me for things outside the office," I confess as tears well in my eyes.

"He did what?" Roman growls, and I swear if I didn't need him now, he'd go inside and hurt Dr. Sanders.

Which is insane. Because my hero isn't violent.

"He's horrible. He's always made me uncomfortable, but it's never been this bad," I confess. I never considered telling Roman about Dr. Sanders because what could he even do? But now I wonder if I should have.

"Did he touch you?" Roman says softly, but I can tell it's eating him inside.

"Besides grabbing my shoulders, no. He's never touched me," I assure him. Some small part of me wonders if I just saved Dr. Sander's life, then I shake off the thought. Roman may look like he could kill right now, but he never would.

"Good. But just because he didn't hurt you doesn't mean he hasn't been harassing you. He's making you uncomfortable. You have a right to be upset," he tells me.

I hug him even tighter and inhale his lemony scent. I don't know why he only smells like lemons occasionally, but the freshness always brings a smile to my face.

"Come on, sunshine. Let's get you home. I'll order some dinner while you take a hot bath, and if you want to tell me more about it, you can. If not, we can put on whatever movie you want and have a relaxing evening," he tells me sweetly, and guides me down the sidewalk.

I lean into him on the walk home, knowing no matter what I face, my hero will always be by my side.

# Chapter 62
## *Roman*


I follow my mark around the corner.

The doctor shouldn't be out this late. He has no idea what's lurking in the dark, waiting to attack.

He's in the parking lot of a seedy motel. He just rolled around with a prostitute.

It's one thing to cheat on your wife, which is all kinds of fucked up. It's another to pay to do it.

Maybe the sign that no one else wants you should be a hint not to cheat.

Or, you know, the fucking wedding band on your finger.

He's a sleaze, a disgusting excuse for a man.

And he scared what's mine.

For that, he'll pay.

"Dr. Sanders!" I whisper from behind him. As much as I want to shout at him, I don't want to draw any unwanted attention. Even though the parking lot is empty and dimly lit, I can't risk someone looking out their window.

He shrieks and turns around, clutching his nonexistent pearls.

I grab him and drag him behind a dumpster. I already scouted the path, sure to avoid all cameras.

"Please, don't hurt me. Just take it!" He thrusts his wallet in my face. "I'll give you the watch, my shoes, fuck even my wedding band. Just don't hurt me," he cries out.

"Pathetic. It's not like that wedding band means much to you," I seethe. "I'm not here to rob you. And I'll keep the pain to a minimum if you do me a favor!"

"Anything! Whatever you want!" he promises pathetically.

I punch his ribs hard enough to hear a crack. The sound soothes me. If I didn't need him to do this for me, I'd kill him.

He's been terrorizing my sunshine for over a year. He makes her uncomfortable. I would've never known if Cecilia hadn't come to me trembling and pale yesterday upset about Dr. Sanders.

My vision turns red as I picture her scared, and I punch him again and again. I avoid his face, not wanting any visible signs of injury.

This time, his cries do nothing to calm me. Not his. Not the man who terrorized my Cecilia.

I don't care how trivial the acts and comments were.

He made her uncomfortable. Now it's time for him to be uncomfortable.

I knee him in the balls, wanting him to feel inexplicable pain. I know it's a cheap shot. It's one I don't usually go for. It's sick to do that to another man. But he hurt Cecilia. So now he pays.

He howls in pain and doubles over, clutching his crotch. He's shaking and looks close to being sick.

"If you puke on me, I'll make you eat it," I promise him.

It's bad enough he's making me do this next to a dumpster. I'm going to smell disgusting. I swear if I get sick from this, I'm going to come back and kill him.

"Please! What do you want? I'll do anything," he begs, tears streaming down his face.

"I want you to fire Cecilia Rivera. Tomorrow." I demand.

"What?" His brows furrow in confusion, but I don't give a damn. I don't need to explain myself to him.

"Why?"

"So she'll never feel uncomfortable because of you again, you sick fuck," I seethe, and kick him again.

"You're fucking crazy. I don't make any of my employees uncomfortable!" He argues stupidly.

"That's not what her tears said yesterday," I spit out.

"Who are you to her? Why do you care?"

"I'm her fiancé. And I won't stand for anyone hurting her." I tilt his face up so he can see the promise in my eyes. "You don't know who I am. But I'm not a good man. If you don't fire her tomorrow, I'll find you, and I'll kill you. Do you understand?"

"Yes!" he gulps. "How should I do it?"

"I don't care. Just make it quick," I demand.

With one last hit, I leave him bleeding and crying behind the dumpster like the trash he is.

I make a pitstop at one of my offices and shower off the smell.

When I get back to the penthouse, I slip into bed and pull a sleeping Cecilia into me.

I smile as I realize everything is exactly as it should be.

# Chapter 63
## *Cecilia*

I wake up with a pit of dread in my stomach. I don't even get out of bed for yoga. I'm awake, just not moving.

Instead of tea, I ask Roman to make me a cup of coffee. I'm tapping into my Colombian roots to have the strength to go into the office today after yesterday.

I feel sick at the thought, but I can't hide away. I need to go to work.

"You don't have to go in today if you don't want, sunshine. I support you no matter what," Roman tells me for the third time this morning.

His support and understanding is so endearing and helpful, but I have to be strong. I need to face this headfirst.

"I can't run from him. And I won't let him scare me away. I am a strong Latina. He will not make me hide," I tell him in a fierce voice, channeling the strong women in my family. Abuela would never let a man intimidate her, so neither will I.

"Okay, sunshine. I'm just a call away if you need anything. You know I'll drop anything to be there with you, no matter what," he promises, pulling me in for a hug. "I'm so proud of you. You're such a strong woman. You take after your Abuela."

I smile, surprised he made the connection, and honored that he views Abuela and me as strong.

...

When we get in front of the clinic, Roman kisses me fiercely on the sidewalk, and lets me know one more time to call if I need anything.

I go in and start setting up. I say hi to a few of my coworkers but mostly keep to myself. After thirty minutes, Dr. Sanders calls me to his office.

For a brief moment, I wonder if he's going to apologize.

Until I walk in and see Jill from HR.

I can't make sense of the scene. Did he go to HR about coming onto me? Did he turn himself in?

It doesn't make sense.

Until he opens his mouth.

"We're going in a different direction. You'll get paid for today and two weeks' severance," he says in a monotone voice, then glares at my engagement ring with a fury I can't comprehend. "Sign this termination agreement, then you'll be escorted out."

I'm being fired.

I've never been fired before.

I never even considered the possibility that I'd ever be fired.

I contemplate asking why, then realize it won't make a difference. I'm fired either way. And I'd rather not hear what lie he came up with.

I just nod and walk out with Jill. I hand her my badge, but I don't respond when she wishes me well on my future endeavors.

I stand on the sidewalk, numb and confused. It isn't until I grab my phone to call Roman that I realize I'm shaking.

Not wanting to be seen through the clinic window, I walk to the café across the street and call my fiancé.

"Sunshine, what's wrong? Do you need me to come get you?" he asks frantically.

"Yes, please," I whisper through the phone. "They fired me."

As soon as the words leave my mouth, a wave of shame overcomes me. I don't think it's my fault. I've never received so much as a complaint from doctors, coworkers, nor patients. I've assumed this whole time that it's because of Dr. Sanders' advances towards me, but what if I just messed up and the timing is a coincidence? What if it is my fault?

"Oh, sunshine. I'll be there in five minutes. Are you still at the clinic?" he tells me, the worry in his voice evident.

"No, I'm at the café across the street." I murmur.

"I'll be there in four minutes. Stay on the line with me," he instructs.

Over those four minutes, I sit in silence at a table, just soaking in what happened. Roman whispers words of encouragement in my ears the entire time.

I listen to him, and realize no matter what, he'll always love me and stand by me.

Because he's the perfect man.

Because he's my hero.

# Chapter 64
## *Roman*

For the first few days, she was so upset. It was hard to see her that way.

My sunshine should always be shining brightly, never to be dulled by the darkness that prowls the earth. It's not her fault her boss was disgusting and needed to be dealt with. It's not her fault I had to save her from an unsafe work environment.

But even her sadness doesn't make me regret what I did. What I had to do. It was worth it to ensure she's safe.

And now, she's happier. She's started picking up more sessions at the yoga studio. She even smiles more than before. I didn't realize the stress and weight that job was putting on her, but now that it's gone, she's thriving. She's even been meeting with Margot to help finalize her wedding and start planning ours.

The only thing that's missing is Gracie, but she's halfway through the summer semester. She'll be back in a month and a half.

But even without her best friend, she's doing better. It's such a relief having her around. And now that work is out of the way, we can start our family sooner.

As soon as the ink dries on the marriage certificate, I'm pumping her full of me until her belly is round with my baby.

# Chapter 65
## *Cecilia*

It's been a week since I was fired, and I've decided it was for the best. I've never felt happier or freer. And as much as I hate not contributing financially, Roman's wealth helps lessen the feeling of being a burden. I'm not sure what his net worth is, but I'm starting to suspect it's a lot higher than he lets on.

Every day has been peaceful. I get to do long yoga sessions in the mornings, take care of our plants, and even wedding plan with Margot for both of our weddings. It's been incredible. Roman even makes time for me during the day, and we have lunch together most days.

We've been living this perfect life, and I couldn't be happier.

# Chapter 66
## *Cecilia*

I'm in downward dog position in front of the windows. The beautiful view distracts me from all that's around me. I exhale and reach forward further, stretching my back. I sigh in relief and hold the position.

I hear footsteps echo as Roman enters the room.

"Fuck, sunshine. Are you trying to kill me? Waking up to this view…" He sighs as he lets the sentence hang.

I blush and giggle. It's not unusual for him to catch the end of a yoga session, especially since I've been doing them later in the morning.

I go through a few more sequences until I'm in a wide-legged forward fold. My feet are spread apart, my legs are straight, and I'm fully bent in half, my hands resting on my feet and my head resting on the mat. From this position, I'm look between my legs and make eye contact with Roman.

"Cecilia, how long can you hold that pose?" he asks, a wicked grin overtaking his face.

There's a gleam in his eyes as he prowls over to me that sends a shiver down my spine.

"Probably five minutes," I guess.

"I can make that work," he says from behind me.

He gets on his knees, head positioned at my core, and inhales where my leggings press against me.

He kisses the back of my left knee, then slowly trails his mouth, sucking, biting, and kissing, up my inner thigh. Right before he reaches where I need him most, he switches, going to my right knee and repeating the process.

Sweat forms on my forehead, and it's not from the pose. I focus on keeping my breathing even, trying to keep my composure.

When his mouth hovers over my center, instead of kissing me there, he pulls back.

"These are in my way," he murmurs.

Then he rips the seam of my leggings, revealing my thong. Which he rips as well, displaying my core. The cool air makes me shiver, but when he speaks again, his breath warms me.

"Now, time for my treat," he says gleefully, then swipes his tongue through my wetness.

I squeal in surprise then moan at the sensation.

He attacks like a man starved. I don't know who's making more noise. Me at being devoured, or him greedily lapping me up.

He works a finger into me, then another. I squeeze around him, and he grunts.

"Fuck, sunshine. You're always so tight for me." His words are muffled because he doesn't even pull back to speak.

I start grinding myself against him, and he pulls me closer. My legs are shaking so much, I'm not sure how I'm still in position.

He grips my hip with his hand not in me and takes on some of my weight.

"Are you close, sunshine?" he asks desperately.

"Yes, Roman. Yes! Please!" I chant, needing my release.

He thrusts a third finger in me and sucks my clit into his mouth. I explode on him. Bright spots cloud my vision. I'm screaming, but I can't hear it. I can't even function. I'm practically sitting on his face, as he holds me up.

Once I've settled, he leans down between my thighs and kisses me, my taste fresh on his mouth. I don't mind it coming from him.

He tells me to continue my session, as he watches. It must be quite the view with my core on display through the ripped pants and thong.

When I get into the seated straddle, my legs straight out in a middle split, and my torso laying against the floor, resting on my elbows, I feel him approach.

He enters me from behind, practically laying on me, and I find a new sense of relief from yoga. And I know I'll never forget this session.

What an enjoyable start to the morning.

# Chapter 67
## *Cecilia*

We have a wonderful day shopping after our remarkable yoga session.

We went to a nursery and bought plants for the balcony, the ones I loved at our proposal. I'm already planning out how I'm going to arrange them.

Now we're at an estate sale. Roman is... uncomfortable, to say the least. I can tell he's not used to secondhand items. He wrinkled his nose when I found a lovely carpet but gave in when he saw how much I loved it. He did insist we get it professionally cleaned because 'Do you know how many strangers' bare feet and dirty shoes were on it?' He looked a little nauseous at the idea. I can't wait until my normal shopping buddy is back in town.

After we check out, I step outside onto the sidewalk and wait for Roman. He's calling one of his security friends to come pick up the rug for us since we drove here in the convertible.

I pull out my phone, ready to respond to Gracie, when it's pulled out of my hands. Then my purse is yanked on, but since it has a cross-body strap, it doesn't come off. I scream in surprise as the scariest man I've ever seen robs me.

He has short, blonde hair. And blue eyes. His arms are covered in tattoos in a foreign language. He's wearing all black, which looks menacing on him in a way it doesn't on Roman.

And he's holding a gun.

"Give me the damn purse!" he says through gritted teeth. "And shut the fuck up!"

I quickly take my purse off and hand it to him with my left hand. He grabs it then his eyes light up. I follow his gaze, and my heart drops when I find it on my engagement ring.

"Give it to me!" he demands.

A tear slides down my cheek as I gently pull off my ring. I hand it to him shakily, and my heart cracks. He grabs it and races down the street.

I turn, ready to run inside to Roman, but see him running towards me instead.

"What's wrong, Cecilia? Why are you crying?' he asks, frantically checking me for injury.

"He... he took it. He took my ring," I say through sobs, showing him my empty ring finger.

"Who took it? What happened?" he says, cupping my cheeks.

"A man with scary tattoos. He had a gun. He took my phone, purse, and engagement ring," I tell him when I catch my breath.

Roman crushes me to his chest and kisses my hair.

"I promise I'll get it all back, sunshine. I promise," he sighs and pulls me in closer. "But for now, let's go home."

No matter how ridiculous it sounds, I believe him. Somehow, my hero will get my ring back.

# Chapter 68
## *Roman*

I look at the man tied to the metal chair in my warehouse. The man who robbed my sunshine. *At gunpoint.*

It was a stupid mistake. One he'll pay for with his life. No one touches what's mine. No one hurts or scares my woman.

And no one takes what ties us together. The ring I picked out just for her. That shows the world she's mine.

Especially not a lowly Bratva member who shouldn't have been in our territory anyways.

It was easy to track him. Bash was more than happy to help when he heard what this scum had done to Cecilia.

He found his image on street cameras and saw that he's been arrested before for a slew of things. Petty theft, breaking and entering, physical altercations... The list goes on. He's not a good man. And I bet he does worse things for his Bratva.

And now it's time he pays.

I slap him across the face to wake him up. It's demeaning and will offend a man with his ego.

When he opens his eyes, they harden.

"Roman Montclair. Why am I here?" he growls.

I'm pleasantly surprised that he knows me. My face isn't as well known as my name. Only higher ups in the crime families and people I've dealt with before know it.

I guess we've crossed paths.

It's not unusual for me to catch someone more than once. I'll have to check out his scar to see how grave his offense was and how long ago.

"I want to have a chat," I tell him, then slap his face again.

He looks furious but can't do anything about it with his wrists and ankles bound.

"I will not share Bratva secrets," he says stoically.

"Obviously not. You're too low to know any," I tell him with a third slap.

He growls through gritted teeth but continues.

"Then why am I here?" he demands.

"You robbed my fiancée today. I want her things back," I explain.

He pales. He knows that our women are off limits. It's a death sentence to go near one.

"I did not know she was yours. It's all at my apartment. Where you grabbed me. I haven't gone to the pawn shop with them yet," he pleads with me to understand.

"Whether you knew or not is irrelevant. You robbed my woman in my territory. You made her cry. You took the ring that I gave her. That ties her to me forever. For that, you will pay," I tell him.

He nods in resolution. He knows the fate that awaits him.

I grab a knife, cut off his shirt, and see a faint scar, *RFM,* on his side. It wasn't deep enough to scar terribly, meaning his offense wasn't bad. But this time, his offense is unforgiveable.

I grab the knife, and he pales, knowing the ritual.

Instead of going over the scarred skin, I carve my initials into his chest taking up the whole space. The world needs to know what happens to those who mess with my woman. The Bratva is smart enough to figure out what he did. And they'll never touch my woman again.

Then I put a bullet between his eyes. I don't have the patience to drag this out tonight. I want to get back to bed with my sunshine.

I just need to retrieve what's hers first.

# Chapter 69
## *Cecilia*

I wake up, and my heart breaks again when I remember the events of yesterday. I go to rub my eye only to get hit in the head by something heavy.

I look down at my left hand and shriek in glee at the engagement ring on my finger.

My engagement ring.

I look over at a sleeping Roman and shake him awake.

"How? When?" I stutter through the questions, my heart the fullest it's ever been.

"Bash found it in a pawn shop. We all went looking. I told you I'd get them back. I'm your hero, remember?" he tells me with a lazy grin and pulls me into him.

I kiss him frantically, needing to convey how important this is to me.

I don't care if it was Bash that found it. Roman's the one who sent him looking. Roman, my hero. Forever my hero.

Nothing could make me love this man less.

# Chapter 70
## *Cecilia*

I look up at the overcast sky and hope I can make it home before it starts raining. I'm rushing down the sidewalk, keeping my head down when a hand grips my arm and pulls me into an alley.

I look up to see a man cloaked in a black hoodie holding me.

I open my mouth to scream but am cut off.

"Come on, Cecilia. You really don't recognize your best friend?" the man says, and I realize I know him.

I launch myself into Leo's arms and give him a tight hug.

"What a way to say hi after all this time! You scared me! But no matter. How have you been? What've you been doing? It's been so long," I tell him, excited to catch up.

The hoodie is covering his face so he's almost unrecognizable.

"Come with me. We need to talk, and it's about to rain," he says as he leads me further down the alley. We take a turn, and there's a black car with tinted windows. I get in the passenger side, and he gets in the driver's side.

"First, turn off your phone, and give it to me," Leo demands.

I'm shocked by the weird request but do it anyway.

"How have you been? We have so much to catch up on!" I'm excited to tell my friend about my engagement.

"We really do, but we don't have a lot of time, so you need to listen," he says, and I start to wonder if this run in wasn't an accident after all.

"Okay, you're making me nervous. Is everything okay? Are you in trouble?" I ask warily. "We can help you if you are."

"I'm fine. You're the one in trouble." He glances at my engagement ring, then meets my eyes with a hard glare. "Your fiancé isn't who he says he is. You're being tricked, and it's getting dangerous."

I lean away from him, taken aback. What does he know about Roman?

"You don't understand. Roman is the sweetest, kindest man ever. You're mistaken," I correct him.

He laughs bitterly.

"You have no idea. This monster you're with... he's from hell," he says it so darkly, I shrink back. "His whole fucking family are monsters. Every one of them."

"No. You're wrong." I shake my head, knowing the Montclairs are the best people I've ever met.

"You're so fucking naïve, Cecilia. What do you know about the Syndicate? Nothing, I bet, or you wouldn't be with the enforcer," he seethes.

"The Syndicate? Do you mean Syndicate Enterprise, their security and defense company? I know all about it. They help people," I explain, needing him to understand he has this all wrong.

"They don't help anyone. Your precious Montclairs run a criminal organization called The Syndicate. They do so many illegal things. Syndicate Enterprise is just their legal front. The cover to keep up appearances, and Roman Montclair has nothing to do with it." He pauses and grabs my hands. As much as I want to pull back, I don't. "He's the enforcer for the Syndicate. He does the grunt work. The dirty work. He tortures and kills people for a living. And he does it with a smile. Everyone in the underworld knows his name, and we all fear the monster he is."

"That's ridiculous. Roman wouldn't hurt a fly. And the Montclairs are standup citizens. I don't know why you're saying this, but you're mistaken. It must be a different Montclair family," I say gently, not wanting to call him a liar, but I know his accusations are absurd. "I should get going, Roman's going to wonder where I am soon."

I try to open the door, but it's locked.

"You're not going anywhere until you hear me out. I know of Roman's viciousness firsthand. He's tortured me." Leo drops my hands and pulls up the side of his shirt, revealing his ribs. And something more terrifying. "He did this to me. He carved his initials into me to remind me of what he's capable of." He waves his hand in my face, and I realize he's missing his ring finger. "He fucking chopped my finger off! I barely made it out alive. That's why I haven't been in touch in so long. He threatened my friends and family if I reached out to you. He said he'd kill them all then me. He has a warehouse full of torture equipment. He tied me up and almost beat me to death. He's a psychopath."

"Oh, Leo. I'm so sorry you went through that." I grab his hand and rub it soothingly, trying not to look at the nub of the missing finger. "But you're wrong. It must've been someone else. I mean, why would my Roman torture one of my friends?"

"It was him. Right after my birthday at the club. He drugged you, took you home, then found me. He kidnapped me, brought me to a warehouse, tortured me, threatened me, deleted your contact from my phone, chopped off my finger, and carved his name into me." Venom is laced in his voice.

"But why?" I ask, confused. There is no motivation there.

"He wanted you all to himself. He was jealous of our friendship. I bet he even blamed me for drugging you. He probably threatened Gracie into vouching for him. Poor Gracie must've been terrified. We know how skittish and pathetically paranoid she can be." He snorts derisively.

"No. Roman never blamed you for drugging me. He just said it was a stranger. I don't understand. He was with me the full night. I woke up to him sleeping on my floor." It comes out weak, but I refuse to give in to his claims.

"You were drugged. You were passed out all night. He left, tortured me, then came back to you. He's a sadistic fuck. He even used lemon juice to burn the carving worse. He's a sick fuck that gets off on pain. Why can't you see it?"

My eyes widen, and my heart stops at the mention of lemons.

All the times Roman's been gone then comes back smelling like lemons flash through my mind. Over the months, it must have been dozens of times. Sometimes multiple days in a row.

It can't be true.

I can't even fathom the amount of people he could have hurt in that period of time.

"You're starting to understand. But that's not even the worst part. He's manipulated and hurt you time and time again." Leo pinches my chin and lifts my face towards his.

"No," I whisper, begging him not to tell me.

Because I know whatever he says will change me forever. Will ruin Roman and me. And I just can't bear that.

"He drugged you that night at the club. He tortured your friend into abandoning you. But that's not all. He orchestrated the break in at your apartment. He paid the man to show up, scare you, and ransack the place. Wasn't it so lucky that you never saw the robber? That he never hurt you? That Roman came immediately? He arranged the whole thing so you would be forced to move in with him," Leo pleads with me to believe him.

"No," I whisper again, unable to connect the evil monster he's discussing to my sweet, caring fiancée.

"You didn't get fired for no reason. After your boss was a little rude to you, Roman beat him as well. Threatened his life if he didn't fire you. He wanted you completely dependent on him. So you could never leave him," Leo continues.

"No." It's a frail denial.

"I didn't want to have to show you this, but here," Leo hands me his phone.

On it is a video of two men by a dumpster taken from far away. It zooms in, and I realize I know these men. It's Roman and Dr. Sanders.

It's too far away to hear what's being said, but I don't need to hear to understand the fists flying. Roman punches Dr. Sanders repeatedly. He knees him between the legs. Pauses the pounding to talk to him. I feel nauseous. Not even halfway through the video, I turn the phone off.

"How could this happen?" I beg to understand.

"It's okay, Cecilia. You didn't know. You see the best in people, and he took advantage of that," Leo says, rubbing my shoulder in what should be a comforting way. "But that's not all. The man that robbed you earlier this week? Roman tortured and killed him after Sebastian found him. That's how you got that ugly ring back so quickly. It wasn't a work of magic. It was the work of the monster we all hate."

"Killed?" I say, doubt despite reason seeping into my voice.

Leo sighs, grabs his phone, and does something on it.

"See for yourself," he tells me as he hands it to me.

Pulled up is a picture of the robber, clear as day. But his shirt is off. And on his chest are Roman's initials, carved into him just like they are on Leo's side.

I roll down the car window and throw up. Over and over again. I throw up for what must be five minutes. Leo rubs my back the entire time. It isn't comforting. Not at all. It just makes the whole experience worse.

Once I'm done, Leo hands me a bottle of water, and I rinse out my mouth.

"How do you know all of this?" I ask, succumbing to the truth.

"As soon as I recovered from his torture, I started following him. I had to save you from him, but I knew I needed to compile enough evidence so you could see through his charm. His obsession with you runs deep. I didn't realize how far he'd go to ensnare you. And the worst part is, he only wants you because he wants to get one over me. I'm sorry I didn't step in sooner," Leo says, and pushes a piece of my hair behind my ear. I shrink back.

I don't want his comfort. I don't want anyone's comfort. The only person who could calm me is... Roman. But that's not an option anymore.

I don't know what to do.

"What now?" I beg him, needing guidance.

"I have you covered, baby." He reaches into the backseat and hands me a large backpack and some clothes. "Here's a bag full of everything you need. There's twenty-five thousand dollars in cash, clothes, a new ID, a burner phone, and some snacks. It's not enough to last forever, but it's enough to get you far away and to help you build a new life."

He smiles at me, as though he saved my day, but the feeling's wrong. Because the only hero I've ever believed in was Roman. And it turns out he was the villain all along.

"Why are you doing this for me? Where did you even get this money?" I ask, not really caring about the answer. I'm just stalling from what I know I have to do.

"Because you're my best friend. And I can't watch you throw away your life for this monster. He's too evil for your pureness," he tells me. "Now here's what you're going to do. You're going to put on these clothes and headscarf, so when he tries to track you based off what you're wearing right now, he can't. I'm going to drop you off at the train station, and you're going to buy a ticket going somewhere far away. Don't tell anyone. You're not going to contact anyone from your old life. If you do, you put them in danger of Roman. He's going to be looking for you. He'll torture anyone who knows anything. You're going to text me where you end up. I'll keep you up to date on what's going on here. He thinks I'm not in contact with you, so he won't suspect me. You're going to live under this new identity. Don't tell anyone who you are. Do you understand?" he demands.

"But what about my family? What about Gracie?" I ask, not knowing how I could just leave them and never look back. "Can't we just go to the police and report him?"

"The police know, but they look the other way. They don't get involved in the underground crime here. The Mafia is like the police of the underworld. They keep everything in order, so the cops stay out of it. The cops would probably hand you over to Roman to stay in his good graces," Leo explains. "As far as your family and Gracie, you need to leave without a word. Maybe in a few months if Roman's given up the search, you can reach out. But until then, you put them in danger of his wrath if they know anything. Swear to me that you'll leave them out of this."

I hesitate, trying to process everything.

My whole life has been turned upside down in the span of fifteen minutes. I don't even know who I am anymore.

"Cecilia, do you understand?" Leo shakes me, grabbing my attention.

"Yes, I understand," I respond hoarsely.

"Good. Now, I'm going to drive us to the train station. Take this time to memorize your new ID," he says with a smile.

How can he smile at a time like this? I just found out everything is a lie. He's the one who told me. And he's smiling?

I don't think I can ever smile again.

He nudges me, so I pull out the new wallet in the bag and look at the ID.

*Emily Ricci.*

I feel uncomfortable that Leo gave me his last name, but I don't say anything. Other discoveries in the past twenty minutes have made me more uncomfortable.

He pulls up to the train station and stops.

"Good luck, Emily. Remember, text me when you get there," Leo says with a sad smile.

"Thank you, Leo. For everything," I whisper.

"Anything for you, baby," he says, then unlocks the car door.

I get out the car and stare at the train station.

I feel my heart crumble with each step.

I look back at Boston one last time, knowing I'm leaving the remnants of my heart here.

# Chapter 71
## *Roman*

"Sunshine, I'm home! I've missed you," I call out as I enter the penthouse.

It's around six in the evening. so I'm surprised when I don't find Cecilia in the kitchen. She's usually cooking dinner around this time.

I go to our bedroom and bathroom but don't find her in either. She's not on the balcony, nor by the windows doing yoga. I go through each room, looking for her.

My heartrate increases with each empty room. By the time I've established that she's not here, I'm breathing heavily as fear races through me.

I pull out my phone and check the tracking app I have on hers.

*No location found*

My heart stops, and my stomach lurches.

*No.*

*No, no, no.*

I push down my bile and call Bash.

"Hey, man. Now's not a good time," he starts, but I cut him off.

"Cecilia's missing. She's not at the apartment. And her phone isn't showing a location," I say frantically.

"Fuck!" I hear noise in the background that sounds like a window closing, then... *Is he climbing a tree?* After some walking and a gate creaking, a door opens. Then he climbs a flight of stairs, and I finally hear typing.

"Where are you?" I ask, confused as hell.

"I'm at home," he says easily.

"Right. Your new house in the suburbs," I say dumbly.

"Yeah. Now let's focus on Cecilia. What's her last known location?" he says.

"She was at the penthouse this morning. Then she went to the yoga studio. I wouldn't be surprised if she stopped at a thrift store on her way home," I tell him, holding back a shudder at the idea of wearing someone else's clothes.

But she loves going there. Even when I've offered her more money than she can count to go to nice boutiques, she turns it down.

"No. I mean where is the last known location on her tracking app?" He sighs at my stupidity.

"It doesn't say," I explain angrily. How dare he mock me right now from his middle-class bedroom!

"Fuck. What app did you install? You did install an app, right?" he says with a sigh.

"Of course I did!" I tell him which one, and I swear I can hear his eyes roll.

"That's a shitty app. They have ones now that'll track the location and save it, so you can know where she's been."

"Well, I'm sorry I'm not a computer genius like you," I grumble, pissed.

"Whatever, I'll track street cameras. What time was her yoga session and when did it end?" he asks.

"It ended at one fifteen p.m. It's Sanctuary on College Drive."

I look at my watch and note that it's seven. She's been missing for almost six hours.

Fear doubles down in me. Where could she be?

After too much time, Bash makes a noise.

"I see her. She's walking down the street, heading in the direction of the apartment. Everything seems normal... Oh, fuck," he mutters.

"What?" I all but yell.

"Give me a second. I'm trying to find another angle," he says uselessly, not explaining anything.

"Fucking telling me, Bash," I growl.

"A hooded man grabbed her on the street and pulled her into an alley. The alley doesn't have cameras, and she never reemerges onto the street. There's another exit from the alley, but there aren't any cameras. I'm setting up a street camera search looking for her through facial recognition and based off her outfit. It could take days, even with the small search radius. But I'm not finding anything on her or the man. I can't even identify him," he sighs, defeatedly.

"No. No one grabbed her. Why would someone grab her?" I know it's denial speaking, but I can't believe it.

"You've pissed off a lot of people. And you haven't kept your connection to her a secret. Any one of them could've wanted her to get back at you." It comes out accusingly.

I know they've been pissed about me handling the Bratva, but I never thought it'd come to this.

"If you had told her, maybe she could've been prepared," my little brother doubles down on scolding me.

"Keep looking. Tell me if you find anything. I'm calling Dom," I grind out before ending the call.

Anger courses through me because someone took her.

Someone took my sunshine.

And I'll stop at nothing to get her back.

# Chapter 72
## *Cecilia*

*Five weeks later...*

I look around the café I work at, and sigh. After over a month in Marigold Valley, I still have trouble accepting the reality of my new life.

I have a job as a barista. It's not bad, but it's different. I live in a studio apartment and have a sweet elderly neighbor, Mr. Banks. He's my only friend here. I've had some customers and coworkers try to initiate friendships, but I just don't have it in me. I can't let anyone in. I don't know how to trust anymore. Not just others, but myself. I never doubted Roman, not for a minute. And look at how wrong I was.

My days feel meaningless. I work as much as possible, not that I'm desperate for money. With how frugal I've been, I still have plenty of what Leo gave me. He's my only connection to my old life. To Cecilia María Álvarez Rivera. To the ghost of my past. But despite how hard he tries to stay connected, it hurts too much. I barely reply unless it's about the people I care about. My family. Gracie... The Montclairs.

He only updates me on Roman's family when it's pertinent to their search. I know they're still looking. All of them. So, I can't reach out to my family yet.

But I care. More than I should. And not because of the problems they're causing me. But because despite what they've done, despite who they are, I still love them.

I still love him.

I lift my hand to my long necklace chain, lift it from under my shirt, and hold the engagement ring. It's the only thing I kept. I've tried to get rid of it so many times, but I just can't.

Because despite how dumb it is, despite not even knowing the man, he's still my Roman. My héroe.

I still have trouble connecting the monster to the hero.

I still have dreams about him. On the good nights, he's holding me, caring for me, saving me. We're back at the penthouse loving each other. And I wake up only to cry at my reality.

On the bad nights, I watch him torture and kill people I love. People I don't know. Innocent people. And I wake up drenched in sweat.

Because of the dreams, I work every early shift I can. I work doubles most days. Always the one to pick up other's shifts. I need the distraction, or I find myself wallowing in my depression.

After work, I head home every day.

My only joy is cooking dinner for Mr. Banks. He's a kind man, never prying, but always here for me. I know he suspects I'm running from something, but he never asks.

I cook my native dishes almost every night, needing that connection to home. He loves them, always praising the food. It feels good to share that connection to home with someone.

Sometimes we watch old war movies and westerns. I've never been a fan of action before, but so much about me has changed.

I'm not Cecilia María Álvarez Rivera. I'll never be her again. And I've had to sever all ties to her.

I don't do yoga. I run now. Every day. To chase the demons away. Some mornings, if I wake too early, I'm running at three a.m. I don't go shopping or gardening. But in my free time, I crochet. It's a craft I picked up from Mr. Banks. We crochet while watching the violent black-and-whites.

I keep busy. Working. Running. Cooking. Mr. Banks. Just so I can't be stuck in the past.

I know it's no way to live. It's not conducive. And long term, it'll drive me crazy. But I'm still in denial about the permanence of my situation. The only thing keeping me in Marigold Valley is my elderly friend.

"Emily, we need more cups. Go get them from the back," my teenage manager tells me.

"On it!" I yell back wearing a fake smile.

The same fake smile that I've been wearing the past five weeks.

Because I don't know if I'm capable of smiling anymore.

If I'm capable of happiness.

# Chapter 73
## *Roman*

Five fucking weeks.

It's been five weeks and two days since my sunshine disappeared.

Since she was taken from me.

No one has owned up to it.

Despite the dozens of Bratva members I've interrogated, despite the plethora I've killed, no one claims anything.

It's driving me fucking insane.

I'm consumed by anger. I let it coarse through me, drowning out my fear. Because if I let fear rule me, I'll never find her.

Dom storms into my penthouse, and I fume.

"How the fuck did you get in?" I demand.

"Bash got me in. Enough is fucking enough! You're going to start a fucking war. You're banned from touching another Bratva member. I'm taking down your access codes to the warehouses. You're done. You're out of control. It's not getting you anywhere," he says coolly. Levelheadedly. Like he isn't ruining my chances to find and save my sunshine.

"I suggest you rethink that. Because standing between me and Cecilia is the last thing you want to do. I don't give a fuck who it is; I'll destroy anyone blocking my path to her," I spit out.

"Did you just threaten me? Not only your brother, your family, but also your boss? You're forgetting your place, little brother." It comes out as even as always, and it makes me snap.

I swing at him, catching him off guard, clipping his cheek.

He comes back at me, and we fall to the ground, wrestling like we did when we were boys. But unlike then, there's a rage in me that won't be quelled until I get her back.

But he pulls back.

"I'm not fucking fighting you. Get your shit together. I'm meeting with the leaders of the other families to see what they have to say. What if it wasn't the Bratva? What if you've been butchering the wrong group? We can't have that. If you want to be invited to the meeting, you need to get your shit together. Do you understand?" he demands.

"Fine. Make it happen soon, or I'm back hunting. I won't sit around waiting. I will find her!" I growl.

I haven't let my mind wander to where she is. What horrors she could be enduring. I only know she's alive because if they'd killed her, they would've flaunted it by now. But I also know some fates are worse than death. And if she's suffered in any way, I'll burn the world to avenge her.

Because mark my words.

I will find my sunshine.

I will save her.

And I will avenge her.

Nothing can stop me.

# Chapter 74
## *Cecilia*

"Emily dear, what's on your mind? You've passed dicing and now are just mutilating that onion." Mr. Banks says with a concerned sigh.

"Sorry. I'm just lost in thought." I put down the knife and face him. "Do you ever... do you ever miss something that's bad for you? Something you know you shouldn't? Something you know you can't have, but you want more than your next breath?" I ask, needing to share in my misery. I can't stop missing Roman, and it's killing me.

After a long pause, Mr. Banks answers.

"I was an alcoholic for fifteen years. It's why my kids don't visit me. I was a horrible father to them. For the longest time after I got sober, I would crave a sip. That self-control to say no is why I'm where I am today. Alive and finally happy. You just have to keep saying no," he tells me, and I can tell he thinks I'm struggling with an addiction.

"I'm so sorry. I didn't know," I whisper.

"It's okay, dear. I'm better now. Happier," he says with a sigh. "I just miss my kids. But what I put them through was unforgiveable. I was terrible to them. They came second to my addiction. I forgot about them. Stole from them. Even manipulated them on occasions. Being sober for decades hasn't been enough penance. I know my son has children, and it breaks my heart that I have grandchildren I'll never know," he says sadly.

"Mr. Banks, I think your remorse shows that you are ready. I think you should reach out," I tell him, the little piece of Cecilia still in me believes in forgiveness and second chances. "You're a changed man. That has to count for something."

"Have you ever had someone wrong you? Do you think there are any actions that simply can't be forgiven?" His eyes swing to the engagement ring hanging in front of my shirt with a raised brow.

"It's different. What he did... what he did was unforgiveable. He lied to me. Hid so much. He manipulated me in unimaginable ways. I don't even know the man I fell in love with. I don't think he ever truly existed. And I was a fool to believe him," I sigh and turn back to chopping.

"Yet you still wear his ring," Mr. Banks counters.

"I still love him. It's stupid. The man I fell in love with is a farce. A façade. He isn't real. But he was my everything. And he's left me a shell of a person." A tear slips down my cheek, and I suck in a breath.

"Is love enough? You say my children should forgive me for the same offenses, but you can't forgive your husband?" he sighs, and I can tell this conversation is as much about him as it is about me.

"It's different with Roman. He's a monster. And I don't think he regrets what he did. You do. You'd beg for forgiveness," I turn, facing him. Trying to get him to understand.

"Did he ever hurt you? Threaten you? Were you ever in danger because of him? If so, then you're wrong, it isn't different." He looks down shamefully. "Because I did. I hit my sons when they stood between me and my fix. And no matter how much I regret it, nor how much I've changed, I'm not sure I have a right to ask for forgiveness. Even after decades of soberness."

I'm quiet for a minute, processing his confession. I can't connect the kind old man to the abusive drunk he claims to have been.

"He never hurt me. I was never afraid of him. But he did hurt others and hide it from me." I look down before steeling my gaze. "I once believed everyone deserved a second chance. That if someone is capable of change, they've earned forgiveness."

"And what do you believe now? Now that he's wronged you, what do you think?" I can hear the desperation in his voice.

"I think you should reach out to your sons. You should at least try to connect. Even if they don't accept it, you can still offer your forgiveness. And maybe you'll be reunited with them and meet your grandchildren," I say truthfully.

"Then I think when your husband finds you, because there's no way he isn't looking, that you should at least hear him out. He loves you, right?" Mr. Banks asks.

I nod because that's the one thing I can't refute.

"He loved me so much he did unimaginable things to keep me," I confess, keeping the details to myself.

"Then at least hear him out. Men do crazy things for the people they love. *The things they love.*" He shakes his head as he remembers the crazy things he did for his addiction. "At least for me, give him the grace you want my sons to give me. At least listen," he begs.

I just nod again, unable to make any promises.

Some cuts run too deep.

"The empanadas will be ready in about thirty minutes. Why don't you pick out a movie?" I suggest, abruptly ending the conversation.

"I love your empanadas!" he exclaims as he slowly makes his way into the living room.

And we have a normal evening of movies, dinner, and crocheting.

But all the while, my mind remains on one thing.

If he found me, would I be able to forgive him?

# Chapter 75
## *Roman*

I walk into Dom's office expecting it to be filled with the family heads, but freeze when I only see Dom and Lorenzo, the head of the Mafia.

"What is this? Where's everyone else?" I clench my fists in anger.

Viktor, the head of the Bratva, along with the heads of the Cartels and Irish Mobs should be here. I was promised everyone!

"Viktor refused to come after you've desecrated his family. Lorenzo has offered information, so I told the others they weren't needed," Dom explains.

I study Lorenzo, wondering what the Mafia has to do with Cecilia's disappearance.

"Well, what is it?" I demand, stalking towards Lorenzo.

Lorenzo, while a formidable opponent with his reputable Mafia and high intelligence, is double my age. I could easily force the information out of him. But something tells me he has a backbone of his own, and that he wouldn't fold under the worst torture.

"Sit, boy," he commands in a thick Italian accent, pointing at the chair in front of Dom's desk that's next to him. "I come with only the intention of stopping a war you've been determined to start with your temper. It isn't the Bratva responsible for the Latina's disappearance, but one individual acting rogue."

I sit, intrigued and hopeful to finally have some information.

"Please proceed," Dom asks, gesturing politely with his hand to Lorenzo, while glaring daggers at me.

I know the Mafia is our greatest ally. They've worked alongside us peacefully, and they never break our rules. Dom would be furious if I ruined that.

"First of all, I regret to inform you, that the Latina–" he begins, but I cut him off.

"Cecilia," I growl, correcting him.

I won't stand for her to be labeled in any way. She's proud of her heritage, and I love her culture, but I don't appreciate the derogatory way he's saying 'Latina.'

He dips his head in acknowledgement.

"I regret to inform you, no one took Miss Álvarez Rivera. She left of her own volition," he says, studying my reaction. I see his hand hovering over his gun, ready to fight back if I explode at his ridiculous claim.

"That's ridiculous! Why would she leave? We saw a man grab her!" I shout, flying from my chair so quickly that it topples over.

"Sit down," Dom seethes, glaring at me. "Please explain. I've seen Cecilia. She's never been anything but happy. Why would she run?"

Lorenzo eyes me warily and nods at my chair. I reluctantly take the cue, and glaring at him, I pick it up and sit down like a petulant child.

"The man who grabbed her was one of mine." Lorenzo stares at me cautiously. My fingers dig into my arms rest, my knuckles turning white. "He wasn't acting on any Mafia orders though. We have no quarrel with you, Roman. His name is Leonardo Ricci. You may know him as a friend of your fiancée, Leo."

My vision reddens.

*Fucking Leo!*

I should have known.

I grind my teeth as I shake with rage.

He's fucking responsible.

"Who is he?" Dom asks, staring at me.

"He was Cecilia's friend. I met him once, on his birthday, at one of our nightclubs. He drugged her that night." I flash my eyes towards Lorenzo, gaging his reaction at what I confess. "I tortured him that night for what he's done, but I didn't kill him because he was Cecilia's friend. It was all well within code. We are allowed to kill rapists. We don't stand for men who hurt women," I defend myself.

But Lorenzo isn't angry.

"I don't blame you. If someone did that to my wife, I'd have murdered them slowly and painfully. It is true to our code. We would kill even our own for a crime as heinous as rape. But we didn't know this occurred until yesterday. Leonardo never mentioned it. But he's been acting differently for months. Disappearing, unfocused, distracted. We didn't know why." Lorenzo looks up at me.

"He's been obsessed with enacting revenge on you. We went to his apartment yesterday, and it was covered in images of you and of Miss Álvarez Rivera. He's been following you two for months. Tracking you. Compiling a pretty damning case against you. And not all of it is false." Lorenzo shoots me a disapproving glare, and I know he knows the lengths I went through to keep and protect Cecilia.

"What does this have to do with Cecilia disappearing?" I growl, already knowing the answer.

"Leonardo compiled enough damning evidence to convict you, then grabbed her that day. He exposed everything about you to her, effectively scaring her." Lorenzo sighs and runs a hand through his grey tendrils.

"What does he mean, Roman? What did you do?" Dom demands. "I know you didn't tell her about the Syndicate, but was there anything else?"

Lorenzo raises an eyebrow at me.

"Besides torturing Leo, I also may have been the one to orchestrate the robbery on her apartment. But she wasn't supposed to be there. He came at the wrong time." I pause. "I also confronted her boss and demanded he fire her after he sexually harassed her. It was for her safety," I confess, and Dom's gaze darkens.

"He also blamed you for the drugging that night and claimed you tortured him out of jealousy. He claims you threatened her roommate to comply with you. And the Bratva member that robbed her, he showed her a picture of the body with your signature. It was pretty damning," Lorenzo explains.

I feel sick as the pieces fall into place. She fucking left because that bastard framed me as a monster. Which I am, but not to her. *It's his fucking fault.*

"He gave her a new ID as Emily Ricci." I see red at the thought of her with his last name. "He also gave her twenty-five thousand dollars, then dropped her off at the bus station. They've been in contact ever since."

"Where did he get twenty-five thousand dollars?" Dom asks.

Lorenzo chuckles darkly.

"The stronzo stole from us. From his famiglia. To exact revenge on you, Roman," Lorenzo's voice reveals his fury. "He is no longer welcome to us."

"Where is he? I need to find him!" I growl.

"I will hand him over. We have exacted our revenge on him, and while we normally *deal with* traitors personally, due to the unconventional circumstance, we've decided to give him to you," Lorenzo says.

"Thank you, Lorenzo," Dom says, standing up, and offering his hand. "How can we repay you?"

Lorenzo shakes Dom's hand.

"By stopping the unnecessary violence against other families. If you've caused a war, we want no part of it. And since you are solely to blame, we cannot side with you. But we refuse to side with the Russians. You must make amends and restore a treaty with them. I will not stand for any casualties of my people," Lorenzo says.

He dips his head at me and walks himself out.

Dom turns to me, his earlier calm transforms to fury.

"You almost started a war with our worst enemies over something you are at fault for!" He seethes.

"It was a misunderstanding. After what happened to Margot, it was a logical conclusion!" I defend weakly, knowing I fucked up.

"A misunderstanding? Unacceptable. Now *I* have to fix your mistake!" he spits out. His eyes bore into me as the severity of my mistake sinks in.

"I'm sorry," I mutter words I never say. I never apologize. But I know he needs to hear it.

"I don't want your apologies. Let's get this bastard," he says and rounds his desk.

"You're coming too?" I'm surprised. He doesn't usually get his hands dirty. That's my job.

"Of course. This son-of-a-bitch almost started a war. And he drove my future sister away. He needs to pay. And I'm going to be right there with you."

Well, fuck. I guess my cold-hearted eldest brother may actually have a soft spot for his sisters-in-law.

But as we walk through his mansion to collect Leo, a rage I've never known consumes me.

This fucker not only took my sunshine from me, but he turned her against me.

For that, he'll pay with his life.

# Chapter 76
## *Cecilia*

Today's been normal... or at least it would be if I didn't feel eyes on me all day. I'm going crazy looking around the empty café. No one's here. I close in five minutes. But even being the only employee closing tonight with no customers in this empty café, I still feel eyes on me. Which is impossible.

No one is here.

And yet, I glance out the window again.

*Screw it.*

I lock the door, too paranoid to continue. No one comes in this late anyway. I turn off the lights for the main room and head to the back.

I put away some boxes in the back room, then once that room is ready for closing, I come back out to the main room.

And scream.

Because a man stands in the middle of the café.

A man in all black. Tactical pants and a t-shirt.

A man with a buzz cut and tattoos.

A man I'd know in any lighting, even in this darkness.

"Roman," I breathe out, not believing my eyes.

He inhales and closes his eyes, like he's savoring the sound of his name.

"I've found you, sunshine," he says in a voice so lethal, it sends shivers down my spine.

But maybe those shivers aren't just from his wicked voice. Because I don't think my damp panties are either.

"How did you find me?" I ask, still in a daze.

"Your little lying bastard of a friend confessed with his last words," he says calmly as if this is a normal conversation, but it's not. Because there is no normal between us. Not anymore.

"So, it's not true? About you? And your family? You're not killers? You didn't ruin my life?" Hope bleeds into my voice.

If he tells me I have it all wrong, if he can explain it... I'll forgive him in an instant. I'll go home with him, and everything will go back to how it was.

I want that more than anything.

"He lied about a few things. I never drugged you. He did. That's why I tortured him. And his reasoning was wrong with some things. But for the most part, it's true. I am a monster. A killer. And I've done terrible things to get you. To keep you." His face morphs into a wicked grin I've never seen before. It's sinister and evil. Nothing like my gentle giant. "But know this, sunshine. You will never get away from me again. You will never have the opportunity again. Because you're mine."

"You're fucking crazy!" I raise my voice, trying to fight his words.

"Oh sunshine, you haven't seen crazy yet." His face sours, and he tsks. "And don't curse. It's not you. My Cecilia doesn't say foul things."

"Your Cecilia doesn't exist anymore. You ruined her. You ruined me! My name is Emily," I protest.

"Cecilia, you're being unreasonable," he scolds me.

"My name is Emily Ricci!" I scream it this time.

"NO, IT'S NOT! YOU DON'T HAVE THAT BASTARD'S LAST NAME!" Roman roars, then takes a calming breath. "Your name is Cecilia María Álvarez Rivera. And before the day is done, it will be Cecilia María Montclair."

"You're insane," I whisper as I back away further behind the counter, grateful for the barrier. My palms start to sweat as the realization that I truly don't know this man washes over me. My hero would never yell at me. Never curse at me. This man truly is a monster.

He only chuckles at my words then takes a step towards me, and my heart pounds. I don't know if it's from fear... or excitement. But I have to stop him. I can't be near him.

I hold up my hand in a halting motion. "Stay the fuck away, you bastard! Don't take another step!" I demand.

"We've been over this. My Cecilia doesn't curse. And she especially doesn't curse her husband out." He slowly starts moving again, approaching the counter separating us. "And I am insane. Of course I'm insane. You make me insane!"

Then he effortlessly jumps over it.

I back up further, but for each step I take away from him, he takes one double in length towards me.

I turn and sprint, trying to get to the back room.

But in less than a second, he has me in his arms. He turns me to face him, and this close, it's difficult to refuse him. Too difficult.

Because while my brain knows Roman is a monster, my eyes still see my hero.

He loops one of my wavy strands around his finger and glides through it. He tucks it behind my ear, then fists the hair on the back of my head.

I look up and meet his gaze.

It's the biggest mistake I could make.

His eyes glance down at my mouth.

I hitch a breath as I glance at his.

Then he pounces.

His lips descend upon mine in the hungriest kiss we've ever had. It's frantic and harsh. He's claiming me.

He's always been a gentle lover, but this is far from that. It just reminds me that I'm kissing the Monster Montclair.

And despite it all, I wrap my arms around his neck and pull him in closer. I respond eagerly to his kiss. I'm not strong enough to resist the man I love. Not when he's kissing me like this.

His tongue parts my lips, and I greedily grant him entrance. The moment our tongues touch, a shiver shoots down my spine.

Starting from a prick on my neck.

Then the world fades.

And I'm falling into his arms.

"Now, you're coming home," I hear a faraway voice say as I succumb to darkness.

# Chapter 77
## *Roman*

I stare at my sunshine's sleeping form as we travel back to Boston on a private jet. We're in the bedroom at the back for privacy. The crew has strict instructions not to interrupt us.

I told her I hadn't drugged her at the club. And it was true. I hadn't drugged her yet.

But now I have.

She wouldn't have come willingly, and if I had spent another second in that Godforsaken town, I would've been tempted to put a bullet in my brain. She needs to be in our home, in our bed, with me.

And I need her unconscious as I take a few safety precautions for her.

I roll her onto her back and gently move her hair off her neck. I feel around, trying to find the right spot. When I do, I open an antiseptic wipe and clean the area. I uncap the needle containing the high-tech tracker and inspect it. It's not as large as I thought it'd be, so it shouldn't hurt too much. But I didn't want her awake for the pain or the pain that's to come. Also, I need her still.

I pinch her neck and insert the tracker at the base of her skull. Once it's inserted, I wipe away the drop of blood and look at my handy work. You'd never even know it's there.

And now she'll never be able to disappear on me again.

Next, I lift the bottom of her shirt, revealing her lower back. I glare at the high-rise jeans she's wearing in disgust. My Cecilia would never wear denim. She'd be in a flowy skirt or linen pants. Or even yoga pants.

I shimmy them lower until they sit at the top of her luscious ass.

Then I pick up the tattoo gun and get to work.

I smile when it's done, pleased with my art.

I've carved this so many times, I could do it in my sleep. But tattooing it, engraving it into my sunshine, it's almost sensual.

The *RFM* tramp stamp looking up at me brings the biggest smile to my face.

Now, the world will know she's mine.

But there's one more thing I need to do to avoid any possible misunderstanding.

I grab her left hand and glare at her empty ring finger. This won't fucking do. It should always show our union. Just like her back will.

I turn the gun back on and tattoo a small ring around the base of her finger. A wedding band. It's thin enough that when she chooses to wear her ring, it'll cover the tattoo, but it's thick enough to send the message.

That she's taken.

*By me.*

I lift my own left hand and tattoo a band around mine. It's obnoxiously thick, but the world needs to know. Plus, wearing a ring in my line of business could get messy.

I eye myself, wondering where I can carry her name permanently. There isn't much bare skin left, and I need it to stand out. Since from my neck down to my fingers and to my ankles is covered in ink, I have to get creative.

On my left thumb, between knuckles, I tattoo *Sunshine*. It looks poorly done, but I'm simply content to wear her mark.

On my left pointer finger, I tattoo *Cecilia.* Needing her branded on me.

On my left middle finger, I tattoo in all capitals, *HUSBAND.* Now there's no room for confusion.

My ring finger has my band, which is all it needs.

Then on the pinkie, I tattoo her name again, just to double down on it.

I look down at it with a smile. I love her claim on me, even if she doesn't know about it yet.

On my right hand, I tattoo one word per finger, starting with the pinkie and ending with the thumb.

*Cecilia*

*María*

*Álvarez*

*Rivera*

*Montclair*

I make a fist with both hands and enjoy the way her name shines through.

A sick part of me loves that when I throw a punch, what they'll see is my woman's name. And they'll know I'd do anything to protect her.

I look at my arms and fill every empty area with her name.

I continue down my chest and onto my legs.

I fill up dozens of empty spaces with her name.

It'll be like a game of *Where's Waldo* for her. She can spend her time under me and on top of me searching for her name. I wonder how long it'll take her to find them all.

Once I'm filled with as much Cecilia as I have room for, I start cleaning and covering our tattoos.

I got a little carried away. I was only prepared to do her two and my ring finger, so I run out of cleaning supplies quickly. But I make sure hers are taken care of first.

At some point, I wake her long enough to get her signature.

It's on the line right next to mine. Forever intertwining us.

And for the first time in six weeks, I feel at peace.

Because I finally have my sunshine back.

And she'll never get away again.

# Chapter 78
## *Cecilia*

My head pounds as I open my eyes. I'm groggy and sore. The light in the room blinds me.

I try to wipe my eyes, but my right hand doesn't move. It rests on the pillow above me. I try to yank again, but all I feel is pain in my wrist.

My eyes fly open, and I look up.

My wrist is handcuffed to the headboard.

To the headboard in our bedroom.

In the penthouse.

*What the hell?*

"Good morning, sunshine," Roman calls from the doorway of our bedroom, a bright smile on his face.

He's genuinely happy to see me.

I can't say the same.

"You locked me up?" Even though it's obvious, it comes out as a question because of my disbelief.

I knew I didn't know him like I thought I did, but my sweet hero would never have done something like this. I'm too shocked to make sense of it.

"I just need you restrained until I know you won't try to escape," he says calmly, still smiling like this is perfectly normal.

"How did I even get here? I don't remember anything," I ask, shock still numbing my emotions. I know I should be angry, but I can't process anything.

He just grins. It's a victorious grin. And realization shoots through me waking me like cold water.

"Oh my God! Did you drug me?" I screech, furious.

This is how it felt the last time he drugged me. The morning after the club. I can't believe he'd do this. *Again.*

"Of course. You wouldn't have come willingly, and I need you at home with me. I couldn't go another night without your warmth. These last six weeks have been torture for me," he explains as if I should feel bad for him.

"You're fucking crazy!" I shout.

"Cecilia, what have I said about cursing? I don't like this new side of you. My sunshine would never speak so foully. You're too intelligent and kind to waste words on crudity," he scolds me, and my blood boils.

He strides across the room and sits on the edge of the bed next to me. He grabs my left hand and holds it in his.

I glance down.

And am appalled by what I see.

"DID YOU TATTOO ME?!" I scream.

Fury washes away the shock. How fucking dare he? He adulterated my clear skin. Granted, the wedding band ink around my finger is dainty and can easily be hidden by my ring, but I can't admire his handiwork right now.

"You ran away from me. You stopped wearing your ring. So, yeah, you now have a permanent wedding band so everyone will know you're my wife." He lifts my hand to inspect the tattoo, and a sweet smile takes over his face. Then he leans down and kisses the tattoo reverently.

Wait, *wife?*

He said wife.

He's so fucking wrong.

I will never be his wife.

"We're not married. And we never will be. So, don't call me your wife!" I seethe, knowing it's a low blow.

His face crumbles, and I almost regret my words until his expression hardens.

"You already are my wife. I was able to wake you up long enough to sign the paper." He points to a framed certificate hung on the wall that didn't used to be there. *Oh my God, it's a marriage certificate!* "The plane staff were all the happier to be witnesses for a very nice tip."

"You fucking psycho! You can't do this! I hate you!" I cry out as tears well in my eyes.

I've always dreamt of my dream wedding. It would be in a garden. For our wedding, I'd have it in the courtyard at the mansion where he proposed. I'd be wearing a beautiful white dress, and my dad would walk me down the aisle. Everyone I love would be there.

And I definitely wouldn't be drugged and unconscious in a plane with no one around.

A tear slips down my face, and I quickly wipe it away, only now pulling my hand from his.

He took that from me. After all he's done to me, he did this too. I can't forgive him.

When he sees the tear, he sighs and pulls me into his arms. He slides his hand up and down my back comforting me.

"Oh, Celia. You don't hate me. You could never hate me. You don't have a cell in your body capable of hate. Especially not towards your hero. You love me. And I love you, sunshine. More than anything. You should know that by now. Haven't I done enough to prove it?" The delusion is evident in his wistful voice.

The use of nicknames that meant so much to me snaps me out of my trance, and I yank myself out of his arms. His expression falls again, but I won't allow myself to feel bad for him. This is all his fault.

"Don't call me that! Don't use those names! They're a lie. You'll never be my hero again. You never even were. You're the villain of my story!" His face hardens, and he sucks in a breath, but I keep going. "How could you think you love me? You don't even know what love is! All you know is control and manipulation."

"Sunshine, you know that's not true. I did it all for you. Out of love for you. You can argue all you want, but you know this is real." He cups my cheek into his hand, and it takes everything in me not to lean into his touch. Into the touch of the man I loved. "You shouldn't have talked about your problems if you didn't want me to fix them."

I jerk back.

"How fucking dare you! You caused most of those problems! You didn't fix anything! You didn't do any of it for me! It was about control!" I glare at him.

"I saved you. Like I always do. Your boss was harassing you, and you hated your job, so I handled it for you. You hated living alone when Gracie moved out, so I gave you a little push. Which, by the way, you weren't supposed to be there for. I made him pay for that. The man that robbed you, he was a bad man. An enemy of the Syndicate. And he took the ring I got for you. He deserved the death he got. It was a message to all not to come after my woman. My wife." He sighs. "Your life was better once I helped you. You were happier until that bastard got to you. You were living your dream. With me. Because of me."

"That wasn't the right way to do it! And drugging me! That wasn't to save me, you monster!" I throw back, unable to deny the rest.

Because although it wasn't in methods I approve of, he's right. He bettered my life, and I'd never been happier than when I was with him.

"I already told you, I had to get you home. And you would've fought me the entire time. I wouldn't risk hurting you trying to restrain you." He reaches for me, but I scurry away against the headboard.

"No. I mean at the club. Leo said you drugged me. Then you tortured him. And took his finger." The last sentence has me squeamish. It's my last grievance against him. If he hadn't just drugged me, I still would've doubted it.

"I didn't drug you then. You really think I could do that? Leo drugged you. Just ask Gracie. She's the only reason he didn't get you alone when I was gone. She and I fought him off for you. That's why I tortured him. That's why I cut him out of your life. I should've killed him. That's our code, to kill rapists. Your friendship was the only reason he lived past that. I would never do that to you."

His eyes convey truth, and I realize this entire time, he hasn't lied to me. He could easily lie, and I'd lie to myself to believe him. Because I love him that much. But he's been nothing but honest. Even about the worst offenses.

"You literally just drugged me," I counter petulantly. "And why would Leo drug me?"

"You aren't listening. I drugged you to bring you home, not to rape you. There's a difference." He sounds exasperated. *Good, join the club.* "And Leo's a fucking monster. He was going to rape you. He's always wanted you, and he told me it was time you stopped playing hard to get. That he's waited too long." Roman's gaze darkens, and he tenses as he recalls it. The fury radiating off him doesn't scare me though. Not like it should. Because he's angry on my behalf, out of love for me.

"But why would Leo save me from you then?" I ask, desperately needing answers.

"Because he was obsessed with revenge. He was stalking us for months. I'm sorry I didn't realize. I should've known, but I'd been distracted for so long because of you. I wasn't working at the best of my abilities." He runs his hand over his hair in frustration, then grabs my hand again and pleads with me to understand. And I do. I believe him. Even though he's lied about so much, even though he just drugged me, even though Leo was my friend, I believe him.

Then I remember what he does for *work*.

"You still lied to me. About so much. About who you are. You hurt people! Kill them! I don't even know you!" I yell and yank my hand away.

I kick him with my feet, trying to get away from the sick bastard. I only make contact once, before he grabs both my legs and traps them on his lap. He mindlessly starts massaging them, and I internally curse him for still being my Roman.

"Calm down, sunshine. But yes, you're right. I did lie. You, my beautiful, kindhearted goddess, would never have been with someone who does what I do. So, I may have left out a few details. I do what I have to for the Syndicate. And, fuck, I enjoy it. I enjoy avenging my family. Protecting them. Protecting you." His grip on my calf tightens when he says it but loosens when I wince. He starts massaging again. "I would never hurt you. You have to believe that. Me drugging you yesterday is proof. I wouldn't even allow you to feel the pain of the tattoos or allow you to get hurt fighting me."

Mr. Bank's words echo in my head. About forgiveness. About always being safe around him. How he was never a threat to me. How he did everything to keep me. How he–

"Wait, *tattoos*? As in plural? Where else did you tattoo me? What all did you do to me?!" I screech and try to kick my feet free to no avail.

"You have my initials inked at the base of your spine. And a tracker inserted in your neck. Now, I'll always know where you are." The affection in his voice makes me nauseous.

"You sick fuck! That's an invasion of privacy!" I continue to fight against his hold.

"For over five weeks, I thought you were taken. I thought you were being held captive, going through unimaginable things. I was worried sick. I almost started a war over it. I will never allow that to happen to you. This is only a safety measure. It's not to keep you from running. I'm locking you up until you're no longer a flight risk. Until you've forgiven me, and we're back to what we were before that sick fuck told you lies," he tells me tenderly, and his belief in what he's saying makes me even more nervous than before.

He truly thinks I'll just forgive him.

"We'll never go back to what we were, so don't bother trying. There's nothing left of us to fix. You made sure of that when you betrayed me time and time again." I look away, unable to face him as I say it.

Because I don't know if I'm lying. Lying to him. Or lying to myself.

But I need it to be true.

Because how could I forgive him after everything he's done?

How could I be with someone who hurts people and enjoys it?

"As long as you fight me, you still care. You still want me. You never forgot me. It's why you wear my ring around your neck. You hate yourself for it, but you still love me." The surety in his voice infuriates me.

Because he's not entirely wrong.

"Fuck you!" I seethe.

"You know I'm right," he says with confidence.

And fuck him because he might be.

# Chapter 79
## *Roman*

I hate to see her this way. So angry. So upset.

This isn't her.

My sunshine shines brighter than anyone I've ever met. She's the embodiment of happiness, peace, and love. She's kind-hearted and empathetic. She's light and goodness.

Her eyes used to glow as bright as the sun, but she's lost herself.

I may have dulled her for now, but I will reilluminate her. I'll bring her back to who she once was. Because my sunshine deserves happiness.

And I make her happy.

So, I'll stop at nothing to keep her.

# Chapter 80
## *Cecilia*

It's nighttime. The sun set hours ago, and I can't help but be happy about it. About finally going to sleep. *Next to him.*

Roman undid the handcuff after our conversation so I can freely roam the room and bathroom. I noticed that everything that could be used as a weapon is gone. Even the lamps are screwed into the nightstands.

Not that it'd be much use to me.

I may have changed, but I still can't harm someone. Not even him.

Maybe especially not him.

Roman's kept me fed all day. Eggs and sandwiches. All he knows to make. It makes me wonder what he's been eating since I left. I wonder if he's been okay without me.

*It doesn't matter. I don't care if he's been taking care of himself!*

But I bet I'll only last another day before I insist on using the kitchen.

And as if thinking of him summons him, he walks in.

"Hey, sunshine. How're you holding up?" he asks with genuine concern in his voice. As though he's not the reason I wouldn't be doing well. As though this isn't completely his fault.

"I'm dandy. Why wouldn't I be?" Sarcasm negates my words.

"Sunshine, we're going to break you of this negativity. It's not like you, and it's concerning me," he says softly as he makes his way to the bathroom. "Come on, let's get ready for bed."

I follow him to the vanity and make note that everything of mine is exactly how I left it. It's as though I was never gone.

I just stare at it all.

"I never gave up hope. I knew I'd bring you home," he explains, his voice rough.

I look at him and see the fear in his eyes. He truly believed I'd been taken. That I was being held against my will. And it terrified him.

Guilt flashes through me, and I have the urge to hug him.

I step forward towards him, then come back to reality.

No. *No.* He doesn't deserve my hugs. He deserves to feel scared. He did this. It's all his fault.

*And Leo's,* a small voice in my head reminds me.

My friend used me to get back at Roman for protecting me when he tried to hurt me. My friend betrayed me long before Roman ever did. And if I really reflect on it, if I weed out all the lies Leo told, then what Roman did really wasn't so bad. He truly was just trying to help me. In his twisted way.

I know he loves me. He's gone through great lengths to protect me. He's never been a threat to me. And he makes me happy.

But he lied.

It'd be so easy to forgive him. To go back to the paradise we were living in before. To forget all he did.

But I just don't know if I have it in me.

I don't know if I can go back now that I know what he is. What he does when he leaves for work. When he comes back in the middle of the night smelling like lemons. I don't know if I can ignore knowing the pain he caused when he comes back to cuddle me.

But I also know I may not have a choice. He won't give me another opportunity to run. And even if he did, I couldn't get far with the tracker in me.

I silently brush my teeth, change into pajamas behind the closed door of the closet, and get under the covers.

Roman comes in and starts stripping in front of me.

I watch as he loses his shirt.

Then he undoes his belt and slides it out.

He unzips his pants. They drop to the floor with a thud.

He grabs a pair of boxer briefs, and steps into them.

*All in front of me.*

I can see his raging cock bobbing as he steps into them.

My core dampens, and I curse myself for having a response to him. I tell myself it's only human nature, but I also know no other man could make me feel this way.

I turn away from him, listening as he deposits his dirty clothes in the laundry hamper. As he walks to his side of the bed.

I feel the bed dip as he climbs in and gets under the covers.

Then he slides to the middle, and pulls me towards him, so that I'm resting on him. He brings my right arm over his chest, and my right leg over his thighs. Positioning us how we always sleep.

And I just can't bring myself to pull back.

It's been so long since I've had human contact. Since I've felt loved. And he makes the loneliness fade away.
So, for tonight, I'll steal his warmth.

# Chapter 81
## *Cecilia*

I wake up to his warmth surrounding me. I breathe him in, loving the feeling. I know it's wrong, but I can't help it.

I had a great dream that none of it ever happened. That we were happy. That we were in love.

The dream turned dirty quickly, and now I'm burning with desire.

And I hate myself for it.

I crave intimacy. His touch. Our love.

I slide my leg up against his hardness. I press into it, and he groans.

"Sunshine, after the noises you were making in your sleep, I'm barely hanging on. If you keep touching my cock, I'm not going to be able to restrain myself," he grunts out.

His hands abandon me, and he raises them above his head, as though every touch tempts him.

And damn it, I feel the same.

I know I shouldn't but at the same time, I'm being forced here against my will. And I'm so needy. And he knows how to make me feel good. What if I use him just this once? Just to get some relief. It doesn't have to mean I forgive him.

I trail my hand down his chest and slide it under his boxers. I grip his cock.

"Cecilia, you're playing with fire," he warns me darkly.

I stroke up and down once, then again.

That's all it takes for him to flip us over so he's hovering over me.

"I can't take you soft and sweet like usual. It's been too long. My hand can only give me so much relief," he warns, and I smile.

"Do it. I want it hard and rough," I tell him.

That's how I need it. I can't make love with him. It'll break me. This is purely physical.

He groans then leans down to kiss me.

I turn my head away, not able to give in to that intimacy.

"Sunshine, you can pretend to hate me. You can use my body to get your release. But you will kiss me while doing it. I won't let this be meaningless for you. Because it never is for me. So, when you use me, you're going to know it's your Roman, your hero," he growls then dips his head.

The moment his mouth locks with mine, I lose all sense of control.

I run my fingers through his short hair and press his lips harder to mine. He nips my bottom lip, demanding entry, and I comply. His tongue duels mine, and it's a fight for dominance. A fight he easily wins.

I slide my other hand over his shoulders, down his back, then over his chest.

He groans at every touch.

When I finally try to pull back, desperate for air, he trails his lips down my neck, biting, sucking, marking me. It feels like the first breath after being underwater for too long.

He keeps going, past my collarbone, to the swell of my breasts.

He rips open my nightgown, fully exposing me down to my panties.

With my breasts on display, he attacks. He leaves marks on the soft tissue, then plays with my nipples, nibbling and sucking them. I can't hold back my moans. I push his head down, needing more. One of his hands finds my other breast and starts tweaking the nipple.

His other hand travels down my body and into my panties. He finds my soaked center and groans.

"Fuck, sunshine. You're so wet for me. I knew you missed me. Let me get you ready," he slides a finger in me.

As he fucks me with his finger, his mouth follows the route his hand just took. Kissing its way down my body. When he gets to my center, he pulls my panties down, reveling in how much I need him.

"You're so fucking perfect, Cecilia. You're gorgeous. Breathtaking," he sighs out.

Then he pounces. He starts lapping at my core. A moan slips from beneath my lips. Then he slips in a second finger and focuses his mouth on my clit.

It's been so long since I've had his touch that I don't last long. After less than a minute, I'm falling over the edge.

He groans into me as I scream his name. The ecstasy I feel is unmatched. But it's not enough.

I need him. All of him.

He pulls back just enough to strip off his boxers, and I see it. The wet spot on the front. I raise an eyebrow at him, shocked that he found his own release simply from giving me mine.

"Hearing my name on your lips as I send you over the edge with the taste of you on my tongue and your pussy choking my fingers..." He shakes his head. "I'm only human. I can't resist that. It's really for the best. I would've only lasted seconds inside of you."

He pumps his dick twice in his hands, then crawls back up me, and captures my mouth. I can't even be upset at my taste on his mouth because he thrusts into me in that moment.

I scream even though he prepared me for it. The fullness is everything I've needed. It's everything I've been missing.

I look up, and he's staring into my soul. I turn my head away, trying to break the eye contact, the intimacy. But he doesn't let me. He grips my chin and forces my head towards him.

"My wife will look at me when I'm fucking her. You will know it's your husband making you feel this way," he growls.

And it infuriates me.

It reminds me of what he's done. That he orchestrated our marriage while I was drugged. And I'm blinded with rage.

"I'm not your wife," I seethe.

"Yes, you fucking are. You're mine. And I'll never let you go." He smirks. "Get used to it, *wife*."

He emphasizes *'wife'*, and it has me seeing red.

Like a woman possessed, I bring my hands around his neck. And tighten.

I choke him.

I choke my husband.

When I realize what I'm doing, I start to loosen my grip, horrified by my actions.

"Tighter," he gasps out.

I look up and see the feral gleam in his eyes.

He fucking likes it. The sick bastard actually likes it.

But it feels too good to have an outlet for my rage, so I tighten my grip and choke my husband. I take my fury out on him.

And all the while, he continues thrusting into me. In fact, it's spurring him along. He's even more relentless now, shoving me into the mattress with each thrust.

It's feels euphoric.

When his face goes from red to purple, I drop my hands, not wanting to kill him. Not yet at least.

Then I turn my head to the arm holding him up next to me. And I bite him.

He groans, and I feel his cock twitch inside of me.

I bite down harder, wanting him to feel my pain. Wanting him to feel my anger.

"Yes. Fuck, sunshine. Make me hurt. Take your revenge," he groans in pleasure, and I know the sick bastard is getting off on the pain.

And I know it's the only thing that allows me to keep going. If I was truly hurting him, I would stop immediately, unable to cause anyone real pain. Not even him. No matter how angry he makes me.

But since he's loving it, I can guiltlessly continue.

I bite him. Up his arm, to his shoulder, over his pecs. His neck. Everywhere I can reach. Then when I raise my arms ready to choke him again now that he's a normal color, he reaches down. And circles my clit.

With my hands tightening around his neck and his fingers on my needy nub, we both tip over the edge.

And as I fall, all I see are two brown orbs looking lovingly down at me. And a part of me breaks. Because despite all the pain I've caused him, despite all the nasty things I've said, he still loves me.

And maybe Mr. Banks was right.

Maybe love is enough.

# Chapter 82
## *Roman*

It was the best sex I've ever had. It may have been hate sex to her, but it was cathartic. She needed to hurt me. To take out her hurt and anger. And fuck, I never knew I was into pain. I've never had someone choke me or bite me. And fuck if it isn't arousing.

I pull out of my sunshine, and watch our combined release pour out. Before it can hit the mattress, I push it all back into her. I plug her with my finger, and make sure nothing can leak.

I need it all inside of her.

I need to increase our chances.

To keep her forever.

# Chapter 83
## *Cecilia*

When I realize what he's doing, my eyes fly open, and I swat at his arm.

"Oh my God! Roman, you need to stop! I didn't have my birth control with me when I was gone. I'm not on any protection!" I freak out, needing him to understand what's at risk here.

"I know," he chuckles.

"What?" I whisper.

"It was still in your nightstand when you left. It's the only thing of yours I got rid of," he says, and criminal smile forming on his lips.

"Why... why would you do that?" I ask, at a loss for words.

"Because you're not leaving this penthouse until you're pregnant with my baby," he says with assurance, and I almost pass out.

"What?" I whisper.

I can't help but feel elation at his words. It's all I've ever wanted. A baby. With this man. My only stipulation has always been that I need to be married first, and although it wasn't how I wanted, technically we are married in the eyes of the law.

"Sunshine, it's the only way I can ensure you won't leave me. Plus, it's our dream. A house full of babies. And now that we're married, it's time," he says with his finger still inside of me.

"But we're not happy right now," I argue weakly.

"I am. I have you back. My sunshine is home, safe and healthy. It's more than I could hope for. We're going to be a family." He smiles so brightly that I can't help but join in.

When he raises my legs, letting gravity help, I realize what this really is.

I kick him and scurry away, trying not to care that I hit his face.

"What the hell, Cecilia?" he grunts out, grabbing his cheek.

I scurry across the bed, then across the room.

"No! You can't do this! I won't let you!" I cry out, betrayed once again.

"What are you saying? This is what we planned. This is what we wanted." he retorts.

"No! You can't use my dreams against me. I won't let you manipulate me in this way. I won't have a baby with you. Not with the man I hate." I shout at him as tears stream down my face, and my already broken heart fractures more.

"Cecilia, you know that's not what this is. I'm just trying to get us back on track to live out our dreams," he says calmly, trying to convince me.

But we both know it's not the full truth.

He just admitted it. He knows I won't leave him if I'm pregnant. I would never take my baby away from a loving father.

"You're the biggest mistake I've ever made," I whisper, knowing it's the truest statement and simultaneously the biggest lie I've ever told.

He's my damnation and salvation.

His face crumples at my words. He opens his mouth to respond, but I flee to the bathroom and lock the door. I can't hear him out. I won't give him the chance to manipulate me with sweet words and kind gestures.

I feel the liquid dripping down my inner thighs, and I turn on the shower and try to get it all out of me.

As tears stream down my face, and sobs echo from my throat.

Because despite his intentions, this is our dream. Our dream future of our home overflowing with our children. And I want nothing more than to have it.

*But not like this.*

And I hate him for making me say no to it. For ruining what was once the happiest I've ever been. For making me fight against my dream. And for making me fight him too.

The whole time, he's trying to soothe me through the bathroom door.

I'm sure he could easily get through the lock, but he doesn't. And I'm grateful for that. Because despite being the only one who can calm me down, he's also the only one who can hurt me this way.

And that's what makes the pain so much worse.

How could I ever forgive him?

But how could I not?

How could I live without him?

How could I live with him knowing how he manipulated me?

# Chapter 84
## *Roman*

Her words break me.

I know she's hurting. I can hear her sobs through the bathroom door.

I don't leave. I sit on the other side, professing my love to her.

I respect her privacy. I don't break in. I don't hold her like I want to. I don't do any of it. Because for once, I'm giving her space. It's going to be her choice. She gets to decide when she wants me back.

It was wrong of me to try to trick her into staying.

I realize a baby won't fix the foundation that was broken. We need to heal our relationship before we add to it.

But I'm not giving up on our dream. One day, we will have a cottage full of love and children. And we'll never want to spend a day apart. And we'll look back at these trying times and realize we came out stronger.

I'll stop at nothing to get there. I will get my sunshine back.

Because she once loved me. I know she can do it again.

But for now, I'll love her enough for the both of us.

# Chapter 85
## *Cecilia*

Every day that passes, I feel my heart mending.

It's gotten to the point where I realize the only thing holding me back from forgiveness is my own hurt. I'm holding myself back from my happiness.

What he did was horrible, but his intentions were pure. He only wanted to help me. To keep me.

He lied about who he was because he was scared I wouldn't accept him. And that's the only part I'm having trouble coping with. I have it in me to forgive him for his offenses against me, but what about all the people he's hurt? All the people he's killed? I don't know if I can be with a man like that.

But my heart yearns to forgive him. I want my héroe back. And I know he's in there. He's just as much a part of Roman Montclair as the monster is.

He's proved it every day.

He lets me out of the room now. He caters to me hand and foot. He treats me with love and respect. He's even wearing condoms, which he's never done with me before. I know he hates it, but not because of the physical barrier but because of the emotional one it represents between us.

He's been honest with me. Every question, no matter how terrible, he answers truthfully. He told me he'll never lie to me again. He'll never risk our relationship like that.

He still firmly believes we can recover from this, and I'm starting to believe it too.

Because sometimes, love is enough.

# Chapter 86
## *Cecilia*

Roman comes home smelling like lemons.

It crushes me.

I've been able to ignore this side of him. I've been able to pretend it doesn't exist, but now I have to face it. If we want a chance at a happy life together, I need to know everything. And I need to hear it from him.

"Where were you?" I ask, even though I know the answer.

He meets my gaze, and his face drops. He knows I know. And it breaks him just as much as it's breaking me.

If he lies to me now, we have no chance of ever getting back together. But if his answer is worse than I can handle, we also have no chance.

We stare at each other, the silence choking me.

Finally, he walks to me, grabs my hand, and leads me to the couch.

"I was at a warehouse. A Bratva member was snooping around one of our clubs, and I needed to question him," Roman tells me.

"Did you hurt him?" I ask, hoping despite reality that he didn't.

"Yes. I didn't kill him, but if I needed to, I would've." He sighs and grabs my hand.

I inhale sharply, hating every truth he gives me.

"Ask your questions, Cecilia. I don't want any more lies between us. I promise you I will answer every question honestly. But please understand that sometimes ignorance truly is bliss. So only ask questions you want the answer to," he warns me.

"I don't want any of the answers, but I have to know," I plead with him.

"Ask. You have my word. No more lies."

"Did you carve your initials into him like you did Leo and the robber? Like what's tattooed on my back?" I ask hesitantly.

I hate that I love the tattoo. It's his signature on me. It's a visual representation of our ties to each other.

And I've noticed the additions to his own ink. His fingers decorated with representations of what I am to him. I've even noticed my name where there used to be blank spaces on him.

"Yes. It's my tagging method. When I interrogate someone, I carve my initials into them. The worse their offense, the bigger their carving. It's how I keep track of who I've caught before. If the mark is recent, then I know they're a frequent offender." He sighs and rubs his hand down his face.

"The tattoo on you, it wasn't to associate you with them. I would never want to do that. It was to tie you to me. If anyone sees my signature, they'll know you're mine. They'll leave you alone. It's for your protection. My name will keep you safe..." He hesitates. "But I also wanted my claim on you known. I want the world to know you're mine because I'm a jealous and possessive man when it comes to you. I'm sorry for not asking permission."

I nod silently, unable to accept his apology just yet.

"Why do you interrogate people?" I ask, focusing on the first explanation he gave.

"I'm the enforcer for the Syndicate," he explains, looking away from me.

"What's the Syndicate?" I ask. Leo explained it, but I now have doubts about his honesty.

"It's the criminal organization my family runs. We have clubs all over our territory and run a few illegal operations. We don't deal with drugs or weapons though; we have a moral code. We're like the police of the underworld. We enforce the laws, and if someone breaks them, we handle it. But we're held to the same standard." His eyes shine with pride as he explains what his family does.

"Oh," I say, at a loss for words. "Who all is involved?"

"My dad started it years ago. His father was involved with many of the families and was a casualty to a war that broke out among them. Dad created the Syndicate to ensure and enforce the peace between the families. Mom was never involved. Dad kept her out of it, just as I plan on keeping you out of it." He grabs my hands and rubs his thumbs over the backs of them. "Dom is the head. He took over when Dad retired. As the oldest, it made sense. Matthias isn't really involved. He actually does run Syndicate Enterprise, but I have nothing to do with it. I'm the enforcer for the Syndicate. My crew and I enforce the rules, typically by violence." He winces when he says it. "And Bash is our tech genius. He works for both the Syndicate and Syndicate Enterprise. There's nothing he can't do with a computer."

I feel a pang in my chest at the realization that his entire family knew and never told me.

"Does Margot know?" I whisper.

"Yes. She had a bad run in with the Bratva last year. Matthias keeps her out of it now." Roman's eyes sadden when he mentions Margot's incident, so I don't pry.

The betrayal that Margot knew and kept it from me feels like a punch to the gut. I thought we were friends.

"So, they all knew you were lying to me, and never told me?" I choke out.

"Yes, sunshine. But every single one of them demanded I tell you. They cursed me out for lying to you. Margot almost hit me when she confronted me about it. She was fuming. My dad's the only one who didn't push, but I think it's only because he wishes he could've shielded Mom more." He sighs then cups my cheeks. "They love you. You're part of our family. Please don't think they supported me in any way. And when you were gone, every one of us was out looking for you. Even Matthias and my parents got involved. You're a Montclair. We love you and would've stopped at nothing to find you." His eyes plead with me to understand, and I'm starting to.

"Okay, I believe you. Is there anything else I should know about the Syndicate?" I ask warily, not sure how much more I can handle.

"We've made an enemy out of the Bratva. They're the Russian crime family. We don't have a great relationship with them. Well, *I* made an enemy out of the Bratva. When you were gone, I thought they took you. So... I attacked them. Brutally. I had many victims. I was hellbent on finding you and couldn't see reason through my fear of what might be happening to you. We narrowly avoided a war. Only Dom's diplomacy was able to protect us," he confesses, unable to make eye contact. His shame heals a little part of me. I can tell he regrets his actions even if only because they didn't help him find me sooner.

I squeeze his hand.

"You didn't know. I'm so sorry. I didn't mean to cause any issues," I try to explain. I can't bear that people are dead because of me.

"It's not your fault. I am solely responsible for my actions. Everything from keeping things from you to how I handled your disappearance. But to be honest, if you went missing again, I'd go just as crazy, and everyone would be a suspect."

"I understand. I promise I won't ever leave without an explanation ever again. I didn't realize how complex everything is," I vow.

"It's not always safe, Cecilia. I will protect you as much as I can. But you have to understand, I'm a dangerous man. I have many enemies. I've gone after so many people. You being my wife innately puts you in danger. It can't be helped, I'm sorry. I will always keep you safe, but you have to trust me and listen to me. Do you understand?" The fear in his eyes terrifies me.

"I understand."

And I do. He lives a dangerous life, but he'll always protect me.

He looks devastated by the conversation. He has no idea what I'm thinking. And honestly, neither do I. I need time to think about this.

But still, I climb into his lap. He wraps his arms around me and holds me close. I melt into him. He kisses my hair and rubs my back, keeping me comfortable.

"I love you, Cecilia." His voice breaks.

"I need time, Roman," I whisper, upset that I can't give him more. Not after what I've learned. Not after what he's done.

"I know," he whispers again. "If you need space, I can get you an apartment. If you want your job back, I'll make it happen. If you... if you want an annulment, I'll do it. Fuck, I'll help you get the tattoos removed. I'll get you on birth control.

I'll do anything if you just give me a chance to win you back. Let me undo my mistakes. Let me make it up to you," he begs.

I lean back to look in his eyes and am surprised by the tears welling.

"Do you mean that?" I ask, needing to gage his sincerity.

"I hate it. I hate everything I've offered you. I don't want space. I don't want to end our marriage. I don't want to lose you. I just want you to be happy with me. But I know I fucked up. I did it all to get you, but it backfired and now I'm losing you. If giving you freedom will make you happy, then I'll give it to you. It'll crush me. Destroy me. But for your happiness, I'd do anything. Just please give me a chance. Once I right all my wrongs, let me earn you back. Please, just give me a chance. I'll never be happy without you," he says with a tremor in his voice.

I'm taken aback. This is the first real conversation I've had with my héroe where he's shown true remorse, and now, he's offering me my freedom. I've seen so much of the Monster Montclair. But here's the man I love offering me everything I should want.

And it hurts more than anything.

The thought of ending things, of leaving him, creates a pit in my stomach. I know I should want to get away from him. I should hate him. I should take him up on his offer and never look back.

But I can't even entertain the idea because it makes me ill.

"I don't know," is all I can say.

Because I can't bring myself to forgive him, not yet. But I also can't leave him. It'd be like leaving my heart.

"Okay, sunshine. You have all the time in the world," he whispers into my hair.

Then we lapse into silence.

In his arms is where all is right in the world, while so much is wrong in our world.

Deep down, I know what I've chosen, I just need time to accept it.

# Chapter 87
## *Roman*

I look down to see Matthias calling me.

I've been avoiding my family since reuniting with Cecilia. When I told them she ran away, they were furious. Not only because I almost started a war, but mostly because they love her, and I drove her away.

"Hey, Matthias. What's up?" I greet him dryly, already wanting to get off the call.

"'What's up?' What the hell do you mean, 'what's up?' I'm getting married in two days, and you've been MIA since Cecilia came back. What the fuck?" he snaps at me.

*Oh shit.* I completely forgot about their wedding.

"I'm sorry, man. We'll be there. Just tell us when and where." I wince even as I say it, knowing I've severely fucked up... again.

I hear muffled noises from the other side then the phone being handed to someone.

"ROMAN FRANCIS MONTCLAIR! YOU SON OF A BITCH. No, sorry, Evelyn's done nothing wrong. YOU

ASSHOLE! HOW FUCKING COULD YOU? I TOLD YOU SHE'D BE UPSET WHEN SHE FOUND OUT! YOU'RE THE WORST! YOU'RE FUCKING LUCKY YOU'RE STILL INVITED TO THE WEDDING! AND IT'S ONLY BECAUSE WE WANT CECILIA THERE." Margot yells at me. The fury in her words cuts me but also brings a smile to my face. Knowing she'd choose Cecilia over me warms me. I love Margot like a sister, but so does Cecilia. I'm glad she'd have her.

"Speaking of which, how is she?" Margot continues, softer at the mention of Cecilia. "We want to see her. She probably hates you! I would too. You're the fucking worst."

I can tell she's about to ream into me again, but Matthias must calm her down, because she changes the topic.

"Your tux and Cecilia's bridesmaid dress will be delivered to your apartment today. Make sure they fit the same as two months ago at the appointments. You are to be at the library courtyard by noon. Cecilia is exempt from helping me get ready due to having an unfortunate fiancé. Unless she wants to, of course. Do you have any questions?" she orders me like a drill sergeant.

"No ma'am," I don't bother correcting her on the whole fiancé thing nor do I ask about snacks. I'm scared to set the bride off again.

With that, she ends the call.

And I head to my wife to tell her the good news.

# Chapter 88
## *Cecilia*

I take a deep breath as Roman navigates traffic.

We're on our way to Margot and Matthias's wedding. We're getting there hours early because I still wanted to help Margot get ready. That was the original plan, and I don't want to mess with her wedding day.

Despite how close we were, I'm nervous to see her. We were becoming great friends, but then I left. Roman mentioned how they thought I was taken, and they all were searching for me. Because I ran instead of talking to Roman, his whole family was worried about me for over a month.

Also, I'm still hurt that no one told me. I understand why the Syndicate needs to be a secret, but they all lied to me. Roman lied about so much, but they knew and never told me.

I don't know how to act around them. I'm upset that they lied to me. They're probably upset that I abandoned them after they welcomed me into the family. It's going to be a mess.

And all too soon, we pull up to the library where the wedding is being held. The building is beautiful. It's not one I've been to before. I'm not big on reading, but I know Margot is. She's even an audiobook narrator.

I close my eyes and start doing box breathing exercises to calm myself while Roman parks. When he opens my door, I feel his hand grab mine.

"Just take deep breaths, sunshine. Everyone is so excited to see you. They missed you so much. There's no need to be nervous," he says softly.

I open my eyes and see the truth in his. Despite it, I still have my doubts.

"But how could they forgive me for running away? They wasted so much time and almost caused a war looking for me. When all along, I left of my own volition. They have to be upset with me," I counter.

"Cecilia, look at me." I do. "They love you. Yes, they were worried about you and searched for you, but when they found out the truth, they weren't upset with you. They were relieved you weren't suffering. And they were pissed at me for being the reason you ran away."

"Promise?" I ask, needing reassurance.

He lifts my pinkie finger in his and shakes.

"I pinky promise," he says with a smile.

Then he kisses the top of my head, and I hug him. His warmth settles me, and I decide I'm ready to face the Montclairs.

Roman helps me out of the car and leads me inside. He brings me to a room in the back and kisses my hair one more time.

"This is as far as I go. I think Margot might hit me if I bother her. I love you, sunshine," he says sweetly.

I shoot him an awkward smile, and shuffle inside.

I still haven't told him I love him. I know where my heart lies, and I know how I feel, but I just can't fully forgive him yet.

And until I've forgiven and forgotten everything, I won't confess my love for him. Even if it's still there.

I look around and see a frantic Margot. She's in a gorgeous classic wedding dress. It's pure white with off the shoulder sleeves. It drapes across her chest beautifully and dips in the center, displaying her cleavage perfectly. It falls into a full skirt with a train. The back fastens in a row of buttons.

Mrs. Montclair is behind her with a crochet hook, trying to button them, but when Margot sees me, she flies forward and launches herself in my arms.

"Cecilia, I'm so glad you're here! Everything's been so hectic, and I need you to calm me down. Our day-of coordinator didn't show up, so the boys have been running around with a list. At this point, as long as Matthias is waiting for me at the end of the aisle, I'm calling it a success." She sighs dramatically with her hand on her forehead, then drops to the ground theatrically.

"Margot! You're going to get your dress dirty! Stand up. I know it's been crazy, but sweet Cecilia is here, and she'll help," Mrs. Montclair scolds Margot in a maternal way, then shoots me a pleading look.

"I'm here for whatever you need," I assure her.

I can't help the smile that forms. Everything feels normal with them. It's like I never left.

"I'm sorry for–" I start, needing to get it off my chest.

"You're not allowed to be sorry for anything. We're so sorry for keeping everything from you. We all told Roman multiple times that he needed to tell you about the Syndicate. And I know more than that happened to make you leave, but Matthias won't tell me. I think he's scared I'll actually murder his brother if I find out. Fucking Roman! He's lucky to be here, at the wedding and alive. We were so worried when you were gone, but now that you're back, he's on my shit list." Margot stops her rant to get off the ground and holds my hands. "If you want to get away from him, we'll help. We've all been talking, and we'll keep you from him if that's what you want."

"Damien and I will help too. You're a daughter to us, and that won't change even if you leave Roman. We love you," Mrs. Montclair tells me.

I'm moved by their loyalty to me. I didn't expect it at all, and I take a moment to process it.

"I'll kill him if you want. Rat poison in his champagne tonight. What's a wedding without a little homicide?" Margot whispers in my ear.

I laugh, caught off guard, but am cut off by Margot's serious expression.

"No! You can't!" I start, then glance at the engagement ring I'm wearing.

"You're forgiving him? After all he's done?" Margot stares incredulously.

He's held true to his word. He hasn't mentioned his offer to me again, but I see the hesitation in his eyes. His longing glances. He knows I could call it at any moment.

But I won't.

"Despite all he's done, he's still the man I love. I'm working on forgiving him. He's been remorseful and patient. He's been perfect," I tell her.

"Good. He better be kissing the floor you walk on. If you ever need to get away from him again, Matthias and I will house you for as long as you need," Margot offers.

The door opens, and an unfamiliar woman scurries in.

She's short, with dark curls, and brown eyes. She looks just like her daughter.

"Margot, the florist finally arrived, and all the flowers are set up. The only thing left to do is get you ready," Margot's mother says.

"Thank God!" Margot shouts.

Her mother turns to me.

"Hello, dear. You must be Cecilia. I am so relieved you're here. Margot kept saying if Matthias can't be here to put her at ease, that you could." The sweet woman says.

Margot's mom pulls me into a hug which I return. I guess they're all huggers.

Margot frets around the room some more, while Mrs. Montclair and her mother chase her down with crochet hooks in hand.

I grab my jade green gown and change into it. I already did my makeup and hair at home, so I'm set to go.

Mrs. Montclair comes to me when she's finished buttoning Margot's gown and straightens my dress.

"You look beautiful, dear. We're so happy you're here. And I can't wait until we're doing this for you, if you'll still have my son," she says kindly, then goes back to the bride.

I don't have the heart to correct her. To tell her it's too late. That her son tricked me into marriage, and neither she nor my family were there to witness it. I was barely even there.

After another thirty minutes, only thirty out from the wedding, an older woman walks in. She's old enough to be my grandmother. Mrs. Montclair greets her as an old friend, and even Margot's mother seems to be acquainted with her.

"Dotty!" Margot squeals. "Thank you for stepping up! How is everything back there?"

Dotty relays that most of the guests are here. From what I gather, the list was rather small. Even though Matthias has many business associates, he wanted to keep the wedding intimate with only loved ones.

Dotty's been acting as the day-of coordinator. Her boyfriend, who's a doctor, has also stepped up.

She's also in a jade green dress, and I realize she must be in the wedding party as well.

When it's time to start the wedding, we walk to two big wooden doors. I'm busy admiring them when I hear what sounds like hyperventilation next to me.

I look over and see Margot practically wheezing.

"Let's do some box breathing," I tell her as I grab her hands.

I talk her through the count and, after a few rounds, she's back to normal.

"Huh. So that's how you do it," she says in wonder.

I don't bother asking because the music starts.

And I get ready to walk down another woman's aisle, knowing I'll never get to walk my down my own.

But despite that, I'm more than happy for Margot.

# Chapter 89
## *Roman*

Music starts, and the wooden doors open.

My back straightens. Because standing there, like a mystical goddess, is my sunshine.

Her hair is in a braid wrapped around her head like a crown and the rest of her waves fall down her back. Her face looks beautiful and radiant. She's in a light green one-shoulder dress that hugs her breasts and falls in small pleats to the ground. It brings out the color in her skin.

She's breathtaking.

And as she floats down the aisle towards where I'm standing, my heart hammers, and I see it. I see a vision of her in white. Glowing radiantly. As she walks down an aisle, towards me.

And it's in that moment, I realize what I've taken from her.

She didn't get the wedding of her dreams. The one she already started planning with Margot. The one she was so excited for. None of her family or friends were there. Fuck, she doesn't even remember signing the marriage certificate.

And I vow to myself that she will get that wedding. I'll make sure of it. Because she deserves that and so much more.

She shoots me a bright smile, and I'm transfixed.

The entire ceremony, I can't take my eyes off her. I don't see anything outside of her. I couldn't tell you what Margot's dress looked like or what Matthias's vows were. Because I'm too consumed with this perfect goddess.

The ceremony passes quickly. Or maybe it's that I could stare at my sunshine forever and it still not be enough.

We follow the happy couple down the aisle. Cecilia takes my arm, and all feels right in the world.

The smile she flashes me on the way out gives me hope.

Because it's the smile of a woman in love.

And she wouldn't fake that, right?

# Chapter 90

*Cecilia*

The ceremony was beautiful. Margot was glowing, and Matthias was a man in love. The vows were beautiful, and tears were shed.

But I was distracted. By the loving gaze of the man I shouldn't want.

We're at the reception, and I'm seated at the Montclair family table.

After the ceremony, Bash gave me a big hug. He told me he'd fight Roman for me. When I politely declined, he chuckled and told me he was glad to have me back. Then, he took me by surprise by defending Roman. He told me that men in love do crazy things. I asked if he'd ever been in love, and he quickly changed the topic. He left to go talk to some people, and I found it odd that he didn't flirt with a single woman since I had heard he was a player.

Dom gave me a tight nod, and a firm handshake. He told me he was glad I wasn't taken, and that I had the Syndicate's protection. It was the most empathetic I'd ever seen him, and yet, he still barely showed any emotions. The way he glowers around the wedding, the slight look of disgust on his face, confirmed my hypothesis that he'll never get married. I don't think the man has enough emotional capacity to be in love.

Mr. Montclair hugged me and shared the same sentiment as Mrs. Montclair. They've been kind to me all night.

Margot and Matthias have been so caught up in themselves that I haven't been able to talk to them much. I can't adequately express my happiness for them. They deserve this and everything more. Their wedding is just as beautiful as their love.

And Roman. He never leaves my side. He lets me mingle and talk, but he never gives me space. Even when I'm talking about things that don't interest him, he's still mindful of the conversation.

When I glance longingly at the dance floor, he startles me by putting a hand on my back.

"Please, do me the honor of a dance, Mrs. Montclair," he says flirtatiously.

I smile, then freeze as his words register.

He freezes as well, then pales.

"I'm sorry, Cecilia. I've been thinking of you as my wife since I proposed months ago. I didn't mean it like that... The offer still stands. If you want to end the marriage, you can. I don't want that, but I'll respect your choice," he replies quietly.

"I'd love a dance," is all I say as I shoot him a smile.

I can't deny the sparks that warm my chest when he called me his wife.

And I realize, despite how I got here, I'm exactly where I want to be.

# Chapter 91
## *Roman*

We've danced to countless songs, but I have no intention of stopping.

I've never been one to dance, but you couldn't pry me away from Cecilia.

We've been slow dancing with her head resting on my shoulder and her arms around my neck. She's pressed against me with my hand wrapped around her back.

It's more intimate than our time on the club dance floor despite it not being sexual in any way. I'm not sure she notices, but I haven't initiated anything since that first day back, so every time we've been together, it's been because she's sought me out.

She still wants me. Or at least my body. But even if she didn't, I'd respect her wishes.

Cecilia looks up at me and just stares in wonder.

I look down at her, letting my walls fall, wanting her to see all my emotions. I've never been so vulnerable with someone before. But she's my wife. She'll always be my wife, even if she ends our marriage. And if I want to keep her in my life, I need to be open. And I need her to feel my love for her. To never doubt it.

"Roman, I lo–" she starts, and my heart races.

My brain stutters, so caught up in what she was going to say that it takes me a second too long to process what cut her off.

The *bang* that cut her off.

The bang of a gunshot.

Then another.

I throw her to the ground and crouch in front of her, ready to protect her with my body. In an instant, one of the guns in my waistband is in my hand.

I watch in horror as my brother's wedding reception is ambushed.

Men in black with rifles and bulletproof vests storm in. Men who came prepared. Men who came to kill.

Then they speak.

*Russian.*

And I know.

I know *I* fucked up.

I know these are the consequences of *my* actions.

I didn't almost start a war. I *did* start a war.

And now everyone I love is in danger.

I look over as Dom fires off two headshots, taking out the first two who enter. He's on the left side of the room. He turns over a table and uses it as protection.

Bash is doing the same on the right side. He's helping guests take cover. He's playing defense, taking out any of them that come too close.

Matthias is guarding Margot, a look of pure fury in his eyes. He swore she'd never have to deal with the Bratva again, and now, on their wedding day, here they are.

Dad is guiding people out the back exit, gun in hand. He's protecting them.

Mom is helping Dotty out, whose boyfriend leaves her to help us. Dr. Richard is the Syndicate doctor. But I forget, he's still a part of the Syndicate and is familiar with fighting.

I fire off three shots, taking down one man.

I hear a whimper and turn to Cecilia.

We're in the middle of the room. I need to get her to Dad. There's no cover here, except me. And I'll cover her with my body if I have to. I'll get between her and every bullet. I'd let her use my dying corpse as her shield if needed.

I look up and see a Bratva soldier approaching, and he smiles.

"Roman Montclair, you wanted a war. Here it is," he says with a thick accent. "Maybe I'll take the slut with me. Afterall, she caused all this, so her cunt must be worth it." He gestures to a trembling Cecilia behind me, and I see red.

I unload my clip into him, still going even once he's down. Then I take his rifle and shoot him again. I'm so busy shooting him that I don't see the man approaching in front of me until it's too late.

The bullet flying through my left shoulder knocks me down. I shoot the man, and he falls. I shoot him again from where I've landed on top of Cecilia, and he dies.

"Fuck," I growl, my arm already going numb.

I look down and see blood staining my white shirt. My vision blurs, but I force myself to stay in focus. There are still more here. And I won't go down until Cecilia is safe.

Even if protecting her kills me.

# Chapter 92
## *Cecilia*

Roman falls on me, still shooting the man who said those horrible things.

His claim that this is my fault just as much as Roman's sound in my ears, and I know it's true. If I had confronted Roman instead of running, he never would've attacked the Russian crime family.

I look up when I hear Roman curse only to see blood seeping through his shirt.

Right over his heart.

I cry out, and he turns to me.

"Are you okay?" he shouts frantically.

"You're hurt!" I cry out.

"I'm fine, sunshine. We need... to get you... to Dad," he says, slowing throughout the sentence.

I can see he's fighting to stay conscience, and my stomach plummets.

He's dying.

But I won't let that happen.

I've seen enough of Gracie's crime documentaries and Mr. Bank's action movies to know I need to put pressure on the wound.

I try to pull his jacket off, which he fights until it dawns on him what I'm doing. With it off, I press into his wound.

"Fuck," he groans in pain.

"Stay with me, Roman!" I demand.

His eyes start to flutter, and I slap him across the face.

He winks at me weakly, then says, "It's not as fun outside the bedroom."

Despite the situation we're in, I still blush and look around, making sure no one heard.

It's in this moment that I see a soldier's gaze land on us.

It all happens in slow motion.

He's approaching us with an evil grin on his face.

Roman's too unfocused to see what's happening.

I eye the big gun at Roman's feet.

And make up my mind.

I lunge on top of Roman and grab the gun. Still acting as a barrier between him and the man, I lift the gun.

My arms shake with the weight, but I hold steady. The man laughs at me, and I can tell he doesn't think I have it in me.

"Shoot me, little girl. I dare you," he mocks.

It must wake Roman because he roars and tries to push me off him.

But I hold steady, take a deep breath, and pull the trigger. The first shot misses him, but as his eyes narrow, I fire again. A bullet flies through his shoulder holding his gun, and he drops it. I pull the trigger again and again, until finally he drops too.

All the while, Roman is trying to get out from under me.

Another Russian is drawn in by the commotion and laughs at me holding a gun. But I don't care. I shoot at him, but not before he fires too.

Somehow, by the universe's grace, he misses. But so do I.

We both shoot again, and this time, my bullet flies through his neck. His shot barely grazes my arm, but only because Roman moves me.

I look around, still holding the gun, and realize all the other Russian's are down.

But it's not enough to convince me to put the gun down. I keep it up, trained on our surroundings. My head is on a swivel, unable to believe it's over. That we're safe.

Suddenly, someone's shaking me, and I quickly turn the gun on them. It's thrown out of my hands, and it's only then that I realize it's by Dom.

"You're bleeding! Where are you hit? It's a lot of blood" he asks frantically staring at my torso.

I look down and realize my once green dress is now stained a deep red.

But it's not my blood.

Without answering him, I hop off Roman and get on my knees. I press his jacket into his shoulder and desperately try to stop the bleeding.

"Roman, please, wake up. Look at me," I frantically beg him.

Dom presses into a second wound on his left arm, and I realize the bullet that grazed me actually hit him. He took another bullet for me.

Roman's eyes fly open, and he glares at his brother.

"Héroe, don't you dare die on me. After all you've done for us, you're not allowed to leave me!" I demand, tears streaming down my face.

He lifts his uninjured arm slowly and cups my cheek. I press my hand against his, keeping it stable.

"Roman, my hero, I love you! You can't die on me. Please stay," I plead desperately. I look down as my tears dance with his blood.

"You still love me?" he asks incredulously. "Will you stay my wife if I live?" His eyes start to droop as he says it.

Dom and Dr. Richard are doing something while he talks to me, but I can't comprehend it.

"I'm your wife no matter what. I'm Cecilia Montclair. I just killed two men for you. Please, you can't leave me," I cry.

Suddenly, a paramedic is next to me, trying to bandage my arm.

"No! I'm fine! Save him!" I demand, shrugging her off.

"Miss, I have to help you too. My partners are helping your boyfriend," she explains.

"My husband," I correct her, needing someone to know.

As they put him onto a gurney, he wakes up.

"CECILIA! CECILIA!" he shouts my name.

I break free of my paramedic and run to his side.

"I'm here, héroe. I'm not going anywhere," I promise him.

When they load him in the ambulance, I'm with him the whole time.

And only when they send him back to surgery do I let the doctor handle my wound.

And the entire time he's in surgery, I cry.

Slowly, one by one, his family trickles in.

Some have it worse than me, others are unharmed. But no one is in as critical condition as my husband. They tell me none of our people were killed. And that the Russians took the brunt of it.

But I don't have it in me to care.

Because my husband is in surgery.
Fighting for his life.
And I can't cope with that.

# Chapter 93
## *Roman*

An incessant beeping wakes me. Opening my eyes hurts, and I feel nauseous.

I look around at the white walls surrounding me and realize I'm in a hospital.

The events of the wedding reception come back to me, and I'm yanking cords out of my arm, ignoring the pain in my shoulder.

"CECILIA!" I shout, needing to find her. "CE–"

"I'm here, Roman. I'm here," the soothing voice of my whole world calms me.

I look to my right and see her at my side. Tears stream down her face, and it breaks my heart.

"Sunshine, why are you crying?" I ask, needing to make whatever it is better.

"You almost died! You almost died, and it scared me. You were in surgery for hours, and then you were unconscious even longer. I had to fight to get in this room with you." She continues to sob.

"Oh, sunshine," I console her. I grip her waist and lift her into my bed.

"No! I can't be in the bed with you! You need to heal!" she scolds me, and I just chuckle.

"If you think a measly gunshot wound is going to keep me from you, you're crazy," I assure her.

"Two gunshots wounds!" she obstinately corrects me.

"Whatever." I roll my eyes at her dramatics. "I'm fine. This isn't the first time I've been shot, and it won't be the last."

Tears well in her eyes again, and she wheezes in.

"Don't say that!" she cries out.

I go over my words and wince when I realize my mistake.

"I'm sorry, sunshine. I promise I'll be more careful in the future," I assure her. It's the truth. I won't let anything keep me from my wife. I need to always be here to protect her.

I grip her arm, pulling her to my chest, and she winces in pain.

"What's wrong?" I demand and pull up her t-shirt sleeve.

To reveal a bandage covering her arm.

A fucking bandage with red seeping through.

She's fucking bleeding!

And I see red.

"You're hurt!" I growl out, fuming.

"It's just a scrape, thanks to you. You're the one who took the bullet for me," she explains stubbornly.

I sit up, ignoring the pain, and turn her gently to face me.

The memory of the ambush comes to me suddenly.

And I'm even angrier than before.

"How fucking dare you?" I demand, beyond furious.

"What?" she asks confused.

"How fucking dare you put yourself in harm's way? How dare you come between me and a man trying to kill? How fucking dare you?" I'm blinded by my fury.

"Excuse me! I'm the reason we're alive. I took out TWO of them! I shot and killed two men." The last line comes out a whisper.

Tears well in her eyes as she soaks in what she did.

I pull her into my chest, grimacing when her head hits my wounded shoulder.

"Sunshine, you saved us. You did what you had to do. If you hadn't shot those men, we'd be dead," I console her.

When she finally evens out her breathing, she jumps back, realizing her head has been resting on my shoulder.

"I'm so sorry. We can get you some morphine if you need it," she offers.

"No, we're talking first. Look at me!" I demand. Only when her eyes find mine do I continue. "Don't you ever do that again! Don't you ever put yourself in any position that could get you hurt. I don't care if the only protection you have is me, you use me until the danger passes. I don't care if I die saving you. You use my body as a shield. I won't live in a world where you're gone! Do you understand me?" I shake her gently, needing her to realize how serious I am.

"But–" she tries to argue.

"But nothing! Promise me you'll never do that again. I'm here to protect you. My job is to make sure you're safe! Promise me!" I'm begging at this point, but I don't care.

She lifts my pinky finger in hers and shakes.

"I promise," she whispers sadly.

Then she leans forward and kisses me deeply.

I respond quickly, loving every minute of it.

"Do you remember what I said before you passed out?" She blushes as she asks.

I work hard to keep my face neutral when the smile fights so hard against me. I remember her forgiving me and telling me she loves me, but I want to hear it again.

"It's fuzzy," I tell her, and it's not technically a lie. My memories of the reception are a little hazy.

"I love you, Roman. So much. I know you messed up, but everything you did, you did for me. While I don't approve of the methods, you made my life better. And you've more than made up for it. I've never been happier than when I was yours. I don't want to move out or get an annulment. I want to stay your wife. I forgive you. So please, please don't ever try to leave me like that again!"

Tears stream down her face as she professes her love.

I pull her in for a hug, and despite the pain, I wrap both arms around her.

"I love you. And I'll never stop loving you. You are my sunshine. I'm sorry I did some crazy things, but you make me crazy. I can't change who I am, that I'll do anything to keep you. Just don't ever leave again," I beg.

"I accept you for who you are. If the Syndicate keeps the city safe from the men that attacked us, then I understand." She pauses then giggles. "I'll never run away again. Plus, you'll know if I do."

I freeze, only now remembering the tracker I put in her.

"I can take it out if you'd like. But it really is a safety measure. The Bratva has taken our women before. I can't risk losing you," I confess.

A look of fear crosses her face then she burrows into me.

"I know you'll always protect me, but I want to keep it in. It makes me feel safe knowing you're looking out for me," she sighs.

I exhale in relief.

I keep her buried in my arms, and when the nurse comes to put my IV back in, I let him, but I refuse to let Cecilia out of my bed.

She falls asleep rather quickly after staying up all night worrying about me.

I just watch her sleep, holding her to my chest.

Where she's safe.

Where she'll always be protected.

And I process what could've happened. How I could've lost her. And I vow to never let anything come between us again.

# Chapter 94
## *Cecilia*

I wake to kisses on my neck.

"Roman! We can't do this here!" I whisper-shout at him.

I feel his smile against my neck.

"Sunshine, don't you know? We're Montclairs. We can do whatever we want," he responds mischievously.

"I'm not even supposed to be in this bed with you. We definitely can't be making out in it!" I scold.

He continues his attack on my neck. One hand trails up to my face and turns my cheek so I meet his gaze.

He leans in and kisses me deeply. He's relentless. I can't stop myself from giving in. When I pull back for air, he stares at me adoringly.

"Oh sunshine, I don't intend to just make out," he says slyly, then slips his hand under the covers.

I moan when he invades my panties, still trailing lower. He meets my core and hisses a breath.

"Already wet for me?" he says with a grin.

"Always. Even just a kiss gets me there for you, my hero," I whisper against his lips.

He pushes a finger in, and I groan at the intrusion.

I grip his arm, but don't make a move to stop him. Because I know if I said the word, this ecstasy would stop. And despite my protests, that's the last thing I want.

With his injured left arm, he hikes my left leg over him, opening me further.

He continues thrusting his fingers into me, grinding his palm against my clit. I'm panting on the edge of my release.

And when he leans in and bites my neck, I fall over the edge.

He covers my mouth with his, swallowing my cries. I'm too consumed by my release to consider the consequences of being loud.

I reach under the sheet and grip his hard dick. I slide my hand up and down, squeezing at the base. He starts lifting his hips, meeting my strokes.

I tsk.

"No, sir. You're injured. I'll be doing all the hard work this time," I scold him, tightening my hold on him in warning.

He hisses a breath and swallows hard.

"Yes, ma'am," he says with a wicked smile and brings one arm over his head and lets the other fall over his stomach.

I continue stroking until I feel precum bead at his tip.

I look back at the hospital door, debating for a moment. They checked on him an hour ago, so we should be good for at least three hours. But it's the night shift, so the halls are quiet.

After a moment of hesitation, I steel my back. Then, under the sheet, I shimmy down my thong, hike up my skirt, and pull up his hospital gown.

"Cecilia! What are you doing?" Roman asks, completely shocked. His eyes are wide, and his jaw hangs open.

"You started this!" I remind him. "Just, hold still. Don't move that left arm."

I climb on top of him and line his dick with my entrance and slowly lower myself.

I look up and meet his gaze. He's staring at me in wonder.

"I didn't think you had this in you, naughty girl." Roman's smile spurs me on.

I rock onto him, up and down, until I feel him tighten.

He tries to put weight on his arms to lean forward to kiss me, but I push his right shoulder to the mattress. He's not hurting himself doing this.

"If you move, we stop," I threaten.

"Fuck, sunshine," he groans. "I'm learning so much about myself."

"Huh?" I can't comprehend his words through the ecstasy.

"I didn't know I loved it when you boss me around. Fuck, you're so hot, sunshine" he gasps out.

I involuntarily tighten at the praise, and he groans.

He raises his right arm around my neck faster than I can track and brings me down to meet him.

His lips come crashing down on mine. His tongue slips into my mouth, and despite his claim to like me in control, he takes over. His hand on my neck prolongs the kiss, and his hips start moving to meet me.

"I thought you liked me in control?" I lean back just enough to tell him.

"Yeah, but there's only so long a man can last," he pants.

I sit down on him and stay there. I pry his arm off my neck and pin it above his head. He could easily overpower me, but I know he won't. And from the look in his eyes, he loves this just as much as I do.

"I'm in charge right now. And you are going to lay here and take it like a good boy," I tell him with a wicked smile on my own.

"Fuck, Cecilia. I'll listen, just please don't stop," he begs.

I start moving my hips again. I speed up, unable to control myself. Especially not when he's looking at me with so much love and adoration.

I feel my release building, and Roman groans against me, his whole body tensing.

"Sunshine, I'm close. You need to get off me," he warns. "We're not wearing a condom."

And his concern for my wishes is my last straw.

"Come in me, Roman. Put a baby in me. Please," I beg him.

"Are you sure?" he rasps, barely holding on.

"Yes. I want our dream together. I want a family!"

"I love you!" he grits out as he falls over the edge.

I feel his release in me, and I follow quickly. I fall onto his chest, and his arms instantly engulf me. He holds me to him, and I don't move. I can't move. I don't want to move.

Because I'm exactly where I want to be.

"I love you too," I tell him.

# Epilogue I
## *Cecilia*

"Make a left here!" I instruct, and Roman listens, turning the car into a lot.

"Sunshine, I know where your doctor's office is," he teases.

I laugh, knowing he tracks me every time I leave the house. I don't mind. In fact, I prefer it. I feel safer this way. So, yes he tracks me, but it's with my permission. Well, that's only when he doesn't come with me.

He thinks we're here for an IUD, and that I'll need a driver afterwards.

But he doesn't know the surprise I have for him.

He holds my hand the entire way through the building, then I check in at the counter. We sit in the waiting room, and I have to hide my grin at his solemn face. I know he wants a baby as much as I do, and I hate lying to him, but I wanted it to be a surprise. I also didn't want to tell him until I knew for sure.

"Cecilia Montclair!" a medical assistant calls from the doorway.

We make our way in, and I step on the scale. I note the few pounds I've already gained, but Roman smartly doesn't comment on it.

We go through the regular questions. Roman pays close attention the entire time.

"When was your last period?" she asks.

"I don't know." I try to hide the glee in my voice.

"Is there any chance you're pregnant?" she asks, then glances at Roman and winks at me, obviously realizing with Roman as my husband, there's a big chance I'm pregnant.

"Yes," I tell her.

Roman sucks in a breath, and his knee starts bouncing anxiously.

She hands me a cup to pee in. I head to the bathroom and do my business. I give it to her, and she leaves.

As soon as she's out the door, Roman's on me.

"Cecilia, is there really a chance you're pregnant?" he asks, and I can hear the hope in his voice.

I reach into my purse and pull out a zip-block. Sitting inside are two pregnancy tests.

"There's more than a chance," I tell him as I hand him the bag.

He inspects them, and I can tell the moment he registers what the two pink lines on each one means.

*Pregnant.*

He lifts me in his arms and twirls me around. Then drops me immediately, with a look of concern.

"Wait, shit! Did I hurt you? I don't want to give the baby vertigo!" he freaks out, then bends down to look at my stomach.

I'm barely showing, but he still stares at the slight bump in awe.

"Is this really our baby?" he asks full of disbelief and hope.

"I think so. That's what we're here to find out," I tell him as I grip his hand.

He kisses and hugs me, then picks me up and places me on the table so gently. He frets, making sure I'm comfortable. That I'm not too hot or too cold.

And I realize this is going to be a long pregnancy.

Roman's already protective of me, to an insane extent. Now that I'm carrying our child... I wouldn't be surprised if he locks me in a bubble-wrapped room.

Dr. Lane finally walks in with a bright smile and gives me a hug.

"Great news! You're pregnant!" She gives us a moment to process it.

Even though the tests came back positive, I needed confirmation from her. Tears well in my eyes, and when I glance at Roman, some have already fallen down his cheeks.

"Sunshine, we're going to have a baby," he says softly.

"This is our dream," I say through tears.

"Do you want a scan done to see your baby?" she asks.

"Yes!" Roman says, instantly.

"We can also run a non-invasive prenatal testing to see the sex, if you'd like. It's a blood test," she offers.

Roman looks at me in question this time.

"Is there no other way to tell the sex?" he asks.

"Not this early. At eighteen weeks, we can tell with the anatomy scan," Dr. Lane explains.

"If you don't want to have your blood drawn, I understand," he says disappointedly.

"Roman, a little needle isn't going to stop us from finding out the sex of our baby." I'm shocked he would ever think that.

The ultrasound tech comes in and starts setting up.

I lay down and roll up my shirt. Roman stands next to me and holds my hand.

"This is going to be cold," she warns, but I don't care.

She pours the gel on and starts moving the wand on me.

Then, we hear it. A drumming. And tears stream down my face.

"That's your baby's heartbeat!" she says excitedly.

"It's too fast! Why is it so fast?" Roman asks, his hand squeezing mine nervously.

"Fetuses and infants have faster heartbeats than adults. Your baby is perfectly normal." She shoots us a patient smile.

Roman exhales and looks to the ceiling.

I'm watching him when the ultrasound tech gasps.

"Would you look at that!" she says, excitedly, pointing at the screen.

I stare in amazement.

"Is that...?" I ask, unable to finish the sentence.

"Yes!" She smiles at me in excitement.

"What? What is it?" Roman asks, confused and worried.

"That's Baby B," she responds.

"I don't understand." He's somehow still confused.

"The first was Baby A. This is Baby B. We're having twins!" I say, both nervous and thrilled.

I don't know how to feel about twins. Two babies is a lot.

I spare a glance at Roman, and he's smiling widely.

"This is perfect!" He leans down and kisses me.

"Twins," I say with a sigh.

"Erm, actually..." the tech says nervously. "Meet Baby C."

Silence, except Baby C's heartbeat, falls through the room.

"Are you saying there are three babies in my wife?" Roman demands answers.

"It would appear so." She swallows, looking nervous.

Roman pales as his eyes shoot to mine.

"Triplets," he whispers. Then he cups my cheek. "Are you okay, sunshine?"

"Yeah, it's just... a lot."

"It is, but it's our *a lot.*"

He's so supportive that tears well again.

"We're having three babies," I repeat.

"Yeah. Three of us running around," he says.

Then he pauses.

"Three little ones. We need to make changes! We need to baby-proof the house. We need to move into the house! I need to buy bullet-proof minivans. We need to get you your license. No, we're going to get a driver. Oh my God! How are we going to take care of more babies than there are us? How are you even going to feed them? You only have two boobs!" he starts pacing, looking more anxious by the second.

"Héroe, it's going to be fine. We'll do this together. And your family and mine will help for sure. It's going to be okay," I calm him.

Once he's settled down, we continue with the ultrasounds. Then we get the labs done, and they tell us they'll have the results uploaded in seven to fourteen days.

...

My phone chirps with an email.

My phone chirps with *the* email.

"Roman," I call him from the kitchen room.

He comes running into the living room so quickly, he skids across the floor.

"Are you okay? What's wrong?" he freaks out, as he's done every day for the past week. I fear he's not going to get any better throughout the pregnancy. I wonder if he'll be even worse once the babies are here, if that's even possible.

"We got the email," I tell him.

"Okay. I'm ready. Are you?" He takes a deep breath.

"Of course! Remember, it will only tell us if there's at least one Y chromosome or none. We won't know the individual sexes," I remind him.

We still wanted to do it, even if the only answer is there's at least one boy.

He sits next to me and holds my hand.

We pull up the link and sit through the longest video of my life. Until finally, the results.

'*You're having a girl!*' pops up on the screen.

"So, we're having at least one girl?" Roman asks, even though I can tell understanding is dawning on him.

"Héroe, I think it means all three are girls. There's no Y chromosome detected," I tell him with a smile.

Having only sisters, I'm used to girls. I'm excited that they're girls. I would've loved them just as much as sons, but daughters are easier.

Roman slowly looks at me, then looks down at my belly, then back at me.

"Girls?" he breathes out. "All daughters?"

"Yes, héroe. We're having three daughters," I explain slowly.

"I need air. No, I need water. Wait, it doesn't matter what I need! What do you need? What do our daughters need? Oh my God, three daughters! Three little girls to keep safe. In this dangerous world." He's pacing as his hands run through his buzzed hair. "Cecilia, I think we need to move somewhere remote. Somewhere without evil boys. I don't trust anyone with my girls. Maybe I can buy an island or something. You like the beach, right?"

I stand up ready to calm him, but he's on me in an instant, helping me back onto the couch.

"You're growing our daughters right now. Whatever you need, I can get you," he insists. There's a tremor in his voice, and his hands are shaking.

"I just need you to be okay. We can't move to an island. Our families need us, and we'll certainly need them," I remind him.

"Okay. But can we at least home school them? They're never allowed to talk to boys," he decides.

"No, héroe. Our daughters will be educated by people who know how to teach. Plus, they'll have to talk to boys. They're going to live normal lives. And you're going to let them. And one day, they'll go on dates and have boyfriends," I tell him, needing him to accept this in the next decade before it happens.

"I think I'm going to be sick," he says, looking rather green.

"It's okay. You're going to be such a great girl-dad," I reassure him.

"Oh my God. What are we going to do?" he mumbles, then pulls me into his chest.

"We'll figure it out together. We'll love our daughters and give them great lives. It's going to be magical," I soothe him.

"Okay. I believe you. As long as we have each other, we're going to be okay," he says. But I think he's trying to convince himself.

I lean into him, and he hugs me.

And all is right in our world.

# Epilogue II
## *Roman*

I stand nervously at the end of the aisle. It's ridiculous to be nervous. She's already my wife, and this is only our vow renewal. Margot and I planned the whole thing based off what Cecilia started planning before... she left.

It's in the garden where I proposed, and it melts my heart that she wanted it to be here. I look around, finally at peace that our family and friends get to witness our marriage, even if it's our second one.

I look around the room and see everyone we love. Well... everyone we love and *Katerina.*

Dom's wife, the Bratva princess, sits in the row behind my parents while my brothers stand beside me. Despite our insistence of treating her as family since she technically is family now, Dom has forced separation between us. We barely know his wife, and it's his fault.

Dom obviously doesn't trust her, evident by the Syndicate guards flanking her. I could entertain the idea that it's for her protection after the events of the last wedding if it weren't for the hostile glares they shoot each other. I wonder if Dom's slight limp has anything to do with their animosity and the guards. Is he trying to protect her or us from her?

Unlike Dom, the rest of the family has been nothing but kind. I, however, have trouble even looking at her. Guilt overwhelms me. Dom only entered an arranged marriage with the enemy's young daughter to force an alliance to end a war I unjustifiably started.

If it weren't for me, Dom wouldn't be married to a woman he hates. I swear he's aged a decade since their wedding. But as I study him, I realize he doesn't look miserable, he looks angry... and passionate. Under the ruthless glare, there's almost something close to admiration in his eyes as he stares his wife down.

It takes me by surprise. I've never seen so much emotion on Dom's face. Hell, I don't remember the last time I saw any emotion from him. But now, he aims so much towards her. Granted, most of it is negative, but I still find it interesting that he cares about the woman he didn't choose.

And the way Katerina looks at him... She looks at him like their marriage is a game she's already won. I can tell she's more intelligent than she lets on. I wouldn't be surprised if she has Dom running in circles.

I just pray they don't kill each other. Because I don't have it in me to step up and run the Syndicate. Oh, also, I love my brother and don't want him dead.

I glance at my brothers standing next to me, and try to see what's going on with them. Matthias is happily married. Dom is... unhappily married. And Bash, I have no idea. He's been distant.

Soft music starts playing, stealing my attention to the doors. They swing open, and I'm disappointed to see Margot instead of my wife standing at the entrance. She walks down, staring at her husband the entire time.

Then Cecilia's sisters walk out. They're smiling happily for their sister.

Then it's Gracie, Cecilia's maid of honor. She's glowing with pride. I know she's excited with how things turned out between Cecilia and me. I also know that Cecilia kept a lot of our issues from her, but I suspect Gracie knows more than she lets on. She winks at me then stands next to the sisters on the other side of the aisle.

Then, my world freezes.

The breath is knocked out of my lungs worse than any punch I've ever experienced. Because being led down the aisle by her father, is my beautiful bride.

Looking like the goddess she is in a white billowy dress that hugs her breasts, flows over her swollen belly, then falls delicately down to the floor, she floats towards me.

When they reach me, her father kisses her cheek and with tears in his eyes, puts her hand in mine.

"Cuídala, yerno. Es lo más precioso que hay en este mundo. Pronto lo vas a entender," he whispers to me. "Take care of her, son-in-law. She's the most precious thing in the world. You'll understand soon." He nods to her protruding belly after the last part.

And I already understand. Despite my daughters not being born yet, they and their mother are the most important things in my life. My world revolves around them now. And I know I'll feel it even more when I finally meet them.

"I will, Señor Hernando. I swear," I tell him, my eyes also rimmed with tears.

"Call me, suegro," he says, then takes his seat.

I lead my beautiful bride in front of the officiant. As he starts the ceremony, I don't hear a thing. Because all I can do is stare at my glowing sunshine.

I didn't think it was possible, but since becoming pregnant, she's become even more gorgeous. It shouldn't be possible. You can't improve your perfection. But somehow, she has.

I feel an elbow in my back and turn to see Dom gesturing me to proceed.

I look at the officiant and realize it's time for my vows.

Which I wrote.

I do a few rounds of box breathing as I take the carefully folded paper out of my tux pocket.

"Cecilia María, from the first moment I saw you, concussed and lying in my arms, I knew I wanted you. All too quickly, I fell in love with you. I mean, how could I not? You're the sun, brightening my every day. I would do anything for you. I know I didn't always make the right moves, so I want to make some vows to you.

I vow to never lie to you again. You deserve only honesty, and a foundation built on lies will crumble at the slightest wind.

I vow to protect you every day. You will always be the most important part of my life. You will always be safe with me.

I vow to be the best husband to you. I'll take care of you and provide for you. You'll never know a day without love.

I vow to be the best father to our daughters and all the other children to come. They're already a priority to me, and I haven't even met them yet. I love them like I love their mother.

I vow to be the best man I can be, because you make me want to be a better man for you. Every day, I will work hard to earn you. Because you're too good for me, but instead of letting that keep me from you, I'll let it drive me to be better.

I love you with everything that I am. You are my heart outside my body. You will forever be mine, just as I am yours. Because, sunshine, you own me. Mind, body, and soul. It all belongs to you. I'd do anything for you, and I will do everything for you."

I stare into her eyes as I profess my love. I almost feel bad about the pregnancy hormones causing her to sob at my words, but I know she'd be emotional even without them. She hiccups, then pulls out a sheet of paper delicately folded.

"Roman Montclair, when I first met you, you were my héroe. You saved me countless times. Even when I found out about the unconventional methods you used, the core sentiment was to help me. You'll always be my hero. My savior. And I know you'll do the same for our children. I'm honored that our daughters get to call you 'Dad'. I couldn't hope for a better man to have a family with.

I vow to always hear you out. I'll listen before coming to any conclusions. I'll trust in you as my husband and as my héroe.

I vow to come to you when I'm in need. And to trust that you'll take care of me, as you've done countless times.

I vow to raise our daughters and all to come in agreement with you. I'll be patient and hear you out. However, they will be allowed to date before they're thirty," she says teasingly, bringing up a conversation we've had many times.

I growl in disagreement. Meanwhile, Margot and Gracie snicker behind her. The crowd cheers. But my brothers, to my surprise, make noises of disapproval, clearly as rationally protective over their nieces as I am.

"I vow to be your perfect wife. I'll be whatever you need me to be. Your friend, your confidant, your calm, your ally, your wife... I'll always be here to support you.

And I vow to lead you to the light. No matter what you do in the darkness, I vow to always be your sunshine. Your peace. Your happiness. I won't let you succumb to the night, because I'll be your sun always lifting you to the daylight.

I love you. And I will always love you. You're my héroe. I'll never take you for granted, nor all you do for me. I love you greatly. Please know, you're my life. And I wouldn't be happy without you."

She smiles at me through her tears, and I have to swipe my palms over my eyes to see through my own. I don't care who sees the ferocious Roman Montclair cry. I'll do as I damn well please for my wife. And they'll take this as a warning of how much she means to me. Of how far I'll go to protect her.

When the officiant finally lets me kiss my bride, I don't even wait for him to finish. I pull her towards me and lean over her belly. I thread my hand through her hair and kiss her fiercely. It's not as innocent as it should be for this setting. But my wife just married me, so I can't help it. She's irresistible.

...

We're sitting at our table at the reception. After the first dance and the father-daughter dance, my pregnant wife needed to get off her feet.

In fact, I grab her feet, take off her shoes, and start rubbing them under the table. She shouldn't be in pain carrying our children.

"Roman," she moans out, and I shift as my cock hardens. "That feels so good."

I curse under my breath and continue the task at hand.

All I can see is her. My sunshine. She's my life. We didn't need a wedding to prove it, but she deserved one. And I know from her smile, she's happy she got it. Pride fills my chest as I look at that brilliant smile.

"Do you think Dom and Katerina will survive each other?" Cecilia asks worriedly, nodding to a corner.

Katerina is talking to one of Cecilia's male cousins. They're a respectable distance apart. Nothing seems amiss. But the furious Dom striding across the room towards them doesn't seem to agree.

Dom pulls Katerina even further away from Mateo and against his chest. Dom then says something to Mateo that has him paling and scurrying off to the other side of the room.

Katerina breaks free of Dom's grasp, the fury on his face reflected in her own. They get into a heated discussion, and for a second, it looks like she might stab him. I see her eyeing the cake knife on the table next to her. He intercepts her hand as it sneaks out to grab it and uses it to pull her into him. She huffs and rolls her eyes.

I hear Cecilia's swift inhale, matching my own worried anticipation. I've never seen someone act so disrespectfully and defiantly towards Dom. I've seen him enact violence on his own men for much less.

I sit up in my seat, ready to intervene if needed, but Dom just grits his teeth and pulls her back into his chest. She fights him, but I suspect she could get out of his hold if she wanted.

He drags her onto the dance floor, and they fall into step easily. With every turn, the distance between them seems to diminish. Until they're chest to chest, and their lips are mere centimeters apart.

It's at that moment I wonder if he's even touched his wife since they married. They seem so inexperienced with their proximity. Horror overwhelms me at the idea of staying away from my Cecilia.

Although the anger is still palpable, there's passion in their eyes. A level of emotion I've never seen from Dom. If I wasn't sitting down, I'd be on the floor from shock.

I watch as Katerina glances at his lips then back to his eyes and lifts her chin ever so slightly. His eyes widen then a wicked grin takes over as his hand trails up her back, pulling her in. He leans down to kiss her, and when their lips are a breath apart, she pulls back and cackles.

She says something to him that has his gaze hardening, and he pulls her back in. He doesn't go for the kiss this time, but I can feel how much he wants it. How much he needs it.

Poor Dom.

Sucks for him though. Because I'm going to bed my wife tonight, and it'll be amazing. I love her so much.

"I think they'll be alright," I assure Cecilia.

But in the back of my mind, I fear that someday soon, it'll be too much. They'll either implode or explode. I just pray the fallout is something devastatingly good. Because the alternative could be horrific. I pray Dom and Katerina don't destroy each other.

Watching them, I realize what a formidable opponent Katerina is for him. And what a strong ally she could make.

If he plays his cards right, the Queen of the Syndicate could be something to behold.

# *Dear Reader*

Thank you for reading *Deceptive Desires.*

This is my second novel and the second in The Syndicate Series. I'm honored that you've stuck by me and continued reading my works. I know I can't take all the credit; those Montclair brothers have no trouble getting women. My author journey has been incredible, and it wouldn't be possible without readers like you.

If you enjoyed this story, I'd be truly grateful if you left a review on your favorite platform(s). Reviews are one of the best ways to support an author. Each one makes a difference.

Dominic and Katerina are just beginning.
Stick around for their story: *Vengeful Vows*

Much love,
Ellie

# Acknowledgements

There are so many people who have supported me in my author journey. So many of you read my works and have stuck by me. *Deceptive Desires* wouldn't be possible without all the positive feedback I received from *Innocent Intentions.* From the bottom of my heart, thank you.

Katelyn, thank you for being my alpha reader. I loved every comment you made. Hearing your reactions made me so excited. And your help in scheming my books helps so much. I'm eternally grateful to have you in my corner. I'm so glad you loved this book as much as I do.

Maggie, my dearest older sister, thank you so much for everything you do for me. From being my guiding light to beta reading this book, I appreciate it more than you know. I love your every comment, even if its "Ew ew ew! I LOATHE this! Change it now!" (Direct quote from Maggie). They make my books even better. I'm so lucky to have an older sister like you. Thanks for always putting up with my dramatics and being my best friend.

Parker Drue, you angel sent to Earth, thank you! Thank you! Thank you! I cannot express how important you are to me, and how big the smiles you bring to my face are. Whether it's watching a God-awful movie with you or reading your hilarious comments, you never cease to amuse me. There's no one's thoughts on my books that I look forward to more. Your crush on Bash will never not entertain me, and I promise to do you justice with him.

Mom, my dearest Momma, thank you. Even though my books are outside your comfort zone, you never cease to support me. You're my biggest cheerleader. I'm honored you recommend my books to your friends, even if they're a little risqué. Thank you for editing my books and being my last line of defense. Unfortunately, you weren't on a plane going across the ocean for weeks when I gave you this one, and I had to hear your thoughts in person. I do appreciate those thoughts, but please, please, please, don't ever bring up the spicy scenes to me again.

Kenzie, you rascal, I love you, girl. You support me in every way except actually reading these books, which I love. You listen to my ideas and help me plot. You'll listen to the most detailed, hours-long description of each scene. You gave your mom a copy (that pic of her reading *Innocent Intentions* had me simultaneously cracking up and cringing). You even help make the men even more dreamy. I'm so lucky to have you in my life and as a best friend. I will continue to write our dream men since real-life men don't seem to be living up to our stringent standards.

Mrs. Amy, thank you so much. You've always been someone I look up to. You've watched me grow and become the amazing (smut-writing) woman I am today. Thank you for supporting me in all my journeys and always encouraging me. I appreciate it. You told me to be proud of my works and of my accomplishments in writing, and that meant a lot to me. And thank you for how you've spread the word and advertised my book. I appreciate you so much.

To my Mimi, my lovely 83-year-old grandmother, thank you for supporting me. I gave you a copy of *Innocent Intentions,* and I am mortified by it every day. I love you and appreciate your support, but the dirty jokes you now make to me have me dying. Kidding, but in all seriousness, thank you. I love you so much.

To Ashley, Chloe, Mrs. Katrina, Aunt Lana, Nanny, Ms. Julie, Mrs. Barbara, Uncle Ned (I don't want to know if you ever read my books), Aunt Keri, and everyone else in my life who read my books even though it's outside your comfort zone. Thank you.

Sammi, you beautiful and kind woman, thank you so much. You were the first book friend I made. You supported *Innocent Intentions* to an insane degree. I couldn't believe how many posts you made. When we talk, you always support me and have great ideas. I couldn't be more grateful. Go follow her on TikTok at @tapisammi.

My ARC readers, you are the heart of this. I live for your reviews. I had many ARC readers from *Innocent Intentions* return for *Deceptive Desires.* It was an honor that you guys loved my writing enough to come back again. I'm eternally grateful to you. I've made some dear friends in my ARCs. Thank you guys from the bottom of my heart.

To every fan who wrote a review or made edits of *Innocent Intentions,* thank you. I hope *Deceptive Desires* gets the same love. You guys blew me away with your support. I didn't expect so much positive feedback. And when I saw that first edit, I almost cried. I couldn't believe people loved my writing enough to take time to do that.

To my readers, thank you so much. I couldn't be more grateful to you. I am so honored that you took the time to read my words. I was beside myself with how many people not only read but loved my debut novel. Thank you for continuing on with the series.

# About the Author

Ellie Hallaron is an author and lifetime storyteller, always turning ordinary moments into something worth retelling.

She fell in love with books early on, and growing up, the only punishment that ever stuck was having them taken away. Novels have always felt like home to her, first as a reader, and now as a writer.

Ellie writes emotionally charged romances with depth, intensity, and heroes you probably shouldn't fall for... but absolutely will.

When she's not writing, she's usually with friends and family who patiently endure her spirals over fictional characters, or she's dreaming up the next story.

She's thrilled to be sharing her words with readers, and there's so much more to come.

# Let's Stay in Touch

If you fell in love with *Deceptive Desires* and want more of the Montclair Brothers, come hang out with me online.

I share exclusive updates, upcoming releases, spicy teasers, unreleased scenes, and more!

You can find me here:

Tiktok:@Ellie Hallaron.Author

Instagram: @EllieHallaron.Author

Goodreads: Goodreads.com/EllieHallaron

9 7 9 8 9 9 9 0 3 9 7 2 9